Patricia Brown

Under a Dying Moon

GladEye Press

Springfield, OR

Under A Dying Moon

PATRICIA BROWN

For April , Kathryn, Suzanne, and the memories we share.

Eleanor Penrose woke to a clear winter morning in the village of Sand Beach. As she lay in bed she looked out her windows at the Pacific Ocean that washed the shore below with the rhythmic ebb and flow of its waves. The mornings along the Oregon coast were cool this time of year with just a hint of spring in the sea air. It was her habit to inventory each day before rising. It was Friday, Walter was gone, Angus was visiting his son, it was coffee group day and the ladies were going to an estate sale in the valley. Eleanor eagerly rolled out of bed and readied herself for the day ahead.

Feathers, her African Grey parrot, greeted her enthusiastically as she uncovered his cage and opened the door, granting him free run of the house.

"Good morning, Ellie," he mimicked Walter's voice. It always sent a spear through her heart to hear her late husband's greeting emanating from the body of a bird, but Eleanor was getting used to life without Walter. Her life was truly wonderful—full of friends, family, and a little romance. She never thought she would feel the excitement of a new love in her seventies, but so many things were uncertain. The one thing that didn't seem to change was her affection for her friends in the coffee group.

She arrived at the Boat House, their regular meeting spot, just as Cleo pulled into the parking lot. Bubbling with energy, Cleo moved briskly from her car sweeping her wind-blown hair out of her eyes.

"Cleo, you have something blue on your face," Eleanor spoke as she peered at the smudge that covered her friend's forehead above her carefully drawn brow.

"It's probably just paint," Cleo said as she rubbed at the offending spot. "I couldn't sleep so I was up early and decided to work on my latest masterpiece."

"So what are you painting?" Eleanor was a retired English teacher and published poet who admired Cleo's artistic abilities because she lacked them herself.

"It's an ocean scape. I'm hoping to find some beautiful frames today at the estate sale. I'm preparing for my show at the Bayside Art Center." Cleo stopped rubbing and asked, "Is it gone?"

"Pretty much." Eleanor took a tissue from her pocket and wiped the last remnants away. The Boat House had few customers. It had been a stormy winter and tourist season hadn't begun yet. A fire crackled in the stone fireplace as Eleanor and Cleo took their usual seats and waited for the others while Cleo continued to describe her latest works of art. Josephine and Pearl came in together and sat down. It was unusually quiet.

"What's up?" asked Cleo suspiciously.

"Josephine thinks I need my hearing checked," Pearl answered sullenly.

"I simply asked her if she liked my new gray pants and she . . ." Josephine began, but was interrupted by Pearl.

"I was sure you said grape ants and I've never tried them. I've never even heard of them," Pearl huffed.

"Don't worry," comforted Cleo. "We've all done that. For years I used to go into the confessional and tell the priest I'm hardly sorry when I should have been saying heartily sorry."

Dede, the mayor of Waterton, joined them just in time to hear Cleo's confession. "You probably were hardly sorry," she quipped as she sat down. Dede was still practicing her faith while Cleo had long ago fallen away.

The waitress appeared to take their order. "Could I have some ice water, please," asked Eleanor.

"I'd like some nice water too," Pearl added. "Is it different from your regular water?"

Dede raised her eyebrows and gave the others a look that said "What the heck!" Josephine sighed and they gave the waitress their usual orders for breakfast.

"It isn't easy getting older. Steve and I often had conversations just like that before he got his hearing aids. We just laugh and say "duck fur" now. I can't even remember what he misheard that sounded like duck fur." Cleo paused trying to recall the phrase. "I guess my memory's shot too."

The ladies in the coffee group were all in the youth of old age and dealing with the gifts it brought, as well as its curses.

"Look at that symbol over there on that sign for the daily special. What do you think it is?" asked Josephine pointing to a drawing that looked like a gnome.

"I've seen that before," Cleo added. "It was sprayed on the tourist train in Garibaldi. I thought it was some kind of graffiti."

"It does look like a gnome that someone doodled in the margins," Pearl said.

"I wonder what it means." Dede raised her brows and tapped her long fingernails on the table.

"Probably nothing," Josephine added logically. "Not everything has to be a mystery."

"I like a good mystery," Cleo stated. "I wonder if it is a gnome and what it could mean."

"Several garden gnomes turned up on the lawn of city hall the other day. I thought it was one of those fundraisers like the flamingos that showed up on people's yards a few years ago," Dede said.

"I remember that," Pearl said. "A bunch of flamingos along with a sign that said 'You've been flocked' were put in people's yards and they had to pay to have them removed and sent to someone else."

"How fun!" Eleanor said. "Where did the money go?"

"I don't remember," Pearl confessed.

"The downtown businesses could use some help this year," Dede said. "With all the road construction blocking their entrances and taking away parking, they've had trouble making ends meet."

"Just what is hen's meat and who is making that?" asked Pearl. "It certainly doesn't sound appetizing."

"Maybe you should get your hearing tested," Eleanor said kindly, but Pearl acted as if she didn't hear. Fortunately, the breakfast orders were delivered and the conversation turned to other things.

"Is it my imagination or are these pancakes shaped like gnomes?" asked Cleo.

The ladies left their cars at the Boat House and climbed into Dede's SUV. It would take them at least an hour to get to the estate sale from Waterton but it took that long to get almost anyplace from Waterton. Time went quickly as they chatted about their families and events in their neighborhood.

"When is Angus coming back?" asked Josephine.

"Where is Angus?" asked Pearl. "I didn't know he was gone. Is he on vacation?"

Angus McBride was a retired homicide detective who had became a special friend of Eleanor's after Walter became ill. Angus's love of Eleanor's cooking had turned into a love of Eleanor, complicating her life and sweetening it at the same time.

"Life is full of surprises and Angus is enjoying the fact that he has a son he didn't know about until recently. He's with him now, probably bonding over fishing or some other manly endeavor." Eleanor missed Angus's company more than she cared to admit. She was happy for him, of course, but couldn't help but worry that he might replace her with his new-found family. Family was something he'd always wanted but never thought he'd have.

"Isn't that DNA testing fabulous?" Cleo commented. "Angus may never have known he had a son who had a wife and three children who also had children making Angus a great grandfather. I wonder how he feels about it all."

"I think he loves it," Eleanor sighed. "He sent me several pictures. His son looks just like him and so do his grandsons and great grandsons. The McBride genes are very strong."

"That's a good thing." Pearl remarked. "He's the handsomest man I know over seventy."

"I can only imagine what a hunk he was in his youth," Dede sighed. "Let's see those pictures."

Eleanor took out her phone and passed it around while her friends oohed and aahed over the hunky handsomeness of Angus's offspring.

"This one has those deep dimples just like Angus," Cleo noted. "Oh to be that young and good looking! I don't think I ever appreciated my youth."

"We're not old," protested Josephine who worked hard at staying in shape and took pride in her appearance.

"No, we're not old, but we're not young either," Pearl said.

"I heard somewhere that 40 is the old age of youth and 60 is the youth of old age. Do you think that is true?" asked Cleo.

"If that is true then we are old," reasoned Dede who had just turned seventy.

"Age is just a number. If we feel young then we're young." Josephine ended the discussion with her voice of authority.

The road followed the winding Wilson River and the evergreen trees flanked the highway on both sides as they drove to the estate sale.

"What are you looking for at this sale?" asked Eleanor. "I know Cleo wants frames for her art."

"I'm looking for deals I can sell on eBay," Pearl said. "Last month I found a beautiful Hermès scarf that I bought for five dollars and was able to sell for one hundred."

"I just like to look," said Josephine. "I already own too much stuff. It's going to have to be something really special for me to buy anything."

"I don't need anything either, but if I see a beautiful book, I might be tempted," Eleanor said.

"You never know what you'll find at an estate sale," Dede added. "This one is supposed to be really varied and rich. It's at one of those old established homes in the West Hills. The

Grant House, I think it's called. The entire family is dead now and some agency is selling off all their stuff. We may get lucky and find a treasure."

"It's probably all overpriced," Pearl lamented.

"Maybe not," Josephine countered. "Family members usually have an emotional attachment to heirlooms and think they are worth more than they are. An agency might be more reasonable."

The Grant House was huge and impressive. After circling the residence several times, Dede finally found a parking spot and the ladies walked up the stone steps and through the massive wooden doors. "Just getting inside this house is a treat," Cleo whispered as they were met by a sophisticated lady with short blonde hair wearing a chic black suit.

"Please take your time looking around," she suggested as she handed each of them a small book. "Most items are listed in this booklet along with the prices. Feel free to ask me if you need any assistance."

Several other people meandered through the magnificent rooms that were filled with beautiful furniture, rugs, and fine pieces of art. Eleanor found her way to the library where she browsed happily among the books. Dede went immediately to the kitchen and discovered various serving dishes and lovely glassware. Pearl headed toward the bedrooms in search of name-brand clothing, and Josephine tagged along with Cleo, who inspected several paintings that hung on the walls. It didn't take long for Cleo to decide the paintings in this house were beyond her budget and the frames extremely costly, although beautiful.

"Let's check out the jewelry," Josephine suggested.

In one of the bedrooms they discovered a large jewelry closet set into the wall that was lined with an assortment of rings, earrings, necklaces, and bracelets. The jewels were divided into genuine gems and costume pieces. Cleo and Josephine tried on several rings and admired most of the pieces, but left without a purchase.

After some time, they found the other ladies gathered in the living room around an interesting statue of a naked man. His penis had been touched so many times the patina had rubbed away leaving it a bright golden color.

"Do you think this would look good in my office?" asked Dede, who as mayor of Waterton had just been given an office after several years working in a closet.

"You didn't tell me you were looking to decorate your new office," Pearl exclaimed. "I saw just the thing in the study. There's a beautiful pen and ink set in there that would look splendid on your desk."

Pearl and Dede scurried away to look at it while Cleo, Eleanor, and Josephine puzzled over the statue's function. "It says in the booklet that the statue was a gift from Italian friends," Josephine said. "It is supposed to bring good luck to those who rub his penis."

"That's disgusting," Eleanor began and looked up to see Cleo rubbing the golden appendage with delight.

Josephine and Eleanor quietly turned their backs as if they didn't know her and giggled as they followed Dede and Pearl into the study where Eleanor found a set of Russian dolls that she knew would delight her granddaughter, Addie.

While Dede debated on whether to purchase the silver and rosewood pen set, Eleanor also discovered a leather-bound first edition, first printing of *To Kill A Mockingbird*. It was from the Franklin Library and in near perfect condition. Individual books were not listed in the booklet so she took it quietly to the lady who'd greeted them at the door and asked the price.

"I'm not really sure," she paused, "Let's just say fifty dollars." Eleanor knew the book was worth at least five times that much and purchased it on the spot. Dede bought the pen set and Pearl left with several scarves and some Eileen Fisher clothing while Josephine and Cleo left with nothing.

"So sad, I guess rubbing that statue didn't bring me good luck," moaned Cleo as they drove away discussing where they would go for lunch.

"Look here," Pearl pointed to an estate sale sign merely blocks away from the one they just left. "Let's stop. Maybe Cleo will find some frames here. It's not as fancy as the other house."

Dede pulled over and in they went. Pearl was absolutely right that the house was not as fancy, but the items inside were both interesting and desirable. Cleo went immediately to several empty frames and paintings leaning against the wall and was amazed at the low prices. She quickly gathered them together to make what she thought was a great deal.

A few people wandered through the rooms, and a man who seemed to be in charge greeted them. "It's a going out of business sale," he explained when asked and hurried away before they could ask any more questions.

"It must be a very eclectic business," Pearl said, "I've seen a variety of items."

"I can't believe this price," Dede remarked as she held up a lovely sandwich plate. "I'm sure this is Fostoria and they only want two dollars for it."

"What do you think of this necklace?" asked Pearl holding up a string of brown beads.

"Those look like Buddhist prayer beads," Josephine said. "Sort of like your rosary, Dede."

"I believe it's called a Mala," Eleanor added.

Josephine took them from Pearl, "I feel a strange energy coming from them. I'm sure I'm supposed to take them with me."

"This is the strangest sale," Cleo noted. "Everything seems priced way under value. Look at this sideboard. They are asking seventy-five dollars when it is easily worth three or four hundred."

"Please don't tell me you want it," Dede said. "There's no room in the car for it."

"No, I'm just taking these pictures and frames, but if I needed a sideboard I'd be all over that." Cleo wandered off to check out the rest of the deals and buy her treasures.

By the time they finished, Dede had purchased the sandwich plate and several other pieces of glassware she didn't need as well as three garden gnomes. Pearl found a lovely engraved wooden box; Eleanor wore a new ring, and Josephine owned the Buddhist prayer beads. "That's what I call an estate sale!" Pearl was high on endorphins from shopping.

"I think there was something very suspicious about it. It was as if they were trying to get rid of those things in a hurry and they were perfectly good treasures. They certainly didn't know the worth of it all," Cleo worried. "What if it was all stolen?"

"That would be a shame. We wouldn't have to give it back though because there's no proof that we bought it. How would we ever know if it was stolen? The owners couldn't contact us," Pearl said.

"We didn't buy that much, just a few trinkets," Eleanor said.

"Right, but I do feel like we took advantage somehow," Josephine added. "It had too many different items for any one business."

"We're perfectly innocent. Stop fretting," Dede said as she drove down the road toward a restaurant called Karma where they enjoyed a delicious lunch of Indian cuisine.

By the time Eleanor got home the sun was setting over the glistening ocean in bright orange and yellow rays. Feathers greeted her by landing on her shoulder and pushing his parrot face against her cheek. She kicked off her shoes and poured herself a glass of zinfandel. They had eaten a late lunch and Eleanor wasn't hungry for dinner. It was entirely too quiet so she turned on the television and the next thing she knew the phone woke her from a deep sleep.

"Hello," she answered groggily.

"Ellie, it's Angus. Are you in bed already?"

"No, of course not." She glanced at the clock and was surprised at the lateness of the hour. "I think I fell asleep on the couch. The coffee group went on an excursion today. I guess I was more tired than I realized."

"I just called to check in."

"How's it going?"

"Good, it's all good. I think I'll be home in a few days." Angus didn't sound right. Eleanor wondered what he meant by good when it sounded otherwise.

"You've been gone longer than usual. You aren't planning to move there are you?" she asked, just a little afraid of the answer.

"No, I miss your cooking too much," he teased.

"What have you been doing up there all this time?" Eleanor suddenly felt like a prying busy body.

"Nothing much, a little fishing, some projects, and a lot of talking."

Eleanor thought he was being vague on purpose. There was a long, silent pause. "Michael's mother showed up this week," Angus admitted sheepishly.

"What does that mean?" Eleanor suddenly had a number of questions that begged to be answered. Who was this woman? Did Michael know her? Why was she there while Angus was visiting? Did Angus want to rekindle a relationship with her and piece together the kind of family he had always wanted?

"It's messy. I'm not sure it means anything." His words did nothing to reassure Eleanor, who was now sitting on the edge of the couch with her heart in her throat.

"Who is she, Angus?"

"She's a girl I used to know when I was in high school. Actually she was one of Fiona's friends." Fiona was Angus's older sister and the only family he claimed until he learned about Michael through a DNA testing kit Eleanor had given him for his birthday.

"What kind of relationship does she have with Michael? Did Fiona know that you had a son?"

"She doesn't have a relationship with Michael. She was in graduate school and moved away when she learned about the pregnancy. She gave him up for adoption and hasn't seen him since. Fiona hasn't seen her since then and she just learned about Michael the same way I did. It's very awkward."

"Indeed. How are you?"

"Tired, Eleanor, I'm just tired. I better go. I'll call you later." Angus hung up. He didn't say goodbye or I love you. He just hung up. Eleanor felt something eating at her heart and realized it was fear.

When Eleanor woke the next morning it took her an entire minute to get her bearings and remember the events of the day before. Angus was in Washington State visiting his newly found son and family. Michael had invited his biological mother to visit and she had come while Angus was there. This was a woman Angus had known when he was young, found attractive, and fathered a child with. Suddenly Eleanor needed to get out of bed and move. She found most of her problems could be solved with a long walk. Instead of getting the morning paper and completing the crossword puzzle with her coffee, Eleanor dressed for weather and left the house for a walk down her hill to the beach below.

The morning was clear but cold. As she strode by Angus's house she began to think logically about what was happening. She loved Angus and was certain he loved her too. He had told her often enough but she had held back those words. He had proposed marriage but she refused. He let her know many times how much her family meant to him and how he enjoyed the times they spent together and how much he loved her cooking. Now he had the possibility of a family of his own. She had to be happy for him. Everything was out of her hands because all the decisions were his to make. Eleanor sighed and walked a little faster, just to keep her heart beating.

On her way back home Eleanor stopped in at the local restaurant, Suzanna's, to warm up with a cup of coffee. A small group of older women known as the Do Nothings were seated at their usual table drinking coffee and chatting.

"Good morning, Eleanor," greeted Mattie May. "Sit down and join us."

"Please do," added Sibyl Wendt. "We've run out of things to talk about."

"Quite right and if you don't join us I'm afraid we'll have to talk about you," threatened Mavis Bench.

"Charming, I'm delighted to join you and avoid being the object of your gossip." Eleanor was fond of the older women. She slipped off her jacket and sat at their table.

"What's new?" Mattie asked.

"Where has Angus McBride gone?" asked Sibyl.

"Who bought Henry Ott's house?" asked Mavis.

"I didn't know anyone bought Henry's house," Eleanor admitted.

"Well the sign says SOLD, so someone must have bought it," Mattie stated.

"I've heard it's a family from the east coast. The man is supposedly an artist or something," Sibyl offered.

"I'm afraid I don't know anything about it," Eleanor repeated. The ladies appeared disappointed.

"Perhaps you should get out more, Eleanor," Mattie suggested.

"What about Angus? Surely you know where Angus has been. He hasn't made an appearance here in several weeks," Sibyl pried. "He hasn't moved has he?"

"No, he's visiting people in Washington. I'm sure he'll be home soon." Eleanor wasn't sure how much information Angus wanted anyone to know about his new family so she left it for him to share.

"I don't know, Eleanor, you don't have much to offer and things have been rather dull this winter," Mattie lamented.

"Is that a new ring?" Mavis spotted the sparkle of Eleanor's latest purchase like a crow that was drawn to shiny things and grabbed her hand to inspect it closely. "It's beautiful. Is it a ruby?"

"Did Angus give it to you?" Mattie asked. "It's huge!"

"I bought it for myself at an estate sale," Eleanor said. "I have no idea what it is, but I'm sure it's a simulated stone of some kind. It didn't cost much."

"Really," Mavis was doubtful. "It's certainly a beautiful gold setting and the stone looks authentic."

"I didn't know you were an expert on gems," Sibyl chided.

"I know quality when I see it," huffed Mavis. "You should have it appraised. You may have stumbled onto a real steal."

"Thank you, I think I will. I'd like to know what kind of stone it is too," Eleanor said.

The ladies sipped their coffee and chatted about the weather and other mundane things until Eleanor decided it was time to go home. Her curiosity piqued, she walked past her place and then took a detour down the lane that led to Henry Ott's house. Long before she reached it she could see the moving van parked outside. Someone not only had purchased Henry's house, but they were moving in that very day.

As she drew closer she could see it was only the moving people and there was no sign of the new owners. Eleanor turned around and headed home.

Several days passed with no word from Angus. Eleanor refused to call him, reasoning that he was most likely off somewhere enjoying himself, getting to know his son and she didn't want to interfere. She decided it was time to invite some people over for dinner. The weather had been foul and Eleanor needed some color in her life. Planning a dinner party was just the thing. She pored over recipes and made some phone calls, made lists, and planned to drive into Waterton to shop, but before she could leave, Feathers flew through the house warning of intruders as the doorbell rang. Eleanor was surprised to see her 10-year-old friend Bootsy Greenwood standing on the porch wearing a raincoat and sporting a backpack.

"Bootsy, what a pleasant surprise!" Eleanor exclaimed as she looked for Bootsy's parents, but found no one else outside. "Please come in."

"I hope I'm not being a nuisance, Eleanor, but I just had to get away," Bootsy explained. She dropped her backpack on the floor and slipped off her coat.

"How did you get here, dear?" Eleanor asked as she found a spot for Bootsy's things.

"I took the bus and then a nice man gave me a ride to your house. He said he was coming this way and it was no bother."

"Oh, Bootsy, was he a stranger?"

"He was at first, but I think we're friends now. Remember when we first met, you said strangers were just friends you hadn't met yet."

"I see." Eleanor didn't want to lecture the girl about the dangers of hitchhiking. She would leave that to her mother. "Are you hungry? I might have some cookies and milk in the kitchen."

"Absolutely starving," Bootsy admitted as she watched Eleanor make a sandwich to preface the cookies.

"These are delicious," she said as she dipped her cookie in her milk and daintily dabbed her mouth to wipe the crumbs away.

"Is there no school today, Bootsy?" Eleanor prodded.

Bootsy gazed into her milk to avoid looking at Eleanor, "I skipped school and I've run away from home."

"So your mother and father have no idea that you are here?"

"That's right," Bootsy admitted.

"Do you want to tell me about it?" Eleanor asked.

"I'm sure they won't miss me. They're always so busy they never know what I'm doing or where I am. I don't think they even care." A tear rolled slowly down Bootsy's cheek.

"I'm sure it must feel that way sometimes, but I don't believe your parents don't love or care about you. They'll be sick with worry when you don't come home from school. Why don't I call them before they alert the police and call out a search party?" Eleanor knew she needed to tread carefully. She didn't want to lose Bootsy's trust or alienate her parents.

"I'd rather just stay here with you, Eleanor. Ever since Granny Scattergoods died I've missed Sand Beach, and then when Walter died, you stopped visiting Rosewood Manor and I've missed you too."

"I agree that a visit would be lovely. I've missed you as well," Eleanor soothed, "but you should be in school. Perhaps

I can convince your parents to let you visit during spring break. You could spend Easter with us. Addie and Elise are very fond of you.”

Bootsy smiled and her entire countenance changed. “I would love that! I’m sure we don’t have any plans for Easter.”

“I’ll call your mother right now and set it up.” Eleanor picked up the phone while Bootsy continued to eat her cookies.

Judy Greenwood was a busy woman. Her work consumed her and Bootsy was right about the time her parents spent with her. Even when they were together as a family they were not present for their daughter. Phones, tablets, and computers took center stage. Fortunately Eleanor was able to get through to Judy. She wasn’t happy and insisted Eleanor put Bootsy directly on the bus back home, but she did consent to a visit during Easter which helped soften the blow. Eleanor wondered what the consequences of running away would be for Bootsy. If there were none, would Bootsy consider this to be more proof that they didn’t care?

“It’s all set, but I have to put you back on the bus, Bootsy. I promise to call and plan a visit for later.” Eleanor was surprised that Bootsy took it so well. Perhaps the child just needed something to look forward to. As they drove into Waterton, Eleanor instructed Bootsy about listening to her instincts when meeting strangers. Then they sang along at the top of their lungs when Lady Gaga’s *Bad Romance* came on the radio.

The day before the party Eleanor whipped up a mocha chocolate chip cheesecake and put it in the refrigerator to chill, and then left for a walk east of her house along the lane that led to Henry Ott's place. The day was finally clear but still held a chill from the wind that blew in from the north. Spring was not yet here. As she approached Henry's house, she could see the new owner outside replacing a lightbulb on the porch. He was engrossed in his task and didn't notice the older woman passing, which gave Eleanor an opportunity to study him unaware. As clichéd as it sounded, tall, dark, and handsome in a brooding sort of way was the only way she could think to describe him. His hooded eyes were framed by angry looking brows, but as he completed his task and turned to see Eleanor his face transformed with a brilliant smile. Eleanor was startled by the quick change and stopped in her tracks.

"Hello," she greeted as she walked toward him. "Welcome to Sand Beach. I'm your neighbor, Eleanor Penrose."

"It's nice to meet you, Eleanor Penrose," he said as he closed the gap between them. "I'm Victor Gaines. You are the first neighbor to show. I suppose it's the foul weather that keeps most of the others away."

"I'm sure you're right. The people here are very friendly most of the time," she said.

"And where does the lovely Eleanor Penrose live exactly? Just in case I need to borrow a cup of sugar or something." His eyes twinkled as he flirted shamelessly with her.

Before Eleanor could answer, the door opened and a tall thin woman with blonde hair stepped out of the house just as a gust of wind caught the door and slammed it against the outside wall.

"Victor, invite her inside before she blows away," she ordered.

"Please come inside and meet my wife. I'm afraid she gets extremely jealous when she sees me talking to other women," he whispered, "especially beautiful ones."

Eleanor smiled as she entered the house. It was impossible to resist his charming demeanor even when she knew it was all in jest.

The interior of the house was just as Eleanor remembered it. The beautiful hardwood floors, the vaulted ceilings, and the wall of windows that framed the panoramic ocean view were the same as Henry Ott had left them. Boxes filled most of the rooms and the furniture had not yet found a permanent home.

"This is my wife, Lola." Victor put his arm around her shoulders. "This is our new neighbor, Eleanor Penrose."

"Really! Are you the poet Eleanor Penrose?" Lola asked. "I've read several of your poems and just love them. I'm so excited to meet you. Please excuse our mess. We're still putting things in order."

"Forgive me Eleanor. I had no idea I was in the company of greatness," Victor apologized.

"I have a copy of your latest book here somewhere. I'd love it if you'd sign it for me," Lola said. "I simply adore cats and think the poem 'Elsie' is my favorite. I can recite it from memory.

Elsie, now it's plain to me
You're not what you seem to be.
It took so long for me to see
(Plus a course in sexuality)
What was there so obviously
Beneath your tail hanging free
In a furry clump of secrecy . . .
Hidden masculinity!
We love you just the same L.C."

"Bravo," Victor laughed, clapping his hands while Lola took an elaborate bow.

"Of course." Eleanor blushed embarrassed by their praise. "I'd be delighted to sign your book anytime. I know how difficult moving can be, let alone cooking in a kitchen still in boxes. Would you like to come to dinner tomorrow night? I've invited a few friends over and it would give you a chance to meet people from the area."

"That would be lovely." Lola was obviously pleased.

"Fabulous," Victor said, "I shall wear my new blue jeans and bring a bottle of expensive wine."

"See you tomorrow at six then." Eleanor was quite pleased with the encounter as she waved goodbye and continued on her way into the oncoming storm.

Eleanor spent most of the afternoon prepping for her dinner party. She decided to go with a shrimp theme. The appetizers had been marinating overnight in the refrigerator next to the cheesecake. The table was set with her lovely white and green china, the crystal wine glasses sparkled, and the silver caught the light from the winter sun that would be replaced by candlelight this evening. Everything was ready, including the flowers that adorned several tables throughout her house. She checked the time and hurried to get herself ready before her guests arrived.

Nothing too fancy for a casual dinner with friends, Eleanor thought as she selected a pair of black slacks and a black sweater with white trim. She quickly ran a comb through her silvery hair and admired the way it contrasted with the black to give her a sophisticated look. When the doorbell rang and Feathers began his usual alert that intruders were here, Eleanor was ready.

Amy and Taylor arrived early at Eleanor's request to help greet guests and mix drinks. Eleanor thought it wise to invite her daughter and son-in-law to make the new neighbors feel more at ease with others their age. Most of Eleanor's friends were old enough to be their parents. Amy immediately set up a bar area and Taylor migrated to the baby grand piano and graced them with his musical gifts while Eleanor put the finishing touches on her shrimp curry Leone.

When the guests arrived, candles were lit, wine was poured, and a lovely aroma filled the house. Most of the guests were members of the coffee group and their husbands, along with Eleanor's nearest neighbors, Nancy and Dennis Wilson. The new neighbors were the last to arrive and were greeted with surprise by Amy who recognized Lola from her workout at the YMCA.

"Lola, I'm so happy to see you again." Amy greeted the couple at the door and took Lola's coat. "I had no idea you were the new neighbors my Mom invited to dinner. She never mentioned you by name."

"I brought a copy of your mother's book to sign," Lola said. "I had no idea your mother was my favorite poet!"

Victor stood holding his bottle of wine while his dark eyes took in all there was of Amy Ash. It would have embarrassed her if she had noticed, but she was totally oblivious. "This is my husband, Victor." Lola introduced the tall man next to her. "Amy and I met at a spin class at the Y."

"Lovely," he said as he took Amy's hand and leered mischievously. "I think I may have to start working out at the Y."

"Mom is mingling, let me get you drinks and introduce you to the other guests." Amy shook off the flirtation easily and made the newcomers as welcome as possible.

There was easy conversation with the soft strains of Taylor's rendition of Pachelbel's Canon in D in the background. Everyone seemed to be enjoying themselves.

"Eleanor, you have to give me the recipe for these delicious hors d'oeuvres," Lola said as she popped another marinated shrimp in her mouth.

"Good luck with that," Cleo said, "Eleanor doesn't share."

"It's the shrimp caper mystery," Eleanor smiled, "and the mystery is the recipe."

"So you cook and write poetry? How remarkable! Maybe you could give Lola cooking lessons." Victor gave Lola a squeeze as if to say he was only joking but the look she gave him in return said it wasn't funny.

"Would you please sign my copy of your book, Eleanor?" Lola asked.

"I'd love to." Eleanor got a pen and signed the book with a flourish while Victor secretly admired the red ring on her finger as if it were an old flame.

"And what do you do, Victor?" Taylor rose from the piano and joined the conversation.

"I'm in the import-export business." Victor eyed Taylor suspiciously.

"This is my husband, Taylor," Amy added quickly, wondering if Victor thought he might be a paid performer.

The two men shook hands. "You're pretty good on the keyboard. What is this, a Bosendorfer?" Victor sat down at the piano and began to play Flight of the Bumblebee with a mad intensity.

Everyone stopped talking and looked at the man at the piano as he entertained them with his artful performance. When he finished they all clapped wildly as he stood and took a flamboyant bow, then cocked his head and gave Amy a wink.

"Show off," whispered Taylor under his breath.

"A man of many talents, I gather," said Josephine who always watched and missed little. Victor smiled wickedly at Josephine. It seemed he was an equal opportunity womanizer and was not deterred by age.

"I do what I can with what I have," he said seductively.

"It seems as though you've been given quite a lot." Josephine's gaze sized him up and down. She was no stranger to men of his ilk. "Just be sure you don't use it in the wrong places."

"Have you met my dear friend, Josephine?" Eleanor interrupted. "Josephine, this is Victor Gaines, my new neighbor. The stunning blonde is his wife, Lola."

"My pleasure," Victor cooed.

"Yes, I was just remarking on his . . . gifts," Josephine admitted.

"And this is Cleo, a talented artist who is giving a show of her paintings next week at the Bayside Art Center. You should come." Eleanor introduced Cleo who fidgeted uncomfortably under the dark eyes of Victor Gaines.

"I just putter with paint," she murmured. "Sometimes I get lucky."

"I'd love to see your work. I'll certainly be there if you tell me when and where. I do lots of buying and selling of art pieces in my business. Believe me when I say I have clients who love to discover new talent." Victor took down the pertinent information and left Cleo glowing as she went off to share the information with her husband Steve.

"Will you be opening a business in Waterton?" asked Dede, who had overheard the other introductions.

"Dede is the mayor of Waterton and Mark is her husband," Eleanor added.

"Lovely to meet you both." Victor shook hands with Mark and drew Dede's hand to his lips. "I'll be working mostly from home, but Lola is planning some enterprise. She isn't one to sit on her hands and we are both eager to make our mark on your quaint little town."

Dede's brow rose. "I'll be looking forward to that." She was not usually one to be taken in by a suave and charming demeanor.

The doorbell rang and Eleanor excused herself as Dede and Victor continued their conversation. When Eleanor saw Angus on her doorstep it was all she could do to stop from throwing herself into his arms, but because she was Eleanor, she remained poised and in control. Angus smiled broadly showing his deep dimples and took in the crowd of partiers that filled the house.

"Am I interrupting something?" he asked as he pulled Eleanor close and planted a kiss near her ear.

"I wasn't sure when you were coming home," Eleanor said. "It's just a few friends. Come in. You're just in time for dinner."

"I'm sorry I haven't called, but things got weird. I'll fill you in later." He cut his comments short as Amy approached.

"Welcome Angus, would you like a drink?" she offered.

"Why would such a smart girl ask such a silly question?" Angus looked at her from under his lowered brows. Without missing a beat Amy brought out Angus' signature Crown Royal on ice from behind her back.

"I saw you coming from the window," she quipped as she walked away.

"I always liked that girl." Angus took a sip from the glass and sighed.

"We have some new neighbors here tonight that you might like to meet." Eleanor led Angus over to Victor and Lola who were now talking to Pearl about her mosaic studio.

"I'm a big supporter of the arts," Victor said, "I'm planning to attend Cleo's exhibit as well."

"Excuse me, Victor, this is Angus McBride. He lives in the house just down the lane. Angus, this is Victor and his wife, Lola. They recently moved into Henry Ott's house."

They all shook hands and smiled at each other the way people do who are just meeting. Angus was more curious to know about them than they were to learn about an old man. Eleanor excused herself to attend to the dinner while Angus continued to study the new neighbors.

"What is it that brings you two to Sand Beach?" he asked.

"It's absolutely beautiful here," Lola responded. "Who wouldn't want to wake up to this view every day?"

"True enough. What's your line of work?" Angus continued.

"I'm in the import-export business." Victor offered little other information but kept looking over Angus's shoulder as if to find a better looking conversationalist, or at least one of the opposite sex.

There was an uncomfortable pause and Lola filled it in with unsolicited information. "We used to live in Seattle but thought we might like to try small town living for a while. We've vacationed here before and found it so inviting. Victor can work from just about any place and I'd like to open a little shop of some kind."

"I just left Seattle. My son lives there," Angus offered and noticed Victor's interest return.

"Before that we lived in New York City. I guess we're gradually working our way to smaller and smaller towns," Lola continued.

"I'm sure you're going to enjoy it here. There's a lot to do if you like outdoor activities. Do you fish?" Angus asked.

"I'd like to try more of it. I did a little in Seattle and some while we were here staying with friends, but can't claim to be an expert," Victor admitted.

"I love hiking and it looks like there are ample trails to explore," Lola added as she put her slender fingers on Angus's arm and flashed her round dolphin-like teeth in a sexy smile. "You look like someone who keeps fit. You must work out."

Angus concealed his shock at her blatant flirtation in full view of her husband and simply smiled and raised his bushy eyebrows in amusement.

"I think Eleanor is signaling dinner is ready," he said and walked toward the dining room with Lola still on his arm. They sat at the table and dished up family style.

"If I wasn't already married I would ask you to marry me, Eleanor, just so I could eat your cooking every day," Victor teased.

"You wouldn't be the first to ask," Angus said.

"What is it we are eating exactly?" asked Lola.

"Don't bother asking for the recipe," Josephine informed them. "Eleanor will only give you the name of it."

"Shrimp curry Leone, is the name," Eleanor said. "I'm glad you like it, Lola. I forgot to ask if you were vegan or had food allergies."

"No, we eat anything and everything," Victor said, "but we don't always enjoy it. I hope we'll be invited back."

"Eleanor is very generous with her dinner invitations," Dede added.

"Just don't bore her with talk of politics or religion," Cleo said.

"Right, at this table there is only room for knock-knock jokes and laughter," Taylor said.

"Knock, knock" Victor whispered to Amy.

"Who's there?" Amy said.

Victor whispered back a lewd and inappropriate response.

Amy didn't laugh and her face turned a bright red while Victor chuckled slyly. Fortunately no one else seemed to hear the crude joke. There were multiple conversations going on at the same time.

"What are you, twelve? That's not the kind of joke we tell at this table," Amy retorted.

"Maybe it wasn't a joke," Victor answered. "Taylor seems to like Lola, don't you like me?"

Amy glanced down the table at Taylor who was engaged in an animated conversation with Angus and Lola. She didn't see anything awry. "Taylor isn't like that," she hissed.

"All men are like that," he said absently as he focused once more on his dinner. "Lola and I have an open marriage. Give it some thought. It might be just what you need to refresh a stale marriage."

"Knock, knock," Amy began.

"Who's there?" Victor asked.

"Norma Lee."

"Norma Lee who?"

"Normally I don't consort with crude men like you." Amy quipped without a trace of humor.

Victor just smiled. Amy was so full of bile she couldn't finish her meal. When she met Lola at the YMCA earlier she thought they might be FUDS, friends under development, but now she couldn't wait to distance herself from them as soon as possible. If she could have left the table to wash his remarks off she would have done so.

The other guests continued to eat, drink, and laugh at what Amy assumed were honestly funny jokes and stories, but for her the night was sullied.

After the last guest left, Angus poured another drink and sat on the couch with Eleanor. "I thought they would never go," he said placing his arm around her and holding her close.

"I enjoyed it," Eleanor said as she snuggled into his embrace. "What did you think of the new neighbors?"

"Too early to tell." He didn't want to explain to Eleanor what he suspected after the flirtatious way Lola had behaved first with him and then with Taylor. After years as a homicide detective he had developed a nose for trouble and smelled something fishy about the couple.

"I think they are rather interesting and funny," Eleanor said. "He claims to be a Reformed Druid."

"A Druid?" Angus repeated. "Aren't they dead?"

"I guess not." Eleanor sat up and looked at Angus. "Tell me about your visit with Michael."

Angus sighed. It wasn't so much that he didn't want to tell her as much as he was just weary of it all. "I don't know . . . families are messy. For the longest time I wanted nothing more than to belong to a family like yours. You and Walter did all the hard work raising your children to be the people they are. You did a great job. Now I find a son who was conceived when I was a kid in high school. He was raised by strangers. Heck I wonder what kind of man he would be if I had been a real father to him."

"Are you disappointed in him, Angus?"

"Yes and no. He seems like a good man. He served for years as a fireman, married, and raised three kids. He takes fatherhood seriously and enjoys his grandchildren, but there's something not right there."

"What do you mean?"

"He confided in me that he's having an affair. I met his wife. She's pretty, smart, and loves him, so I don't understand what he's doing. I know it's a little late for me to be giving him fatherly advice, but I don't think what he's doing is right and I told him so."

"Was he angry?"

"No, I think deep down he knows it's a betrayal and not worthy of him, but he'll have to sort that out for himself."

"What about his mother? Do you want to talk about her?" Eleanor was beside herself with curiosity but didn't want to seem too eager.

"I don't want to but I think I need to. There's something disturbing about her. I just don't know what it is. I was hoping Josephine could help me figure it out since she's a therapist."

"What happened?"

"She knocked on the door. I opened it and all hell broke loose. Her name was Virginia Storm when I met her. She was getting her doctorate at UCLA and came home with Fiona. Heck I was just a kid—dumb and inexperienced—flattered that an older college woman would be interested in me. Virginia only stayed a few days, but she was sexually aggressive. Today I'd describe her as predatory. I never saw her again until she turned up at Michael's place.

"He said he told her I was visiting and she should come another time but she showed up anyway. I didn't recognize her of course. She must be pushing eighty years old, but despite that fact she was still sexually aggressive and what was flattering and provocative fifty-six years ago was just sad and slightly depraved. Honestly Ellie, everything about her visit left me feeling soiled, guilty, and embarrassed," Angus admitted.

"Angus, what she did to you then was rape. You were underage and she was old enough to know better," Eleanor soothed.

"Well, it didn't feel like rape to me then and I had no idea I created a life. The fact that Michael was born out of that and I just went on my merry way with no responsibility whatsoever is unacceptable to me." Angus lowered his head.

"Your young brain wasn't fully developed and Virginia didn't let you know, so you have no reason to beat yourself up over this. If you knew, I'm sure you would have acted responsibly," Eleanor reasoned as she rubbed his back. She hated seeing him so upset over something that happened so long ago.

"I was cheated out of all those years, Ellie. I can't help but wonder how things might have been if I'd known him when he was a boy."

"I'm sure you would have been a wonderful father, but maybe not the greatest at seventeen. Michael seems to have done alright with his adopted parents. He chose a profession that helps people. Being a fireman shows he's a caring person. You can be a friend to him now."

"It may take some time to develop that kind of friendship especially now that Virginia has insinuated herself into the picture."

"What do you mean?"

"She seems to think there's a place for her in his life, but Michael wasn't so sure. I can't begin to tell you what being around her is like. She's bossy and controlling and when she doesn't get her way she's downright unpleasant," Angus frowned.

"So it was just a visit wasn't it? Where does she live?" Eleanor asked.

"That's part of the problem. She stayed at a hotel nearby but kept talking about moving from Los Angeles to Seattle to be near her family. She's been married several times but doesn't have any other children or meaningful relationships and was over the moon to find Michael. I guess she's lonely, but she talked about herself nonstop, and would just come over unannounced and uninvited. We all felt the same about her visits and even hid once and refused to answer the door.

"It was awful . . . she pounded on the door and yelled profanities for ten minutes before she gave up. That's not right. I felt bad for Michael and his wife. Once, she found the key they hid under the doormat and let herself into their house.

When they came home she was sitting in their living room watching TV and drinking gin, but she'd snooped through their things and actually taken photos out of frames. After that they moved the key. The woman has no boundaries. What if she never leaves them alone?"

"Was she still there when you left?" Eleanor asked.

"I'm afraid so. I couldn't stay any longer and didn't feel it was my place to tell her to leave him alone. We talked about ways to handle it, including a restraining order if things didn't settle down. I'm not sure Michael has the heart to tell her to get lost, but it was wearing on his entire family. I hope he doesn't use this as an excuse to leave his wife."

"Did he tell you he wanted to leave her?" Eleanor prodded.

"I don't know. He seems conflicted. One day he'd be ready to leave her and then the next day he was in love with her again. Is it possible to love two women at the same time?" Angus asked. "I really didn't feel comfortable giving him marriage advice since I'm not exactly an expert in that area."

"But you know how to be a decent human being, Angus. I'm sure you could talk with him about that and the consequences of leaving a long-term relationship for a fling versus leaving a loveless marriage for something more meaningful," Eleanor reasoned. "He is a grown man you know."

"You're right, Ellie. I'm really glad to be here with you and away from all that drama." Angus let out a sigh and stood up, reluctant to leave. He took her hand and kissed it. The reflected glow from the red ring lit his eye giving him a devilish look. "I'd better go home while I still can."

The next morning Eleanor woke to a bright sunny day and decided to take advantage of the opening to walk the beach. Angus's house looked quiet and she determined he must be exhausted from his visit and the drama of family and was sleeping late. She walked to the village and down the rocky trail that led to the ocean whose waves rolled in steadily and drove the foam up against the sandy shore. The gulls circled overhead singing their discordant tune while Eleanor drew the salty air into her lungs and felt happy to be alive. No one else was on the beach this early. The air was still but held a chill that she easily dispelled by walking quickly along the wet sand.

In her mind she rehashed the dinner party, relishing the compliments about her cooking and the warmth of friendship. Thoughts of Angus and his new relationship with his son came unbidden and she worried about the time he would spend away from her, and then hated herself for her selfishness. She tried to solve the problem of the unwanted biological mother but decided that was a problem that would solve itself over time and distance. She had no real worries.

She stopped to watch a flock of brown pelicans foraging over the ocean near the shore. Amazed by their large size and massive bills, Eleanor stood admiring their brown plumage. They seemed to have only one focus: a school of small fish. There were no family problems for them, no financial woes or friendship issues, but she would be foolish to envy them. They had other worries. Just getting enough to eat was a major concern and one she had never had. She continued on and before she knew it she had walked her usual course and stopped in at Suzanna's for a cup of coffee.

The Do Nothings sat at their usual table but there was a new addition to the group. "Eleanor, pull up a chair and talk to us. We have a new member to our group," Mattie said.

Eleanor did as she was told. "Eleanor Penrose, this is Edwina Potts. She and her husband bought the little cottage at the end of Ocean Avenue." Mattie smiled as she welcomed Eleanor to the table.

"I'm happy to meet you, Edwina. Welcome to Sand Beach. How do you like it so far?" Eleanor asked.

The petite white-haired lady adjusted her glasses, gave Eleanor the once over and smiled as she spoke, "It is so beautiful here I don't know why it took us so long to find this paradise. And these lovely ladies have welcomed me so kindly. I can't believe my good luck."

"We found her wandering around the village. I think she was lost, so we invited her to have coffee and now we can't get rid of her," teased Mavis. They all laughed. It seemed that Edwina did not take offense easily and fit right in with the others.

"Let's hear your story then," prodded Eleanor.

"Nothing to tell, just me and Potsy, retired to a quiet coastal town." Edwina would not be coaxed to talk about herself.

"What do you know, Eleanor?" asked Sybil. "Are you and Angus getting married?"

Eleanor rolled her eyes, "I've met the new couple that bought Henry Ott's house."

"Oh, so tell us everything," ordered Mattie.

"He's dark, handsome, and a Reformed Druid and she's tall, blonde, and beautiful. They both seem very pleasant. He plays the piano even better than Taylor and she's planning to open a shop in Waterton," Eleanor reported.

"How old are they?" asked Mavis.

"Not sure exactly. Younger than us and older than Amy and Taylor. Maybe late forties."

"What does he do? I think I saw an expensive looking car outside their house. He must make a good living," Sybil noted.

"I think he said something about the import-export business." Eleanor realized she didn't really know much about them.

"Do they have children?" asked Mavis.

"I don't know. I haven't seen any and they didn't mention them. I'm sure we'll find out more about them as time goes on," Eleanor said.

"What is a Reformed Druid, dear?" asked Edwina.

"I believe it's a pagan," Sybil answered.

"Aren't they the religious group who built Stonehenge?" asked Mattie.

"Those were the Druids," corrected Eleanor, "Reformed Druids are a new thing created by a group of academics who were required to attend religious services at their university. I don't remember which one, but it was a form of humorous resistance. They called themselves Reformed Druids and held their own religious services somewhere, probably in a field, and that must have fulfilled the requirement. I think the university reversed their mandate after that."

"How clever! Does this mean we shall see the dark man dancing naked in the moonlight?" asked Mattie.

"I hope not," said Sybil.

"Speak for yourself," said Mavis.

They laughed together as a woman entered the restaurant and glared malevolently at them before taking a table by the window overlooking the ocean. "Yikes, who is that?" asked Edwina.

"She must be a tourist. I've never seen her before," answered Mattie as she continued to stare at the older woman with platinum dyed hair who sported a mink coat and high heels.

"Certainly doesn't fit in here," said Mavis who sat comfortably in her knit pants and sweatshirt.

"I hope she doesn't plan on staying," said Sybil. "We don't need any more grumpy people here. Mattie is enough."

"I need to go. It was a pleasure to meet you, Edwina." Eleanor rose from the table and smiled as she left but couldn't shake the feeling that she had encountered something evil as she walked up the hill to her home.

Eleanor kicked off her sandy shoes on the porch and put on the kettle to make a cup of tea as Feathers flew into the kitchen to keep her company. Armed with tea and a cookie, she sat at her desk and picked up her pen.

Mother Moon
You shine with a reflected light
Cool white
Against the indigo night
Humble beacon
You take no glory for your glow
Illuminating the darkness here below
You change your face with every day
Waning and waxing
And yet you stay the same

Complete
You are full and whole through every phase
Nighttime goddess
Bless us with your slivery gaze
So we may see in darkness light
And never fear the demons of the night.

There was an almost full moon that lit the clear sky that night, but Eleanor didn't see any naked men dancing in the moonlight. If someone could have asked the moon what it saw, they might have heard it whisper, "Murder."

Dede bustled into the Boat House with an important tale to tell. The other members of the coffee group sat at their usual table discussing the new item on the menu—chocolate mousse pancakes.

"You'll never guess what happened last night," Dede interrupted. The others stopped mid-sentence and gave her their undivided attention. "A body was found in one of the swales along the construction site down town."

"Oh no, who was it?" asked Pearl.

"It was Gloria Vandorff."

"Who is Gloria Vandorff?" asked Cleo who seldom remembered anyone.

"Gloria Vandorff was a real estate agent. She and her husband, Will handled most of the sales in Sand Beach," Eleanor said.

"Right, I do remember her. Wasn't she tall and attractive?" asked Cleo.

"What happened to her?" asked Josephine.

"I can't say for sure but I think it was a hit and run. No one seems to have seen a thing," Dede said.

"It seems to me that Gloria Vandorff was the subject of some scandal. What was that?" Pearl asked.

"Wasn't she having an affair with someone's husband?" asked Cleo.

"That's right. Everyone said she was taking 'organ lessons' from the music teacher at the high school," Dede chuckled.

"Maybe his wife got tired of the lessons and wanted her 'organ' back," suggested Cleo. "That could be a motive for murder."

"This isn't anything to joke about. The poor woman is dead," Josephine scolded. Silence descended on the group as they looked guiltily into their coffee cups.

"The Do Nothings have added a new member to their group," Eleanor finally spoke to change the subject. "Her name is Edwina Potts."

"Fascinating," mumbled Cleo. "What does she do? Is she very old? Does she drive? Maybe she ran over Gloria."

"She and her husband bought the yellow cottage at the end of Ocean Avenue," Eleanor continued. "She didn't say much about herself, but I gather they are retired."

"I wonder if they bought that house from Gloria Vandorff," Cleo wouldn't let it go.

"I'm sure they did," Dede said. "She sold Victor and Lola Gaines their house too, but I don't think there is evidence of foul play, at least not as far as I know."

"Did you know her, Josephine?" Pearl asked.

"No, but I don't see any good coming from gossiping about the dead," Josephine said. There was an uncomfortable pause.

"Angus told me about the mother of his son. Evidently she is a very difficult person and caused a lot of drama while he was visiting," Eleanor said, once again changing the topic.

"Wait, wait, wait," Pearl said, "There is a mother involved? When did this happen?"

"Probably sixty years ago," Cleo remarked.

"You mean Angus spent time with this woman while he was visiting Michael?" Josephine asked. "How do you feel about that, Eleanor?"

"I'm okay with it. Angus doesn't seem to have any feelings for her other than disgust. He said she was bossy and controlling. She came uninvited knowing Angus was there even when Michael told her not to come." Eleanor continued. "I'm sure he wants to talk to you about it, Josephine, because he thinks she might be mentally unstable."

"Did he tell you anything else?" Josephine asked.

"She's been married several times but doesn't have any lasting relationships or children. Angus thinks she wants to move to Seattle to be near Michael, but Michael isn't sure he wants her in his life. She acted so bad they actually hid when she turned up uninvited one evening and they wouldn't let her in the house." Eleanor tried to remember other details. "He said he opened the door and all hell broke loose, so it sounds like she's a drama queen."

"Sounds like a borderline personality disorder," Josephine said thoughtfully.

"Is that serious?" asked Dede.

"It could be. Remember Glen Close in *Fatal Attraction*? She stalked Michael Douglas, boiled their pet bunny, and then tried to kill his wife. Let's hope she stays away from Angus," Josephine cautioned.

The ladies ate their pancakes and drank their coffee in a subdued manner. Each trying hard not to think about what they knew of the now deceased Gloria Vandorff or the menace that was the mother of Angus's son.

"I have to go." Cleo stood up and put on her coat. "My art exhibition is next week and I still have a great deal to do. I'll see you later." It wasn't long before the others left too.

It was Friday night and Eleanor planned a special evening with Angus. She had shopped for his favorite dishes for dinner and knew he would enjoy an action movie. The table was set, the dinner was ready, and the apple pie was cooling. Eleanor made a last minute check in the mirror to make sure things were in order, plucked a few chin hairs, and poured a class of red wine. Feathers flew to her shoulder and cooed in her ear but when the doorbell rang he sounded the alert, "Intruders, intruders."

Eleanor opened the door and Angus entered with a beautiful bouquet of pink lilies and a box of See's chocolates.

"I occurred to me, that I missed Valentine's Day," he said.

"Lovely." Eleanor gave him a thank you kiss on the cheek. "Help yourself to a drink while I find these beauties a home."

"It smells delicious," Angus complimented. "I can't begin to tell you how good it is to be back. I never seemed to get enough to eat there and I'm starving."

"Let's eat then." Eleanor returned and plated the London broil with buttered potatoes and caramelized zucchini and mushrooms. "Didn't Michael feed you?"

"He's not much of a cook and, unfortunately, neither is his wife. Mostly we ate from the deli down the street. I took them out a few times but I don't think either of them likes food."

"Does Michael's wife have a name?" Eleanor asked.

"Angela. Her name is Angela and she is a sweetheart, just not one who cooks. Ellie, this meat is tender and full of flavor. I'm not asking how you do it I'm just saying I think you are a food magician."

Several minutes passed as Angus ate and sighed with satisfaction. Eleanor watched him and took her pleasure in his. Every now and then he would smile, revealing his dimples and Eleanor's heart would skip a beat. "So what do you know about Gloria Vandorff's death?" she asked innocently.

Angus's smile disappeared as he lowered his head and rested his chin on his chest. How did she do it? Once again he began to doubt that the reason for her dinner invitation was personal and only an attempt to gain information about a murder investigation. Angus was a man with his own demons. He looked at her under his bushy brows and asked, "What do you know?"

"Nothing . . . is there something to know? I just heard this morning that she was the victim of a hit and run. Is there more?"

"You know there's more. Don't play innocent with me," he cautioned.

"How would I possibly know more?"

"I don't know how you know, any more than I know how you make food taste so damn delicious." Angus put his knife and fork down and glared at Eleanor. "I just know you have a way of getting involved with problems that are none of your concern."

Eleanor was shocked by his response. "I really don't know anything, Angus. I was just making conversation." Eleanor's hurt expression cut Angus to the quick.

"I'm sorry, Ellie, I must be suffering from too much family drama. Virginia always had an angle and now I'm looking for yours." Angus shook his head as if to clear it of a nasty vision.

"Was she really that bad?"

"Worse." He began to eat again.

"Well she's not here so you can just put her out of your mind and relax."

"That's just it. Michael called and said he told her to go back to hell where she came from. He's afraid she might come looking for me."

"Does she know where you live?"

"Yes, I'm afraid I let it slip before I realized what she was. I can only hope she didn't remember what I said about the lovely village of Sand Beach on the Oregon coast and the great fishing I enjoy here." Eleanor took another bite of meat and chewed slowly as she thought about Angus's nightmare.

How easy it was for her to surround herself with people of good character! Walter and she had never had friends who cheated or lied. They were always pleasant and fun. Maybe they didn't know everyone's darkest secrets or if they had committed serious crimes against humanity. Their closest friends were those who shared their values as well as their hospitality. Angus's past was different. By loving him, had she opened the door to hell?

"Are you ready for pie?" she asked.

"I think I'll wait until after the movie. My stomach must have shrunk." Together they cleared the table, cleaned up the dishes, and then settled in to watch a movie.

"Ellie, you are the only person I know who thinks *The Princess Bride* is an action flick," Angus commented as he put his arm around her. He didn't really care what movie they watched. He only cared that Eleanor was there beside him.

"When you live alone you have to be careful not to watch scary movies," Eleanor said. "They have a way of coming back to haunt you when you're alone in the dark."

"You don't have to live alone you know," Angus said but knew better than to expect a response. When the movie was over they feasted on apple pie and vanilla bean ice cream. "I guess I'd better be going. Do you want to walk with me tomorrow?" he asked as he put on his coat.

"Sure, I'll stop by on my way down the hill."

"As you wish," he mimicked the dread pirate Roberts. Angus gave Eleanor a deep kiss and looked into her eyes as he said, "There's no way it was a hit and run. She died from severe blunt trauma to the head, but there wasn't enough blood on the scene. Gloria Vandorff was murdered and her body was dumped in the swale."

Eleanor had missed Angus. She woke early and was eager to see him again but completed her daily rituals of coffee, newspaper, and puzzles. Feathers flew to the window as soon as he was freed from his cage and did a parrot jig as he watched the outside world. Before Eleanor left the house she noticed a crow perched on the outside deck peering in at Feathers. They seemed to be having a conversation only they understood. When she opened the door to the deck the crow flew away calling its farewell in crow talk. Feathers simply stepped first one way and then the other on his perch.

"Did you make a new friend?" asked Eleanor as she stroked his gray feathers. Feathers said nothing.

Eleanor left the house and as she approached Angus's she noticed a car parked outside. She knocked on the door but no one came. Just as she was turning to leave, the door opened and a woman with platinum dyed hair peered around the door holding a blanket around her obviously naked body. "May I help you?" she asked.

Eleanor stood in shock recognizing the woman she saw the other day at Suzanna's while she sat with the Do Nothings. Could this be the notorious Virginia Storm? Eleanor regained her composure and pushed her way inside.

"I'm here to see Angus," she said as calmly as she could.

"I'm afraid you've come at an inconvenient time. As you can see we were in the middle of something."

"Where is he?" Eleanor asked. As she looked around the living room she could see the mink coat and high heels the woman had worn in the restaurant hastily tossed on the floor.

"Angus is in the bathroom," she said. "You should leave before he comes back. He won't be happy about your intrusion."

"No, I'll stay," Eleanor sat down on the sofa and began leafing through a hunting magazine.

"I really think you should go," the woman repeated with an edge of impatience in her voice.

"I don't mind waiting. Angus and I have plans." Eleanor did not look up as she continued perusing the pictures of elk and deer as if she were truly interested and there wasn't a naked woman standing nearby with murder in her eye.

After a short time, the woman put on her mink coat and stepped into her high heels, grabbed a small purse, and left slamming the door behind her. Eleanor watched quietly as she got in her car and spun out throwing gravel behind her as she went.

"Is she gone?" asked Angus as he appeared from downstairs.

"Holy cow! Was that Virginia Storm?" asked Eleanor.

"Unfortunately yes, how did you get her to leave?" he asked.

"Why did you let her in?"

"I couldn't keep her out. She just barged in and dropped her coat. She wasn't wearing anything under it, and believe me, it wasn't pretty."

"So you hid in the bathroom?"

"I'm not proud of it," Angus confessed, "I told her I was having some gastric distress and hoped she would get tired of waiting and leave before you got here."

"Coward," Eleanor accused.

"Let's get out of here before she comes back. She's staying at the Sand Beach Inn," Angus said as he grabbed his jacket and opened the door. "I need a plan to get her out of my life."

Eleanor and Angus walked down to the village and on to the beach. The sky was overcast and a cool wind blew from the southwest. Other beachcombers passed them as they strode silently immersed in their own private thoughts. Angus reached for Eleanor's hand and they both began to talk at once.

"I'm sorry, Eleanor," Angus began.

"Sorry for what?" Eleanor asked. "I've brought misery home with me . . . to you. I look at your life and it's neat and orderly and I have a lot of messy baggage. I wish it was otherwise."

"We need to talk to Josephine about what options we have for dealing with someone like Virginia."

"You think it's possible?"

"Is it possible to deal with her? Of course it is. I think a failure to plan is a plan to fail and I won't accept failure for either of us."

"I could run a background check on her. Maybe she's wanted for something and could be sent back to California."

"You do that and I'll set up a lunch date with Josephine when we get back. There must be a solution short of killing her." Angus didn't comment but the look in his eye was deadly.

They decided to meet at the Cow Bell, a little restaurant outside of Waterton where they were sure they would not run into Virginia. Josephine listened intently as Angus told his story while Eleanor picked at her Shrimp Louie. Josephine shivered when Angus reported on Virginia's past relationships.

"She's been married five times and the last guy had his house burned down after he kicked her out. There wasn't enough evidence to arrest Virginia even though she was suspected. So there are no outstanding warrants for her," Angus said.

"She sounds like a classic case of borderline personality disorder," Josephine sighed heavily.

"Is that bad?" asked Angus.

"The worst," Josephine stated emphatically. "Once they get their hooks in you, it's almost impossible to rid yourself of them without dire consequences."

"Is there no cure for it?" Eleanor asked as if Josephine could prescribe a magic pill of some kind.

"Nope, not if she's eighty years old. Therapy for that kind of disorder takes years of hard work. The therapist must build up the trust of the patient and one wrong move can destroy it causing all to be lost and severe acting out to occur, like burning down your house."

"Michael pawned her off on me. Maybe I can get her interested in someone else." Angus pondered the possibilities.

"Fiona comes to mind," offered Eleanor.

"Fiona would be the perfect person, but I couldn't do that to my only sister." Angus sighed. "Besides I think it would have to be a man."

"I would suggest keeping away from her at all costs," Josephine said. "She's visiting here and can't stay forever. You might consider visiting friends out of town or going on a trip and hope she loses interest in you."

"It didn't take her long to find out where I live," Angus said, "and in a village as small as Sand Beach, she's sure to find out where Eleanor lives as well. Even if we left, she might follow us. I feel better staying here where I know my resources and she doesn't."

"Should we alert the police or get a restraining order?" asked Eleanor.

"She hasn't done anything yet except come to my house without invitation. The police can't do anything until she commits a crime," Angus stated.

"People with her disorder tend to create chaos wherever they go. It may not be criminal but it will be unpleasant. If you can remain calm and not feed into her need for drama, that will help," Josephine added. "Don't take responsibility for any of her actions, Angus. Just remember, you didn't bring her here, she came on her own. Don't rescue her if she gets in trouble. Let her work out her own problems."

They ate their lunch in silence while each of them imagined what disquiet Virginia Storm would bring into their peaceful little world.

Victor and Lola Gaines wasted no time inviting several of the local residents to their home for dinner. Eleanor was excited to see what Lola had done to the house now that they had a few days to settle in.

She wasn't prepared to find that there were still boxes unpacked in the front room and there was nothing in the way of food in the kitchen.

When Angus and Eleanor arrived with a bottle of wine, Dede and Mark were already sitting on the boxes drinking Margaritas out of plastic cups and discussing the business opportunities in Waterton with Lola and the city manager.

"Welcome my friends!" Victor smiled and shook Angus's hand and kissed Eleanor on the cheek. "Will you have a Margarita? Lola made a big pitcher of them and they're very tasty." Before they could answer, he was gone, but quickly returned with two cups in hand.

"Thank you, Victor." Eleanor took her cup and wandered into the living room where she saw Amy and Taylor. Angus stopped to talk with them while she discovered Edwina Potts and a man who was introduced as her husband Potsy. They presented themselves as a cute couple, youthful and fit for older people with matching white heads of hair that reminded her of Q-tips. She immediately named them the cute-tips in her mind and smiled at her cleverness.

"It's so nice to see you again, Eleanor," Edwina said as she and Potsy gazed at the beautiful view of the ocean below. "They have such a lovely vista here."

"I think we will have to get a bigger house with a better view," Potsy chimed. "Edwina is always so spontaneous. She will buy the first thing she sees instead of searching for the best thing."

"Always the critic, this one," Edwina said. "If I remember correctly, you were my first. Are you really saying I could have done better? I love our little cottage and it is perfect for us. Maybe if we decide to stay here we'll build the kind of house you want up on the highest point with the best view possible. Only the best for my man."

"That would make me happy," Potsy admitted. "I would like nothing better than to look out over everyone's roof tops and see these waves crashing below me every day, and go golfing, of course."

Edwina shook her head, smiled, and patted his arm. "Have you met these lovely people over here? I believe they are in the real estate business. Maybe they'll sell us some property, Potsy."

Eleanor recognized Louis and Marvel Adler of Adler Reality. They were in competition with Gloria Vandorff and her husband, Will. Eleanor wondered how they felt about Gloria's death or if they even knew it was murder.

"It's lovely to see you again, Eleanor." Marvel nodded her perfectly coiffed head and Louis greeted her with a smile. They were a young and upcoming couple with whom Eleanor had met once or twice at civic functions but couldn't say she really knew. They wandered over to another young couple who Eleanor knew made their living in wealth management. Eleanor began to wonder what this gathering was all about.

Suddenly, Angus was at her side whispering in her ear, "Have we wandered into a Ponzi scheme? Are they suddenly going to ask us to invest in their new business venture? Why are we here?"

"I don't know? It does seem odd," she whispered.

"And there's no food," Angus lamented.

People wandered around until Victor began to play a medley of Billy Joel tunes on his baby grand piano. They gathered round the piano and Lola surprised everyone with a rendition of "For the Longest Time" in harmony with Victor. It wasn't long before everyone was singing and some were even moving what little furniture there was aside to make room for dancing. Amy and Taylor appeared to be enjoying themselves as they swayed together to the music as if in a trance. The margaritas seemed to have a joyful effect on everyone and the volume increased as the evening wore on with more music, singing, and dancing. At one point, Lola presented a bowl of chips and salsa which were quickly devoured and Victor set up his karaoke machine and challenged Taylor to a sing off. Soon the competition was on between teams of enthusiastic singers. Pizza appeared and disappeared but the margarita pitcher never seemed empty. Before Eleanor realized it, the clock struck midnight and she all at once felt exhausted and wanted to go home. She saw Angus dozing in a chair in the corner. When she poked him he jolted awake.

"I was just resting my eyes," he said. Most of the older partiers left at the same time as Eleanor and Angus. As they thanked Victor and Lola for an interesting evening they received warm hugs and sloppy kisses from their hosts.

Angus walked Eleanor home along the path in the dark. A full moon hung in the sky illuminating the waves and the quiet rolling of the surf serenaded them along the way, creating a romantic atmosphere.

Angus held her hand and Eleanor felt a tingle that started in her fingers and spread to the rest of her body.

"What do you suppose was in those margaritas?" Angus asked as he squeezed her hand and pulled her into his embrace. His kisses tasted sweeter than margaritas. Eleanor pulled away reluctantly and led him along on the path home.

"I think we need something to eat," she said as they entered her house and turned on the lights. "There's a roasted chicken in the refrigerator and some fruit salad too."

Angus headed immediately to the kitchen while Eleanor found Feathers roosting in her office and put him in his cage for the night. The romantic spell was broken.

"That was an interesting evening. I must say I enjoyed myself," Eleanor admitted.

"A dinner invitation without dinner isn't exactly my style of entertainment," Angus muttered with his mouth full of chicken.

"I think we were invited out of courtesy for having them over the other evening," Eleanor said.

"That may be, but I think they were schmoozing the mayor and some other people to get something."

"What do you think they want?" Eleanor asked.

"I heard Victor talking about real estate and investing, so maybe he wants tips on properties from the Alders."

"I'm sure Lola wanted to know about starting a business in Waterton. I heard Victor say that earlier. It doesn't hurt to make connections with people who can help you." Eleanor had just finished speaking when she heard the front door open and Amy and Taylor came wandering into the kitchen.

"We need food." Amy got plates and began to fill them with chicken and fruit while Taylor poured water into two tall glasses.

"What kind of dinner party was that?" asked Angus as he eyed their plates.

"That was not a dinner party," Taylor said. "I'm sure it was a swinger's welcome party."

"What!" Eleanor exclaimed.

"Exactly," Amy agreed. "After several guests left, the others started pairing up with people who weren't their mates. It was a little uncomfortable to say the least, so we left."

"I don't think we'll be on their invitation list again," Taylor remarked.

"That's okay with me. I don't know why I let you talk me into going in the first place. Victor Gaines is an amoral sex addict and I'm not into that kind of thing," Amy said, "but I wasn't going to let you go alone."

"I didn't know it was 'that kind of thing'," Taylor claimed using air quotes.

"Do you think they drugged us?" Eleanor asked remembering the walk home with Angus.

"Maybe, they certainly didn't feed us," Angus added. "It might have been those margaritas or that Reformed Druid stuff mixed with the full moon."

"Oooo, maybe they're witches!" Amy teased.

"If not witches, attractive pagans for sure," Taylor said. "I'm kind of regretting my Christian upbringing."

Amy elbowed him in the ribs. "Is it just your guilt and fear of hell that keeps you faithful?"

"No, it's my fear of you breaking my ribs with your elbow," Taylor whined as he rubbed his bruised torso.

"Men, I just don't understand them," Amy lamented.

"Don't try, Amy," Eleanor advised, "just feed them and use them to do the heavy lifting." Angus's bushy brows rose in surprise at an Eleanor he did not recognize.

"I've always suspected it, and now I know for sure," Taylor said. "We love them, work for them, give them everything, and they're just using us for our muscles."

"Better keep working out then," Amy said. "You wouldn't want to outlive your usefulness."

Taylor popped the last of the fruit salad in his mouth and said, "We better get home. It's late and I've got some working out to do." His eyes twinkled with lust until Amy jabbed him in the ribs again. "I meant I have to go to the gym tomorrow."

"Good night and thanks for the snack," Amy said as she pushed Taylor out the door.

After Angus put the dishes in the dishwasher and helped Eleanor tidy up the kitchen he held her and whispered in her ear, "I think you've cast a spell on me. I don't want to leave you. Tell me to stay."

"Stay."

It was a magical night, but neither of them knew a Storm had already been there and the aftermath would be deadly for someone.

Eleanor puttered around in the morning doing the crossword puzzle, the jumble, and Sudoku while she enjoyed her coffee. Feathers wasn't talking to her. She wondered if he was angry about Angus spending the night, but he lacked his usual energy, seeming to give even his arch enemy a pass. Lately she noticed he spent most of his time at the bank of windows that looked out on the deck. As she walked to the windows to check the weather she saw that crow again perched on the railing looking in at Feathers. It cocked its head and looked at her with one eye and then the other as if taking her measure. Feathers did a little happy dance and spoke in Walter's voice, "I love you." She stroked his feathers and watched the crow fly away.

Eleanor had put off going for a walk until the morning fog cleared and now dressed for the cool weather, but before she could leave the house the telephone rang.

"Hello," she answered. There was a long pause and then an unfamiliar voice began to recite: "Tuesday, What am I doing with my life? I just can't be happy eating and watching TV. I really want to travel the world. I want to see it all, swim in every ocean, climb the Pyramids, walk on every continent, dance and sing, and eat in every country. Ahhh, I will explore this planet from pole to pole because I have no desire to go to the moon." Then there was mad laughter and a click.

Eleanor hung up the phone more disturbed than she could say. Something about the message was familiar but she wasn't sure why. She moved quickly into her office and to the shelf where she kept her journals. All of them were gone. Someone had been in her house, had taken her personal journals, and had just called her reading an excerpt to let her know she had been violated. Her private thoughts and feelings were now in the hands of a stranger. Who would do such a thing and why?

Eleanor checked to see if anything else had been disturbed or taken. She looked in her jewelry case and the wall safe behind the picture, but couldn't find anything else missing. All of her valuable books remained untouched. This was not an ordinary thief, but someone cruel and creepy. Eleanor let out a deep sigh, locked her house and walked down her hill to the beach. She passed Angus's house knowing he had gone to the gym early to work out. She marched by Nancy Wilson's house and the hidey-hole and down to the beach, all the while puzzling over who, how, and why.

So intent on solving her mystery, Eleanor failed to see the seagulls circling overhead or the beauty of the blue-green waves breaking off the shore or the watcher at the window of the Sand Beach Inn. By the time she returned to Suzanna's she was red-cheeked and certain the culprit had to be Virginia Storm. Eleanor couldn't remember the last time she even noticed the journals but who else would want to do such a thing and how did she get into her house? She stopped in and sank down at the table where the Do Nothings sat.

"You look upset," Mattie commented. "Is something wrong?" Eleanor took a deep breath and spilled it all. She wasn't sure it was a good idea but she felt better for doing it.

"That's terrible," Edwina commiserated. "Are you quite sure it was this Virginia person?"

"Pretty sure," Eleanor said, "Although I can't prove it."

"Does Angus know?" asked Mavis. "He's a trained professional. Surely he could find a clue."

"I just discovered it this morning and Angus isn't home," Eleanor said.

"How do you suppose she got into your house?" asked Sybil.

"I don't know that either," Eleanor admitted, "Unless I forgot to lock my door. She's staying at the Sand Beach Inn so she's nearby. I have no idea how long she intends to stay here. What if she takes my journals with her or copies them? I don't know what her intentions are."

"Perhaps she came to your house while you were at Victor and Lola's party. Wasn't that a delightful evening? I must admit I enjoyed myself immensely. The singing, the dancing, and watching those young people lusting after each other was quite a thrill," Edwina laughed. "Of course the food was terrible, but everything else was such fun!"

"Did we miss the young Druid dancing naked in the moonlight?" Mattie seemed disappointed. Just then Virginia walked in the door in her mink and high heels. She glared at the ladies and raised her hand in a one-finger salute revealing a ruby red ring that looked remarkably like the one Eleanor purchased at the estate sale.

"There's your proof, Eleanor," Mavis had spotted the ring and recognized it also. "She's wearing your ring!"

"What are you going to do?" asked Sybil.

"The ring means nothing to me. I didn't even know it was missing, but the journals are personal. I'd like to punch her and make her give them back." Eleanor couldn't believe how angry she felt.

"Better to be calm," Edwina advised. "She may be the type to come unhinged. Wait for your moment."

"I'm going home to call the police and report a theft. At least they'll have a record of it if something else happens. Perhaps they'll find my journals in her hotel room and arrest her." Eleanor put on her coat and hurried home, but when she got there she called the coffee group instead and planned an emergency meeting for lunch at the Boat House.

When Eleanor arrived at the coffee group's favorite restaurant, Cleo had her iPad out and the other ladies were studying it intently.

"Look at this," Pearl ordered as Eleanor sat down. Eleanor saw a picture of a young girl who was missing from her family home. She was wearing a ring with a red stone in it.

"Isn't that the ring you bought at the estate sale?" asked Dede.

Eleanor agreed that it did look like it, "Maybe she ran away and pawned the ring."

"Do you think it was stolen?" asked Cleo who still had concerns about the estate sale.

"It was absolutely stolen from my house," Eleanor said. "And what's more, I saw Virginia wearing it at Suzanna's this morning."

"Who is Virginia?" asked Cleo.

Josephine and Eleanor quickly filled the members of the coffee group in on the latest developments involving Angus and his relationship with Virginia Storm.

"Does Angus know any normal women?" asked Pearl.

"It does seem like he attracts the worst possible kinds of women," Cleo agreed. "Present company excluded, of course."

"I'm sure that is why he is so smitten with you Eleanor," Josephine added. "You represent the best of humanity to him."

Eleanor wasn't in the mood for compliments. "I think Virginia broke into my house and took my journals. This morning someone called me and read an entry from one of them, then laughed and hung up. It's very disturbing to think that she can read my private thoughts. It makes me sick to my stomach."

"Are your private thoughts divinely erotic?" Cleo asked.

"Yes, some of them are and some of them are just boring accounts of my days and others are poems that I've written but haven't published yet. I want them back!" Eleanor cried.

"What do you want us to do?" Josephine asked.

"I'm not sure, but I thought you could help me come up with a plan," Eleanor continued.

"Have you called the police?" Dede asked.

"No, I don't want to involve them unless I have to. It won't be as important to them as it is to me. They might take too long to investigate and I don't want Virginia going through them, making copies, or taking them with her if she leaves."

"We just need to break in to her place and take them back. Where is she staying?" Cleo made it seem so simple.

"She's staying at the Sand Beach Inn." Eleanor knew she could count on Cleo to come up with an idea that involved danger. She secretly believed Cleo had a criminal mind.

"We'll have to get her out of her room somehow," Dede plotted.

"I could invite her to dinner and have a talk with her about Angus," Eleanor suggested.

"Yes, but when she finds the journals missing, she'll know you were involved and try to get back at you," Josephine said.

"Do you think Angus could take her on a tour of the city? That would give us plenty of time to get in and out and maybe she wouldn't suspect you, Eleanor," Dede said.

"It would be even better if Eleanor went with them. Maybe Angus could take you both out to dinner. Then she couldn't pin it on you at all," Pearl said.

"I like it!" Josephine said. "Virginia doesn't know us or our relationship to Eleanor so she wouldn't think of getting revenge on any of us."

"Ok, how do we get into her room?" asked Cleo.

"That's the easiest part," Pearl said. "My son manages the Sand Beach Inn. I'm sure I can get a key from him."

"Let's do it tonight. I'll bring the idea up to Angus about dinner, but I won't tell him what we're doing. He wouldn't approve." Eleanor was delighted with the plan. "I'll call you when I've set things up."

The ladies enjoyed their lunches of French onion soup for Josephine, Ceasar salad for Eleanor, and fish and chips for the others.

"Is there any news about Gloria Vandorff?" asked Pearl.

"I haven't heard anything about a funeral, if that's what you mean," Dede said.

"Have they arrested the driver who hit her?" asked Cleo.

"Oh my, I totally forgot to tell you." Eleanor surprised herself with her forgetfulness. "Angus said she died of blunt force trauma to the head."

"So she hit her head on the cement. That's not surprising," Josephine said.

"There was hardly any blood at the scene. The police think she was bludgeoned to death and dumped in the swale," Eleanor explained.

"So it was murder!" exclaimed Cleo. "I bet it was her husband. He must have heard about her 'organ' lessons."

"Speaking of organ lessons guess who is coming to church," Dede said.

"Don't make us guess," Pearl complained, "You know how I hate to guess. Just spit it out."

"Victor Gaines."

"I thought he was a Reformed Druid," Josephine said.

"Well, that's what he claims but he offered to play the organ at church on Sunday morning," Dede explained. "How could I deny him when he plays like an angel?"

"That should bring the younger crowd back to church," Cleo speculated, "Especially if he starts offering 'organ' lessons to the ladies."

"Cleo, you're awful!" Pearl exclaimed.

"I love you too, Pearl," Cleo said. "You are planning to come to my exhibition on Saturday night, aren't you?"

"Absolutely," said Josephine, "You know I love your paintings."

"Are you ready for it?" asked Eleanor, "Do you need any help setting up?"

"I'm ready. The Bayside Art Center people are setting up. All you need to do is show up and drink the wine, eat the hors d'oeuvres, and rave about how fabulous the artist is."

"I think I can force myself to do at least two of those things," Pearl said.

"I'm coming," Dede said.

"Victor offered to play piano," Cleo said. "I think he's invited some of his clients from his import-export business."

"He certainly gets around," observed Eleanor. "What did you think of the party they hosted, Dede?"

"Boy, wasn't that strange?" she said. "I really enjoyed it, but the food was terrible. Mark and I left absolutely starved."

"It was a dinner party without dinner. Angus and I went back to my place and ate. Then Taylor and Amy showed up too. They said the party turned into an orgy."

"What! Why wasn't I invited?" complained Cleo.

"I guess we left too early," Dede lamented. "I've never been to an orgy."

"Maybe if you sign up for organ lessons, you'll get invited to the next one," said Pearl.

"Let's wait and see if it corresponds with the next full moon," Eleanor suggested, "Maybe he's a real pagan after all."

When Eleanor returned home there was a message on her answering machine.

"Epitaph for Ellie

When she left the hallowed halls of learning,

What did she take with her?

Collection of classics,

Enlightened eyes in need of glasses,

Opinions on every topic for each side of every coin,

A gray brain with no white, no black,

No doubt,

Her mind was so open

Everything fell out."

Eleanor recognized the poem immediately from her early days in college. She remembered the title was "Epitaph for Betty Coed." She had to get her journals back! She picked up the phone and called Angus. It wasn't difficult to convince him to take her to dinner, but including Virginia took a little effort. "She might be nice if we are nice to her," she argued.

"What if being nice makes her want to stay?" Angus said. He didn't want to worry Eleanor by telling her about the garbage he found strewn all over his deck when he returned from her house the morning after the party. It had Virginia's style of revenge written all over it.

"I'm sure she won't be impressed with anything around here. It may even convince her to leave earlier."

"I think it's a bad idea, Ellie, but if you want to subject yourself to torture, I'll do it," Angus relented. He found it difficult to deny her wishes. "Just know that if things get ugly and I know they will, I'm taking you home—dinner or no dinner."

"You'll have to call and invite her." There was a long pause.

"Maybe she's got other plans," Angus said hopefully—but, of course, she didn't.

Eleanor watched as Angus walked Virginia from her room to the car. She wore the mink coat and Eleanor wondered naughtily if there was anything beneath it. Virginia's face transformed from smiling Barbie to Wicked Witch of the West when she saw Eleanor in the front seat of Angus's truck. If looks could kill, Eleanor would be dead ten times over. This was not going to be a pleasant evening.

Meanwhile the rest of the coffee group sat huddled in Dede's car waiting for the trio to leave. Cleo wore a black velvet suit with a rhinestone zipper she purchased from the Quaker Factory on QVC. She called it her sneaking around outfit. Pearl dressed herself in a black yoga outfit with a sequined baseball cap, while Dede and Josephine wore black sweats with hoodies. They looked like escaped hoodlums from an old folks home.

"I'll go in the office and get the key," Pearl said.

"Did you see which room she came out of?" asked Josephine.

"It was room 4," Dede said.

They got out of the car and slinked toward room 4 keeping in the shadows while Pearl entered the office.

"How is Pearl going to get the key?" asked Dede.

"I have no idea," Cleo said as they waited for what seemed to be an eternity.

Josephine reached out and tried the doorknob. Surprisingly it turned easily in her hand. The door was not locked. They scurried in as quickly as old ladies could scurry.

"Is everyone wearing gloves?" asked Dede who had no intention of leaving any trace behind.

"Yes," answered Josephine.

"Why did she leave the door unlocked and a light on? Do think this is a trap?" asked Cleo suspiciously.

"She was probably so excited that Angus was taking her to dinner that she just forgot to lock it," Josephine speculated.

"She's from California and most likely used to doors that lock themselves and are opened with keycards," said Dede. "Let's find the journals and get out of here."

"What a lovely view she has here. I can see way down the shoreline," Josephine said as she stood at the window looking out to sea.

"Get away from the window, Josephine. Someone outside might see you standing there," Dede cautioned. Josephine quickly moved away and began searching for the missing journals.

The small room didn't hold many hiding places. They checked the drawers and closet and quickly discovered the many journals hidden under the bed.

"Did Eleanor say how many there were?" asked Cleo.

"I think she said twenty," Josephine offered and began to count them dividing the load between the three.

"Should we take Eleanor's ring back?" asked Cleo as she spied it on the bedside table.

"No, let's leave it here and let the police find it in case Eleanor decides to report it missing. Maybe Virginia will be charged with stealing it and be forced to leave town," said Josephine.

"How unlike you to be so calculating," Dede said.

"Should we lock the door behind us?" asked Cleo as they prepared to leave.

"Yes, let her worry about how someone got into her room. Maybe she'll be so scared when she finds the journals missing she'll go back to the hole she crawled out of," Josephine spat.

Cleo and Dede exchanged a look between them. It wasn't like Josephine to be mean. "I think we should leave everything the way we found it," said Dede who left the door unlocked and casually walked to the car with the journals.

"What happened to Pearl?" asked Cleo.

"I'll go see," said Josephine as she deposited her share of the journals. Dede got behind the wheel and started up the car, but before Josephine got to the office Pearl came out. They climbed in the backseat and Dede drove away.

"What happened, Pearl?" asked Dede.

"A strange person was manning the office. I'm sorry I couldn't get the key," Pearl said.

"What did you tell him?" asked Josephine.

"You didn't ask him for the key to room 4 did you?" asked Dede.

"No, we just chatted. I made a mistake. My son manages the Sandman Inn," Pearl admitted.

"That's the one farther down the street," offered Dede.

"It's okay, Pearl. We got the journals," Cleo said.

"I hope you didn't have to crawl through any windows," Pearl worried.

Angus and Eleanor returned from their dinner with Virginia and were both astounded by the uneventful evening they had shared with her.

"I don't get it," Angus pondered as he poured himself a nightcap. "She was positively on her best behavior. What do you make of it?"

"I don't know. Maybe she has a split personality like Dr. Jekyll and Mr. Hyde. Tonight she was the good one."

"I don't believe it. She's probably plotting ways to make my life miserable right now."

"What did you do to deserve her abuse?" Eleanor asked.

"Nothing I can think of. She's most likely between husbands and needs someone to fill the role. I just happened to be the nearest breathing man." Angus swallowed the last of his drink, gave Eleanor a peck on the cheek, and left for home. He didn't hear the wild animal sounds emanating from room 4 at the Sand Beach Inn or if he did he dismissed it as some creature of the night just like everyone else did.

As soon as Angus drove away, Eleanor called Dede to get the scoop on their latest escapade. "Dede, it's Eleanor. Did you get the journals?"

"Yes, it was as slick as snot. She didn't bother to lock the door so it was easy to get in and find them under the bed. I brought all twenty with me and promise not to read them under penalty of death."

"Thank you so much. I don't know how she got into my house, but maybe I was careless about locking my door too," Eleanor said.

"We saw your ruby ring there but left it because it might be stolen or connected to that missing girl. Remember Cleo saw it on Facebook so maybe it could be used to get Virginia in trouble," Dede offered.

"It is a unique ring. Thanks again, Dede."

The two friends hung up without knowing that Virginia Storm had breathed her last horrible breath and lay dead on the floor in room 4 of the Sand Beach Inn.

The night of Cleo's exhibition arrived and still no one knew about Virginia Storm. The members of the coffee group arrived at the Bayside Art Center excited for their dear friend and surprised to find a broad spectrum of guests they did not know. The crowd was finely dressed and sipping wine as they gazed at Cleo's work with admiration.

"There's Cleo over there," said Josephine as she met Eleanor and Angus at the door. "Victor Gaines is here and seems to have invited a group of his friends who've been monopolizing her."

"Sorry we're late, but Angus had a call from the police this afternoon and they wanted him to help them with a homicide," Eleanor said.

"Oh no, is it about Gloria Vandorff?" Josephine asked.

"There was a body that washed up on the beach," Angus added. "It doesn't seem to have any connection to Gloria's case."

"But it's a homicide?" Josephine persisted.

"Looks that way," Angus was reluctant to say more. "Would you like some wine, Eleanor?"

"Yes, please,"

As Angus wandered away to get the wine, Dede joined the group in time to hear Josephine ask about the body. "Is it anyone we know?" Josephine asked.

"As far as I can tell, it was the body of a young girl," Eleanor whispered. "Evidently it's someone who had gone missing, but no one from here."

"I heard something about that," Dede commented. "A body washed up at Sand Beach and some unfortunate tourists discovered it this afternoon."

"I wonder why they think it's a homicide," said Josephine.

"I can't say for sure, but I overheard something about her hands being bound," Eleanor whispered as Angus reappeared with the wine.

"This is quite a gathering. Cleo must be over the moon," Angus said, handing a glass to Eleanor and greeting Dede with a smile. "We should check out her work. I haven't seen her latest masterpieces." Eleanor and Angus walked away together.

Most of Cleo's masterpieces were landscapes and seascapes of the local area painted in acrylic hues of deep blues and greens. A few were whimsical in nature and documented the dairy industry with cows frolicking on the beach and flying over pastures in hot air balloons. She was not a master by any means, but her friends and family all hung her pieces in their homes—some in closets—and there were a few others who actually paid her for them. She had no illusions about her talent and was reluctant to have a show, but was encouraged by her friends who urged her to take a risk. It was no wonder that this night brought her anxiety and rapture combined.

People milled through the large room and mingled as they studied the art on the walls. At one point, Josephine conversed with a Buddhist gentleman as they stood before a painting of the sea.

"This reminds me of my home," he said.

"Where is that?" asked Josephine.

"In this life I live on the Hawaiian island of Oahu, but I have traveled to many places," he said as he turned his kind brown eyes away from the painting to look deeply into Josephine's.

"What brings you to this place on this night?" Josephine asked as she lost herself in his gaze.

"I was drawn to the event by a strange force. For years I have been searching for my lost Mala from a past life. The universe directed me here to this place."

"That is very interesting to me. What do you know of your past life?" she asked.

"I have lived many lives. Once I was a Lama in Tibet. I fell in love with a courtesan but could not marry her. I gave her a bead from my Mala so I could find her again in another life hoping for a different ending. In my last life, I was a Buddhist nun. I remember having a Mala with a missing bead. The lost bead was a constant irritant to me until a visitor came to the nunnery. He was looking for enlightenment and wore the bead around his neck. We were drawn to each other but once again could not marry. He left the bead and went away. I have had many dreams about the missing Mala and came upon this one bead in a beautifully carved box when I visited a Buddhist nunnery in Tibet on one of my travels. It was where I lived many years as a Buddhist nun in my former life. Unfortunately the Mala itself was not at the nunnery—only this one bead." He pulled the bead from his pocket and showed it to Josephine. It was a small brown bead like a tiny walnut with a hole drilled through it. "This bead has led me here."

"I think I have your Mala!" Josephine said excitedly as she pulled the beads from her purse. Each bead of the Mala was a match for the one he held. "I've been uneasy and irritable ever since they came into my possession—feeling a strange ache and longing I can't explain. I've had strange dreams, too, involving a large terra cotta building with many flags attached to it. Inside were women with shaved heads wearing red and gold robes. I haven't been able to rest. For some reason I put them in my purse tonight. Please take them."

The gentleman took the beads and studied they closely, "Yes these are the very ones I have been seeking. May I ask how they came to be in your possession?"

"I bought them at an estate sale," Josephine said simply.

"And you yourself are happy in your life?" he asked.

"Yes," she answered.

"Thank you, I'm sure your kindness and generosity will be amply rewarded. I look forward to meeting you again," he said as he bowed to her, wrapped the beads around his wrist, and walked away as if nothing out of the ordinary had happened. Josephine felt a sense of great relief, but also sadness as she watched him walk away. She hurried to tell Richard about her strange encounter.

Eleanor and Angus admired all of the pieces and visited with several of the people there. After they drank their wine and sampled some finger foods, they found themselves in a circle of friends that included the coffee group and Nancy and Dennis Wilson.

"I heard a body washed up on the beach today," Pearl said, "Do we know who it was?"

"I saw a great deal of activity on the beach this afternoon," Nancy said, "but I can't say I know any details."

"I suppose you know, Angus," Dennis said.

"The body hasn't been identified yet, but there's speculation that she's one of the missing girls from the valley," Angus offered.

"What missing girls are you talking about?" asked Pearl's husband, Cary.

"There've been several girls missing over the winter months," Josephine's husband, Richard said. "It's been in the *Oregonian*."

"I knew we shouldn't have stopped getting the newspaper," Pearl said.

"There are always missing kids on Facebook," Nancy said. "It's tragic that so many are never found."

"I can't imagine which is worse, not finding them or finding one dead on the beach," Dede said.

Just then Cleo joined the group in a state of elation. "You'll never guess what has happened," she laughed, "Someone has bought all of my paintings!"

Suddenly their distress was turned into joy for Cleo. The wine flowed and the friends reveled in her good fortune.

Virginia's body wasn't found until she had been dead for three days. The stench of her rotting corpse caused the other tenants to complain. Strangely enough, no one missed her. The Sand Beach Inn closed its doors for more than a week while a special cleaning crew sanitized the room. The carpeting was replaced and the walls were repainted but not before a thorough investigation was done by the police.

Angus was especially disturbed by the news, not so much because he cared about her but because he was secretly relieved she was out of the way. Eleanor felt the same but they didn't discuss it. Instead, she shared her feelings with the coffee group when they met at the Boat House. "I can't honestly say I'm sorry she's gone," Eleanor admitted.

"Do you know what happened to her?" asked Cleo.

"You're not thinking murder are you, Cleo?" asked Pearl.

"She was eighty. I'm supposing it could have been a heart attack or a stroke," Josephine offered.

"Angus told me the Medical Examiner thinks she died the night we took her to dinner," Eleanor said.

"You didn't poison her did you, Eleanor?" teased Dede.

"Maybe Angus did it to get her off his back," Pearl suggested.

"Or maybe you four ladies stayed in her room that night and beat her over the head because she caught you in her room." Eleanor could play that game too. It was suddenly very quiet while each of them considered what it meant to them if this turned out to be murder.

"Maybe if I'd locked her door, she'd still be alive," Dede said guiltily.

"Would we have to come forward and testify if it's murder?" asked Cleo.

"I was never in the room so I wouldn't even know if you did kill her," said Pearl. The others gave her what could only be described as the stink eye.

"I'm just saying I wouldn't testify against you so don't look at me like that," Pearl said defending her statement.

"That's one thing I know for sure," said Dede. "We didn't do it."

"Do you think the three deaths could be connected in some way?" asked Eleanor.

"It is odd to have three deaths like that in our small area," said Josephine. "It would be even odder if they all turn out to be murders."

"Then I would suspect them all to be connected," said Cleo.

"What could those three possibly have in common?" asked Pearl.

"The body on the beach was found the same day Virginia's body was discovered," Eleanor noted. "Maybe she saw something and had to be silenced."

"Do we even know where her body was when she was found?" asked Dede.

"She was in room 4 at the Sand Beach Inn," said Pearl.

"No, I mean was she in bed? Did she die in her sleep or was she on the floor? Was there blood?" Dede clarified.

"I don't know anything like that," Eleanor confessed, "but I can find out."

"If these victims were murdered and their deaths are connected, that means there is a murderer here," Josephine reasoned.

"We need to find out what's going on," Dede said.

"Do you think those gnomes are part of it?" asked Cleo.

"Don't be ridiculous," Dede chided, "How could they be involved?"

"Remember that TV series called *Grimm*?" Cleo persisted, "There was a symbol that was used to unite the creatures, or Wesen, and spur them to action. Maybe there is some creepy cult of gnome worshipers that is killing people and using that symbol to communicate in some way."

"Maybe it's the Reformed Druids," Pearl said. "I heard they worship shrubs. Anyone who does that might also worship gnomes."

"What if there is a group that kidnaps young people for sacrifices. Didn't you say the girl on the beach had her hands tied? Maybe she got away and Virginia saw it, so they had to kill them both to keep them quiet." Cleo's imagination was running wild. "We don't know how long that girl was in the water or what condition her body was in."

"That sounds silly but there may be some truth to it," Josephine said thoughtfully as she remembered standing in room 4 looking out of Virginia's window. "Maybe Virginia did see something that night that involved the girl on the beach. She certainly had a view from her room."

"You were looking out her window that night," Dede recalled. "Do you remember seeing something suspicious?"

"I didn't see anyone on the beach," Josephine said, closing her eyes in an attempt to see that night again. "There were lights on the water. Maybe from a boat out beyond the breakers, but that's not unusual."

"What will happen to Virginia's body?" asked Cleo. "Will there be a funeral?"

"I'm sure they will send her back to California," Eleanor speculated. "No one here really knew her."

"Do you think Angus will go to the funeral?" asked Dede.

"I think he will, if only to support his son," Eleanor said.

"What is his son's name again?" asked Pearl.

"His name is Michael Patrick," Eleanor said.

"He didn't really have time to get to know his biological mother," Josephine said, "but you'd expect him to pay his respects."

"Yes," Eleanor agreed.

There was a lull in the conversation, which gave Josephine an opportunity to change the subject and relate her story of the Buddhist gentleman at the art exhibit. "I must admit I wasn't myself while I had those beads, but now I feel at peace."

"That's incredible!" Pearl said.

"Almost as incredible as someone buying all of my paintings," said Cleo. She didn't mention the beautiful frames, but no one seemed to notice.

"So Josephine found a home for her beads, and Cleo found a home for her masterpieces. I wonder where my ruby ring will end up," Eleanor said thoughtfully. "Maybe there is something powerful at work here."

"How about my carved box?" asked Pearl.

"Don't forget my glassware," Dede reminded them.

"Didn't you also buy some gnomes?" asked Pearl.

"Yes, I was hoping you forgot about those," Dede said, "I think I already know where they belong."

Once again, because of his vast experience in the field Angus was sucked into a murder investigation as a consultant. Eleanor didn't mind. It gave her an edge in solving the case with her friends even at the risk of frustrating Angus on many levels. Tonight she would feed him a new steak pie recipe with mashed potatoes and some leafy greens. Then, when he was in a food coma she would extract the information she needed about the possible murders. She felt deliciously devious as she shopped for the ingredients for tonight's dinner.

Eleanor spent the rest of her afternoon preparing an epicurean delight. She happily chopped the beef and seared it in the pan as she listened to Sam Smith's album *In the Lonely Hour* and danced around in her stocking feet. She fried the onions, carrots, and garlic and mixed it all together with cider, thyme, bay, beef stock, and tomato puree and then popped it in the oven to cook for hours while she made the pastry. Soon she was singing along to "Like I Can" while she prepared the apple and potato mash. Feathers danced along with her until something caused him to fly to the window where he perched looking out at the gray day. With most of the preparations completed, Eleanor followed Feathers to the window and saw the shiny black crow perched on the deck railing looking back at Feathers.

"Oh Feathers, have you got a girlfriend?" Eleanor asked. "Are you in love?"

Feathers refused to answer but stepped back and forth on his perch, flapped his wings and making a strange clicking sound. He looked out the window and gave a long whistle.

"Who is this girl? I'm not sure I approve of her. She's a crow for heaven's sake." Eleanor said.

When Feathers didn't answer, Eleanor continued her interrogation, "Does she have a name? I think she looks like Ebony or an Inky. Yes, I think her name is Inky. You don't think I'm anti-crow do you? I just don't know her. Maybe I should introduce myself," and she opened the slider and stepped outside.

With a flutter of wings the crow flew to Eleanor's shoulder and pecked at her shiny gold earring. "Oh my, you're not just any old crow are you, Inky," Eleanor said in surprise. Obviously this was a crow someone had made into a pet. On the other side of the window Feathers continued his clicking and dancing in earnest.

"I think Feathers is quite smitten with you, Inky," Eleanor said. Suddenly the crow flew off and Eleanor and Feathers watched as she disappeared into the cloudy sky.

"That was odd, Feathers," she said, stroking his gray feathers as he rubbed his head against her palm. "I guess you're stuck with me now."

Eleanor checked the clock and decided it was time to get ready for company and put the finishing touches on dinner. When Angus arrived with his gifts of wine and roses, the table was set with Eleanor's finest china and linens and the house welcomed him with the aroma of rich steak pie with apple and potato mash that Eleanor had flambéed with apple brandy.

"I can't wait to eat. Let's just have our drinks with dinner. I'm starving!" he announced upon entering the kitchen.

"Fine with me," said Eleanor, who had already had one glass of Cabernet Sauvignon. They dished up their plates and sat at the table in silence until Angus had pretty much finished off his meal.

"Eleanor, you've outdone yourself! That was delicious. Do you think I could have seconds?"

"Absolutely, I made plenty."

Angus rose from the table with his plate. "Do you want anything from the kitchen while I'm up?"

"Just bring the wine bottle," she said as she finished her meal.

"I don't have to ask what you did today. It's obvious that you went to a great deal of effort making this meal," Angus sighed as if he knew the reason for Eleanor's effort, and it wasn't just because she cared about his health or happiness.

"What did you do today?" Eleanor asked innocently.

"You know, investigating a murder. Nothing exciting," he said and then stuffed his mouth with a big bite of mashed potatoes.

"I wonder what that looks like exactly," Eleanor said. "Do you go around town asking people if they saw anything unusual on the night of such and such, or do you compile a list of suspects and interrogate them under a naked light bulb in a dingy cell?"

"Yes," he said and then filled his mouth with a big bite of steak pie.

"I suppose you can't tell me anything about an ongoing investigation," she sighed.

"No," he said and put the final bite of pie in his mouth.

"Well, are you going to Virginia's funeral?" she asked.

"There isn't going to be a funeral," he replied. "Her body won't be released until the autopsy reports are concluded. "Besides, no one would claim the body. She evidently didn't have anyone."

"Does that make you sad?" she asked detecting a note of sympathy in his voice.

"It does," he said as he put down his fork. "It makes me wonder if anyone would come to my funeral. It makes me afraid of dying alone and forgotten and unloved. I bet you never worry about that do you Eleanor?"

"Are you trying to make me feel bad?"

"No, of course not, I just think how lucky you are to be surrounded by people who love you. I wonder what makes a person so damned loveable. You have no idea how many sad and lonely people there are in this world."

"Of course I do," she protested. "I don't live in an ivory tower. Haven't I been going with you every Wednesday night to the soup kitchen to feed the hungry? I see and I feel for them and I'm happy to cook for them and dish up their soup, but I'm not one of them and I am grateful. Believe me, Angus I know how good my life is."

"I'm sorry, Ellie. I didn't mean to be so dark and moody. I guess I feel guilty about Virginia. I can't say I'm sorry she's out of my life because frankly I didn't like her, but she didn't deserve to die that way."

"What way?"

Angus paused, "Alone and unloved."

"I've given a lot of thought to being happy and I think the recipe for that is to forget about finding your own happiness and focus on making those around you happy. It's an elusive thing—happiness, and it can't be forced or caught. It just happens."

"It happens to you, Ellie, and it emanates from you. I feel it every time I'm with you. You make me happy. I'm not sure I do that for any one."

"You make me happy Angus. You make those homeless people happy and I know you made Walter happy. You have so many friends who love you. I don't know why you can't see it."

"I think I could see it if you'd marry me. I'm tired of being alone. I want to be with you every day and every night."

"I'll think about it," Eleanor said, "but I won't be hurried."

Angus's face lit up like a firecracker on the fourth of July. It was the first and only time Eleanor had even considered the idea and it gave him hope he never dreamed possible.

"What's for dessert?" he asked calmly, afraid to ask for more than her promise to think about marriage.

"I didn't make dessert but I have raspberry ripple ice cream," she offered.

"Perfect!" He smiled like a smug cat and cleared the table while Eleanor sat and poured another glass of wine. So far she had learned nothing about the so-called murders and now there was a marriage proposal on the table she had no wish to honor. She began to think that maybe she wasn't the devious one.

Eleanor came to the realization that Angus would not offer any useful information concerning the murder of Gloria Vandorff or the body on the beach. The only other source at her disposal would be the gossip of the Do Nothings, which she planned to take advantage of after her morning walk. It wasn't the best weather for walking as it had been raining heavily all night, but Eleanor decided a little water wouldn't harm her and took off dressed in her most rain-repellant gear.

She passed Angus's house and hurried down the hill to the village with the rain pelting her face. The wind came from the southwest and felt cold as she walked into it. She didn't take time to enjoy the usual treasures on the beach because of the nasty weather. By the time she had gone less than a mile along the shore, she turned back eager to get out of the cold and into Suzanna's warm welcoming shelter.

"Good morning, ladies," Eleanor greeted the four women who sat at their usual table sipping hot coffee.

"Eleanor, please join us," Mattie said, "you look like you could use a hot drink."

"Don't tell me you've gone walking the beach in this weather," Edwina said. "Surely you'll catch your death." Eleanor shook the chill off along with her coat and sat at the table grateful for the warmth.

"This is the kind of weather for staying indoors and reading a good book," said Mavis.

"Or even a bad book," Sybil added.

"Yes, but then I wouldn't see you and hear the latest news of the village," Eleanor said.

"You need some coffee," Mattie said as she took a cup from the neighboring table and poured coffee from the carafe.

Eleanor eagerly accepted it and drank deeply. "So what's new?"

Mattie sat up straight and spoke in her authoritarian way, "You must know about the body that was found on the beach."

"Yes, but what do you know about it?" Eleanor prodded.

"I heard it was a young woman," Sybil said, "possibly a missing person from the valley."

"Really, what makes you think that?" asked Edwina.

"I overheard Officer McGraw talking with Mrs. Kelly in the grocery store. He said her picture was among those missing girls," Sybil said.

"Has she been identified then?" asked Eleanor.

"There's an article about her in today's *Fish Wrapper*," Mavis said. She reached in her bag and pulled out a copy of the local newspaper. There on the front page was a photo of a young girl under the headline that read: Missing Teen Found Dead on Beach.

"It says her name was Tina Mallory and she was from Beaverton. She disappeared after going jogging one morning two weeks ago. Her parents have been frantically looking for her. She was only 15 years old." Mavis summed up. "The cause of death is unknown at this time."

"I wonder how she came to be here," Mattie said.

"Maybe she was kidnapped," offered Sybil.

"Probably a runaway," Edwina said. "Young girls get the hots for some boy and run off with them."

"And end up dead on the beach?" Eleanor questioned. "That doesn't add up unless the boy is not a boy but a bad man."

"I feel sorry for her parents," Mattie said. "It must be dreadful raising a child and losing them that way."

"Then there was that hideous woman who died in her room at the Sand Beach Inn," Mavis said. "There was nothing in the paper about her, but I heard she wasn't found for days and they had to replace the carpet because there was so much blood and gore."

"For heaven's sake, don't they have maid service at that motel? They certainly would have discovered her if they did," Mattie grumbled.

"Perhaps she had the do not disturb sign on her door knob," suggested Sybil. "The poor woman didn't have anyone to notice she was missing for days. She could easily have hit her head and bled to death, especially if she was taking a blood thinner."

"Wasn't she the one who took your journals and stole your ring?" asked Edwina. "She probably got what she deserved."

Eleanor paused before she spoke, "I misplaced the journals, my bad, and the ring just looked like mine." Edwina's brows moved up and her eyes shifted to Eleanor's naked finger. It was clear that she didn't believe Eleanor.

"Didn't you call the police and report a break in?" asked Mavis.

"No, I discovered the journals when I got back. I just moved them and forgot." Eleanor was a terrible liar and felt guilty for doing it but needed to protect herself in case there was indeed foul play involved in Virginia's death.

"I thought she quoted from your journals, dear," Edwina persisted.

"I guess it may have been from my published poems. Isn't it crazy what the mind is capable of doing?" Eleanor was becoming increasingly uncomfortable with the line of questioning, and in an attempt to change the subject blurted, "I heard that Gloria Vandorff's death wasn't an accident, but a homicide."

"Oh my!" Edwina's exclamation seemed overly dramatic.

"Don't worry, Edwina," soothed Mattie, "this really is a peaceful place. It just seems like there are lots of murders here lately."

"A homicide . . . what did you hear?" Edwina asked.

"That she was bludgeoned to death," Eleanor answered.

"Well she could very well have suffered head injuries in a hit and run," Edwina persisted.

"Yes, I suppose." Eleanor was sorry she had brought up the topic and only wished to get away from Edwina's probes. She had already said more than she should. "My friends like to solve mysteries so they often create them. Forgive me for passing along unproven theories." Edwina obviously had a mind like a steel trap.

Eleanor looked out the window and seeing a break in the weather used it as an excuse to escape. As she hurried home she had an uneasy feeling and knew she had to call her friends immediately. The phone was ringing when she walked in the door.

"Hello."

"Eleanor, it's Cleo. Have you seen the *Fish Wrapper* today?"

"No, I haven't looked at my mail yet."

"We're at Dede's. You need to get here as soon as you can."

"What's wrong?"

"We'll tell you when you get here. Dede made her heavenly lemon angel pie." Cleo hung up. Eleanor's sense of unease turned into dread as she got in her car and drove into Waterton.

The ladies were seated at Dede's dining room table drinking coffee and chatting when Eleanor arrived. "What's the fuss?" she asked.

"You better sit down." Dede pulled out a chair.

"Look at the picture on the front page," Josephine said.

Eleanor studied the front page and took note of the photo of the teen that was found on the beach. She had only glanced at it at Suzanna's when Mavis had recapped the story. Cleo pointed out the missing girl's photo and tapped her finger on the girl's hand. Eleanor's eyes widened with understanding. It was the same photo of the missing girl Cleo had shown them before and on her finger was the ring Eleanor had purchased at the estate sale.

"What does this mean?" Eleanor asked.

"It means that the girl on the beach, Tina Mallory, is the owner of the ring, and she's dead," said Dede.

"Where is the ring?" asked Pearl.

"We left it in Virginia's room the night we took the journals," Cleo said.

"I'm glad you left it there," said Pearl. "Otherwise it could implicate us in her death."

"We may already be implicated," Eleanor sighed. "I told the Do Nothings about Virginia, the journals, and the ring. I tried to backpedal this morning because I didn't want them to think I killed Virginia, but if they see this ring, I'm sure they'll think I'm guilty of wrongdoing on some level."

"I wonder where the ring is now," Josephine said. "If the police found it in Virginia's room, they'll certainly make a connection with it and this photo."

"They won't be able to connect it to you, Eleanor. Will they?" asked Pearl.

"Did Angus see you wearing the ring?" Cleo asked.

"Have you told him about the break in?" asked Josephine.

Eleanor's head was throbbing, "No I didn't report the break in to anyone and I don't know if he noticed the ring. He didn't say anything that I can remember. I don't think I can tell him now either."

"Why not?" asked Dede. "He might be able to help us."

"Don't forget that Angus didn't like Virginia any more than I did. He hates that we stick our noses into places where it doesn't belong. He could be a suspect too if Virginia was murdered. I think we need to solve this by ourselves. Besides that, he has asked me to marry him again. I can't ask him about this or anything right now when I'm thinking I have to end our relationship." Eleanor took a deep breath, "Let's look at the facts that we have and see what we come up with."

Dede got paper and pencil and served up the heavenly lemon angel pie with an aspirin on the side for Eleanor, while Pearl put on another pot of coffee. No one wanted to ask another question about Angus.

After what seemed like hours, the ladies came up with several theories with the facts at their disposal.

Gloria Vandorff was murdered by a blow to the head for unknown reasons and left in the swale. She was rumored to be having an affair, which would make her husband a prime suspect.

Tina Mallory was lost, either because she ran away or was taken by an unknown assailant. The fact that her hands were bound, indicate the latter. Her ring was pawned, sold, or lost and showed up at the estate sale after the picture was taken that appeared online and in the *Fish Wrapper*.

Virginia Storm might have been murdered—Mavis had heard about the blood and gore in her room. Virginia Storm may have seen something from her window that got her killed—possibly Tina Mallory being murdered since they both died around the same time.

The ring was last seen in Virginia's room, but its whereabouts were now unknown.

"Is this all we have?" asked Dede.

"I don't think Tina ran away," Eleanor said. "Her hands were bound, so she was definitely kidnapped."

"Maybe she was the victim of human trafficking," said Josephine. "I've read that it's a big business on the West Coast."

"Do you know anything about that, Dede?" asked Eleanor.

"I attended a workshop on it at the community college a few months ago. I suppose it's possible but in a small town like Waterton it would be obvious if prostitutes were roaming the streets with their pimps," Dede said.

"Maybe it's just a port to hold them until they can unload them," Cleo suggested. "Look at all these missing kids on Facebook. What if they send them away by boat?"

"That would explain why Tina was found on the beach. Maybe she tried to escape and drowned," Dede said.

"How would the traffickers do it without anyone noticing?" asked Eleanor. "If they left any of the boat launches people would see."

"They would have to do it at night," Dede said.

"Then they would need a place to keep them until it was safe to move them," Cleo said.

"Where?" Pearl asked.

"It's only a theory, but it might explain Gloria's part in the mystery. She's a real estate agent. Maybe she found the hide-out," Eleanor said.

"Could Gloria be involved in a bad way?" asked Cleo. "I mean did any of you really know her?"

No one could vouch for Gloria's character, and someone who took "organ" lessons had to be of questionable integrity.

"I remember seeing lights out on the water the night we went into Virginia's room," Josephine said. "It may have been traffickers."

"I wonder what Virginia saw. I'm leaning more in the direction of murder for her too," Cleo said, "Although she could have fallen, hit her head, and bled out. Did she have a lot to drink at dinner?"

"I don't think she drank anything," Eleanor said. "Maybe that was why she was so well behaved."

"I could try to find out more about Virginia's room from my son. It's not his inn but he may have heard something," Pearl offered.

"I'll check around the real estate offices of Gloria and Will Vandorff and see what they were working on," said Dede.

"I'm going to find a new ruby red ring, just in case someone noticed," Eleanor said.

"What about those gnomes?" asked Cleo, "They may be a piece of the puzzle."

"No, I'm sure they're not," Dede answered too quickly. "Does anyone want another piece of pie?"

By the time Eleanor got home her headache had turned into a migraine. She took a dose of pain reliever and went to bed. In her dreams she saw a young and angry Angus throw Virginia against the wall in some dark and dingy hotel room. Virginia's mink coat flew open revealing the body of a young girl wearing a ruby ring on every finger and one large stone in her belly button. When Angus saw her voluptuous body, he threw her on the bed and began to kiss her. Eleanor couldn't bear to watch so she walked to a window that filled the entire wall and saw a boat filled with naked children being cast onto the shore by a stormy sea. When she looked back, Angus and Virginia sat on the bed reading her journals and laughing as they popped her marinated shrimp into their mouths. Eleanor felt light and free instead of angry. She opened the door and walked into the light.

When she woke, it was the middle of the night. Her mouth was dry, but the throbbing migraine had turned into a dull ache. She went to the kitchen for a glass of water and returned to her bedroom where a light on the ocean caught her eye. There was a boat out there moving south just beyond the huge rocks. She went to her telescope in the living room and tried to focus on it but the ship disappeared. It wasn't going fast enough to travel out of sight. It must have doused its lights. Eleanor put on her nightgown and crawled back into bed and slept until the morning light woke her.

Eleanor searched the internet for a ruby ring that might pass for the one she bought at the estate sale. It was harder than it looked. The setting was one of a kind and there didn't seem to be anything close to resembling it. She wondered how many people would notice if she just got a red stone set in gold. Surely Mavis would know. She seemed to have an eye for that kind of detail. Angus would know if he had seen the ring. Being a trained professional meant he noticed almost everything, although he didn't seem to notice the fact that she wasn't comfortable with the idea of marriage. She would have to talk to Angus soon.

She remembered her dream and didn't need her friends to interpret it for her. Angus had brought an element of darkness and baser elements into her life. She enjoyed his company and had strong feelings for him, but she didn't want to marry him. Sometimes love just wasn't enough. They wanted different things. Angus wanted to be married and to experience that sense of belonging to another, but Eleanor had already had that with Walter and now she wanted something else. She wanted freedom.

Eleanor picked up her phone and dialed Angus's number with a sadness she hadn't felt in a long time. "Angus, I need to talk to you, can I come over?" Eleanor thought it would be better if she could deliver her news and leave instead of watching him go.

"Sure. Is everything alright?" He didn't like her tone.

"I'll be right there." As Eleanor walked the short way to Angus's house, she rehearsed what she would say.

"We can still be friends. No, it's better to just break it off clean so you can find someone who will give you what you need. I'm very fond of you Angus, but I'll never marry you. You need to find someone who wants the same things you want. I like my life the way it is. I'm happy but I can't be responsible for your happiness. You have to create that yourself. Maybe you should spend more time with Michael and his family instead of with me."

As she got closer to his house she noticed her eyes were full of tears. Quickly she brushed them away and knocked on the door. Angus opened it and the look of concern on his face made Eleanor rethink her plan. Nothing had been said yet so it wasn't too late to change her mind.

"Hi," she said.

"Come in," he said. "What's on your mind, Ellie?"

"I've been thinking about your proposal," she began.

Angus knew this was not going to go the way he wanted. He was a trained professional after all and was good at reading people.

"You don't want to get married," he interrupted. "I know that already. Just forget that I brought it up. I'm happy just having you in my life."

Eleanor thought for a moment that this might work but she had thought that before. Now she had convinced herself that it was in his best interest to end it so he could find someone else—someone who truly wanted a lifetime commitment.

"I would hate to lose your friendship Angus, but I think you should start looking for a wife. I know how much you want to be married so you're not lonely and I understand that. I don't want to be the one who stands in your way."

"Ellie, you don't understand, I don't want to be married to just anyone. I want you." Angus stepped closer but Eleanor stepped away.

"I won't call or invite you to dinner or pester you about your murder investigations anymore. I mean it Angus. You need to move on."

Angus reached out and took her face in his large hands, "I will tell you everything I know about the murder of Gloria and Virginia and the girl on the beach—just don't walk away from me."

Eleanor considered his words and then hated herself for it. She was not a manipulator. She put her small hands on his large ones, looked him in the eye and said, "Angus, how dare you think that I would break off our relationship or pretend to do so to get information from you! Who do you think I am? I'm appalled you hold me in such low regard."

Angus sighed. Why were women so hard to understand? Everything he said was the wrong thing. All he really wanted was to make Eleanor happy and now he had made her angry.

"I'm sorry, Ellie, I didn't mean it like that. I just want to keep things the way they are. Everything I want is standing in front of me. I love you." Angus wanted nothing more than to kiss her.

"I'm sorry too, Angus, but I think we should have a break and see other people." Eleanor didn't know where that came from. She had no intention of seeing anyone but her words had an immediate impact on Angus. It was as if she had slapped him.

"I see," he said in a hard, cold voice. He went to the door and opened it allowing Eleanor to walk away, miserable and alone.

Eleanor was surprised that life without Angus continued as if nothing had happened. The sun still rose in the morning and set each night. The waves continued their monotonous rhythm and the sea gulls circled in a gray sky complaining in their shrill voices. The mountain of happiness she once felt in his presence was replaced by a deep pit of sadness in his absence in equal measure. She struggled to recover a little bit of equilibrium in her life. Busy keeps the blues away.

Blue Sky Time
Some days I must just sit
I twirl my hair
Gaze out the window at the blue sky

The gray day

    The

                      Falling
                      rain

My body still,
But not my brain.

Eleanor spent the following week researching human trafficking in the state of Oregon. She had no idea how prevalent it was in the United States or on the streets of Portland. Hundreds of thousands of American youths were being exploited here in her own country. It was unbelievable and totally unacceptable but she didn't know what she could do to help. Many of those young people were runaways. She thought about Bootsy, her young friend who lived in the valley, and her own grandchildren and worried that they could become victims. They were so innocent and trusting. Hadn't Bootsy taken a ride from a strange man at the bus stop? It could have been Bootsy lying dead on the beach. The interstate highway and many waterways in the area added to the appeal of traffickers. Perhaps they were moving toward the coast because enforcement was making it more difficult to pursue their activities in the cities. Thinking about it gave Eleanor nightmares.

She walked every day but mostly on the paths to the east of her house because she didn't want to pass Angus. The only time she walked on the beach was on the mornings she was sure he wasn't home. It had been weeks and he hadn't called and Eleanor didn't see him or hear about him until she met with her friends at the Boat House.

"Now that I have these hearing devices I feel like I'm part of the party," Pearl was saying as Eleanor sat down.

"You can't even see them," Dede noted, "but what happened to your eye?"

One of Pearl's usually clear blue eyes was blood red. "I was trying out a special serum that's supposed to make your lashes grow lusher and I poked the wand in my eye. It really hurt but it feels better now."

"Is it working?" Cleo asked as she peered closely at Pearl's eyelashes. "I mean the serum, not your eye." "Will you grow a hairy eyeball now?" Dede teased.

"I hope not, but I can say I'm red-eye for anything now," she chuckled.

"Josephine and I went to see the movie *Book Club*," Cleo said.

"Was it any good?" asked Pearl.

"I'm sure we would never read *Fifty Shades of Gray* in our book club," stated Cleo, "but there were some really funny parts. I loved Candice Bergen's character."

"I like the message that older women can still be vital and even enjoy sex, but I found it disappointing especially at the end where everyone ends up with a man . . . like that's the only way a woman can have a happy ending," Josephine added.

There was an uncomfortable pause as they looked at Eleanor, but said nothing. "What?" Eleanor asked oblivious of their discomfort. "I haven't seen the movie and have no critique of it."

"So what have you been doing?" asked Dede.

"I've been researching human trafficking. I'm almost positive that's what happened to Tina, the teen who was found on the beach," Eleanor said. "What have you found out about the real estate angle?"

"Nothing really," Dede said. "The police have been questioning Will Vandorff. He's a person of interest because rumor has it she was having an affair, but I don't know if they have any solid evidence against him. They haven't found the murder weapon and haven't made an arrest."

"Did you learn anything from Angus?" asked Josephine.

"No," Eleanor said. "We're no longer seeing each other."

"Was it the marriage proposal?" asked Cleo.

"Yes, he needs to be married and I just can't do it," Eleanor said sadly.

"So that explains his recent behavior," Dede said.

"What behavior is that?" Cleo asked.

"He's dating," said Dede.

"Who?" asked Eleanor.

"You don't want to know," Josephine said giving the others a look that said 'Be Quiet.'"

"He's just hurt that you won't marry him, Eleanor. He doesn't care about all those other women," Pearl said.

"All those other women . . . how many other women are there?" Eleanor wanted to know.

"I've seen him with at least three," Dede said, "Cheryl Donald at the movies, Mary Vogel, and Jeanie Davis out for dinner."

"Those are all good choices for wives," Eleanor said thoughtfully. "At least he's not pursuing some slutty bar room skank."

"Well, I did see him with Toni Dupree at the Red Shed Bar. They were both pretty drunk and she was all over him," Pearl said.

"What were you doing at the Red Shed Bar?" asked Josephine.

"I have a secret life you don't need to know about. I like to play video poker and smoke in the back room," Pearl confessed.

"You probably need to know that Angus is no longer being consulted in the homicide cases," Dede said, "because he's a person of interest in the murder of Virginia Storm."

"Really? How could that be?" Eleanor was aghast. "I was with him that night."

"But not all night," Josephine said.

"No, not all night," Eleanor admitted.

"We're no help, because we left before Virginia got home and you saw her alive when you dropped her off, but Angus could have killed her after he left you," Cleo stated.

"You don't believe he could have done it, do you?" Eleanor asked.

"Of course not, but she was a pain in his neck," Dede said, "and he was the only person here who was connected to her or might want her dead."

"It could have been a robbery gone wrong," Pearl said, "Or a passing stranger who was a serial killer."

"Unless it was someone who saw her looking out the window seeing something she wasn't supposed to see," said Josephine.

"What can we do to help him?" asked Eleanor.

"We have to solve this case," said Cleo. "We're in it up to our bloodshot eyeballs."

"We'll have to do it without Angus's help," said Dede.

The coffee group broke up with plans to meet later that evening at Moy's Chinese Garden. They needed time to think about the events and have a little fun as well.

As Eleanor drove home she convinced herself that she was okay with Angus dating other women. That's what she wanted him to do when she told him to find a wife because she didn't want marriage, but the idea was much different than the reality. It hurt and she couldn't deny it. When she got home she went to her computer and searched for missing teens hoping she could distract herself from thoughts of Angus. If she were only a young teen she could set up the traffickers and find out how things were done. What if she tried to buy a young man on the internet? Maybe she could find out that way, but it wasn't likely and could be dangerous. She might even get arrested. Human traffickers didn't deal in young girls only. They sold people of all sorts into various types of slavery. If Tina Mallory was taken to be sold, there had to be a link to Sand Beach. Someone here had to know more about it. She was positive the three murders were related. Angus would be the first to say everything was connected and she would find that connection and save Angus, but first she needed a nap.

As Eleanor slept she dreamed about Victor Gaines and his lovely wife Lola. They were in Henry Ott's house and a big party was in progress. Several people drank and danced to loud music while grown men kissed little girls in dark corners and lured them into bedrooms. Eleanor wandered through the house like a ghost passing through walls and viewing the depravity without being able to stop it. She knew there was a secret room in the house. She passed through the walls and found several young girls locked inside—their hands tied— crying without making a sound. Eleanor watched a man come to take them down to the beach and send them off in boats that launched out to sea in the dead of night. She watched and did nothing. When the last boat left the shore she looked up and saw Virginia's face looking out of her window. Behind her someone with a club beat her until she was nothing but a stain on the carpet. The killer had no face but wore a badge that caught the reflected light of the moon.

Eleanor awoke disturbed by her dream yet felt rested. She looked out the window to see a break in the clouds and the golden sun shining down. Perhaps a quick walk would help clear her head. Walking down the lane by Victor's house she noticed a gray Mercedes with California plates parked outside next to Victor's black BMW. She walked by quickly thinking they must have company. As she came to the end of Ocean Avenue she saw Edwina through the window of the yellow cottage. Her head was down and she did not look out to see Eleanor passing by. Her attention was obviously on something on the table. When she looked up, Eleanor glimpsed a monster whose face changed before her very eyes into a kindly grandmother. It must have been a trick of the light bouncing off the window pane or a need for new glasses she thought as she waved a friendly greeting and walked on.

Eleanor showered and dressed and drove into Waterton to meet her friends for dinner at the only Chinese restaurant in town. They were gathered at a large table near the back and had already ordered enough food to feed the entire city. The coffee group had brought their husbands. It was the first time in a long time that Eleanor had gone out with them alone without Walter or Angus to accompany her. It was the first time she felt like a third wheel. She sat down and was immediately put at ease because that is how her friends treated her—like a whole person not merely half of a couple.

"So Eleanor, what do you like? We have Happy Family, pot stickers, spring rolls, orange chicken, rice, and I don't know what this stuff is," Cary said as he generously passed each dish to her.

Eleanor forgot how loud the men could be. They talked about baseball and golf while the women discussed their children and grandchildren.

"I would like to learn to golf," Eleanor said unexpectedly. "Who do you know that gives lessons?"

None of the ladies in the coffee group played golf. "I'll take lessons with you," said Josephine.

"I'm sports challenged," said Dede, "so I'm out."

"Don't tell us you failed at bowling *and* golf," Eleanor said incredulously.

"As a matter of fact, I did," Dede said. "It was all about scoring. I just never got the hang of it in either case."

"I've tried it and I just spent all my time looking for my lost ball," Cleo said.

"We don't have to be good at it to have a good time," Pearl added. "Let's all give it a try."

"Then we can rent those little cars and drive around the course drinking martinis from flasks," Eleanor said.

"Oh, but it's so hard getting the olives out of those little holes in the flasks," complained Cleo. "We should stick with gin and tonics."

"Joe Bean gives lessons," said Mark. "You can call the club house and see if he is offering a class for groups."

"I'm all over it," said Eleanor.

The chatter suddenly turned quiet as Angus walked into the restaurant and sat down at a nearby table with Molly Fletcher. "Are you all right?" Dede whispered to Eleanor.

It was a shock seeing him with another woman, but Eleanor pulled herself together, "It was bound to happen sooner or later."

Angus looked over at the table and nodded in greeting, but did not smile. A few of the men waved in reply and continued eating. "He looks miserable," noted Cleo. "I bet he wishes he was sitting at the fun table."

"Give the man a break, Cleo," Steve cautioned. "He's got a lot to deal with right now."

Eleanor assumed everyone knew about their changed relationship and was grateful there were no pitiful looks passing her way.

"I've always like Molly," Eleanor said. "She's a good choice."

Steve tossed her a fortune cookie, "Read it out loud, Eleanor."

Eleanor obeyed. "People may doubt what you say but they will believe what you do . . . in bed." The entire table erupted in laughter and so it continued with each of them sharing their fortunes.

"Over self-confidence is equal to being blind . . . in bed."

"People rise to your expectations . . . in bed."

"An alien of some sort will be appearing to you shortly . . . in bed."

"Flattery will go far tonight . . . in bed."

"The greatest danger could be your stupidity . . . in bed."

"Do not mistake temptation for opportunity . . . in bed."

"I think we're too loud," Josephine said. "Maybe we should tone it down a little." She noticed how often Angus looked over at their table trying to catch Eleanor's eye and how Eleanor refrained from looking in his direction at all. Maybe she was through with him as she said, or maybe she found it too painful.

"We're done here anyway," said Richard as he laid his money on the table and scooted his chair back. Everyone did the same until there was enough to cover the bill, plus a generous tip. There was no bickering over fairness among this group. As they left a few gave a friendly wave to Angus but no one approached his table.

After hugs and farewells out on the street, Eleanor got in her car and drove to the grocery store to pick up some coffee creamer and ice cream. While she was there she ran into Jeanie Davis, one of the women Angus had been seen dating.

"Eleanor, I'm so sorry about you and Angus. I'm sure you've heard that he asked me to dinner and I want you to know all he did was talk about you. It was very humiliating for me and I won't make that mistake again. I just don't want you to be mad at me for going with him. Honestly, I was flattered that he asked me out. He's so handsome and such a gentleman. I'd marry him in a heartbeat, but it seems that his heart is taken." Jeanie squeezed Eleanor's arm and walked away without Eleanor saying one word.

As she got back in her car her thoughts turned to the sad man she saw tonight at the Chinese restaurant.

It hurt her to know that he was so unhappy and it hurt her to think of him with Molly Fletcher as well. What had she done exactly and why had she done it? If she was honest with herself she had to admit she was sad and miserable too. Tears welled in her eyes making it difficult to see the road ahead.

She blinked and they rolled down her cheeks. It was the marriage part she didn't want. Marriage meant doing his laundry and cooking for him every day. The special date nights would disappear and the care and effort she put into pleasing him would become a duty—something he would expect instead of something she freely offered that caused him to be grateful. The wine and roses would dry up and those deep lingering kisses would turn into meaningless pecks.

No, she was right to refuse to marry him. If he wanted that he would have to find it with someone else. She would not be responsible for his happiness at the cost of her own. It might hurt now, but later she would be glad. It didn't occur to her at that moment that she wasn't getting any benefits from her break up. There were no date nights, wine and roses, or deep lingering kisses now. Wasn't a person supposed to live in the moment? Was it foolish to worry about a future that didn't exist and might never come to pass? What was that she read somewhere about not your future being bright—but your now.

The lights from the car behind her reflected in the rear view mirror and into her eyes, but just as she adjusted the mirror something leaped in front of her car causing her to brake and veer off the road into the ditch. Her air bag deployed with a jolt. While she sat in her car gasping for breath, the man in the vehicle following her stopped, slid down into the ditch, and opened her door.

"Ellie, are you okay?" Of course it was Angus. Was there ever a time she needed help that he didn't show up?

Eleanor could not speak. Angus unbuckled her seatbelt and she slid out of the car and into his arms thinking this was the end. She was surely dying. Every breath she took was pain.

"Ellie, talk to me. Where are you hurt?"

"I'm- dy-ing," she finally choked out the words.

Angus was smiling, "No, you're not dying. I've seen people who were dying and believe me you're not dying. You just had the wind knocked out of you. Just rest here a bit until you catch your breath." He sank down propping her against the side of her car while he grabbed a blanket from her back seat and wrapped it around her carefully looking for other injuries. After a while she recovered enough to stand up.

"What are you doing?" he asked.

"I've got ice cream in the back seat," she said. "Can you take me home before it melts?"

"As you wish." The ride to Eleanor's house was a quiet one.

"Did you see what jumped out in front of me?" she asked as they drove up the hill to her house.

"No, I didn't see anything but you driving under the influence of Chinese food and a bad fortune cookie," he teased.

"I think it was a deer," Eleanor said, "I'm glad I didn't hit it. Do you think my car is ruined?"

"I didn't get a good look at the damage, but if you want I can go back and pull it out of the ditch."

"No, I'll call AAA," she didn't want to feel overly grateful.

"Are you sure you don't want me to take you to the hospital to get checked out?"

"I'm fine, really. You were right. I just had the wind knocked out of me."

"Let me at least get you safely inside."

Eleanor let him help her out of his pickup, unlock her door ,and come inside. He turned on the lights and searched for intruders while she made a call to AAA.

"All clear except for a very sulky parrot," he commented.

"Oh Feathers is in love," she said casually. "Would you like some ice cream? It's raspberry ripple."

"Are you having some?" he asked.

"Yes," she already had two bowls ready to go.

They sat in the kitchen eating ice cream just as they used to do before the proposal ruined everything.

"You know you'll never find a wife if you get drunk and talk about other women when you're on a date," Eleanor scolded.

Angus looked up under his bushy eyebrows, "I know."

"Any of those women would marry you. All you have to do is show them a little of the real you."

"I don't know, Ellie. You've seen the real me and you don't want to marry it."

There was nothing Eleanor could say that would comfort him that wouldn't also cause him to think there was still hope so she simply finished her raspberry ripple and thanked him for the ride home. After he left she found a fortune lying on the kitchen counter.

"There is only one happiness in life: to love and be loved."

I see you Angus McBride
Your stern and furrowed face
Conceals a wounded boy inside.
Those sure and measured words

Belie the doubt you hide.
I see you
In all your imperfections
The outward and the inner man
The things you fear you cannot do
The things you fear you can.
I see you
In your sublimity
Struggle amid your life's debris
Your shadow self—sinking down
To let your perfect light shine free.
I see you
Strive to make wrong right
 To make the broken whole
Shoulder burdens not your own
Too heavy for your soul.
I see you
Stand alone while lovers pass you by
Too proud to play a minor part
Uncertain where love goes
When it leaves the heart.
I see you

Eleanor's car was in the shop. There was only a little fender damage, nothing major. Nancy Wilson, her friend and neighbor, drove her to the body shop.

"So what's going on with you and Angus?" she pried.

"Nothing, we're just taking a break from each other." Eleanor was trying to put him out of her mind.

"You broke up! I've heard that he's dating, but I must tell you, he hasn't brought anyone home. I've been keeping watch. Are you dating too? Because if you are in the market for a new man, I know someone who would be perfect for you."

"Nancy, I'm not looking for a husband, but I think Angus needs a wife. That's the problem in a nutshell."

"I see."

"I'm thinking of taking golf lessons. You golf. Who should I get to teach me?" Eleanor had forgotten the name of the man Mark had recommended. She thought it was something like Jim Beam, but wasn't that a whisky? Maybe she had hit her head in the accident.

"Well I know the perfect person. I'll call you later with his number."

"Have you heard anything about the death of Virginia Storm?" Eleanor hadn't given her full attention to the case since her break up with Angus and thought it might create a diversion.

"Officer McGraw is handling the case since Angus has a conflict of interest. He was asking people in the neighborhood if they had seen anything suspicious on the night they think Virginia died or the day that body washed up. I can tell he thinks the two are related in some way."

"Angus always says that everything is related," Eleanor commented.

"I've noticed lights off shore lately—even more than usual. I wonder what that could be late at night."

"I've seen them too. It makes me think about smugglers or pirates doing something illegal that must be done in the dark. Do you know much about human trafficking?" Eleanor asked.

"Not much, although I've read that it happens more than we know and in our part of the country. Do you think that's what happened to that girl?" Nancy asked.

"I don't know. I'd hate to think it could be happening right under our noses. Surely the police would know and be investigating that angle," Eleanor said.

Nancy dropped Eleanor off at the body shop where she got an estimate for her broken car and a loaner so she could drive herself home. Once home, before she could pour a cup of tea, Officer McGraw rang the doorbell.

"Hello, Mrs. Penrose, I hope this isn't a bad time, but I need to ask you a few questions."

"Come in Officer. Would you like a cup of tea? I was just about to have one."

Officer McGraw walked into Eleanor's white kitchen where everything sparkled and helped himself to a chocolate chip cookie.

"You did offer a cookie with the tea," he said with a grin.

"Please help yourself." Eleanor poured the tea and sat at the counter waiting for Officer McGraw to finish his snack.

"These are really good. Do you put something special in them? My Gramma always put orange zest in her oatmeal cookies. She said it was a secret ingredient."

"Interesting, I'll have to give that a try some time," she said. "Now how can I help you?"

Officer McGraw took out his pen and notebook and began his questioning. "Where were you on the night Virginia Storm was killed?"

"I don't know. What night was she killed?"

"My best guess is February 21."

Eleanor consulted the calendar that hung on the wall in a wooden frame. "That would have been the night Angus and I took her out to dinner at the Boat House. We ate dinner and dropped her off sometime before eight. Then Angus brought me back here and went home."

"Was that the last time you saw her?"

"Yes."

"How well did you know her?"

"Not well. She'd only been in town a few days."

"Did you know she was harassing Angus?"

"I knew she went to his house uninvited."

"Did you ever hear him threaten her?"

"No. Is Angus a suspect?"

"Unfortunately, we have to consider him since he seems to be the only one who knew her. Hopefully, we can eliminate him as a suspect soon."

"But he's still consulting on Gloria Vandorff's case, isn't he?"

"Those crimes are linked by a common murder weapon so he's off that case too." Officer McGraw paused and wished he hadn't given away that information.

"But surely he's helping solve the murder of the missing girl on the beach," Eleanor persisted.

"That's considered an accident at this time." Eleanor knew it wasn't an accident, the girl's hands were tied but she knew when to quit.

"You said earlier that Angus brought you home that night and then left. Do you remember what time he left?"

"No, not really."

"Did he spend the night?" Officer McGraw looked uncomfortable. "I'm sorry, but I have to ask."

"No," Eleanor answered honestly. She was not the type to lie and would have said otherwise if it had been true.

"Did he say where he was going?"

"I assumed he went home."

"May I ask why you and Angus took Ms. Storm out for dinner? I understand Angus wasn't fond of her."

"It was my idea. I thought we could talk to her and maybe work things through."

"Can you describe that night for me? How did she seem? Were there angry words or any drama?"

"We picked her up about six o'clock. She wasn't happy that I was there—I assume she thought she was going on a date with Angus alone, but she seemed to recover as we drove to the Boat House. We talked about her visit here. Angus was curious about her reason for coming. She said she just wanted to reconnect with him because he was the father of her child. That part did get a little tense. Angus reminded her that their mutual child was a man who didn't need their coparenting and he wasn't interested in 'reconnecting' with her.

They talked at length about their son and how wonderful he had turned out. They both seemed proud of him. Angus made some remarks about her uninvited appearance at his house, which seemed to embarrass her but he didn't threaten her in any way—not even with a restraining order. I could tell she wasn't happy about that, but she didn't react in an angry manner. We ate our dinners and then we took her home. It was a very quiet ride. I think she was sulking in the back seat."

"Were either Angus or Ms. Storm under the influence that evening?"

"No, we didn't have anything to drink with dinner. I couldn't say if Virginia had something before we picked her up or after we left her. She seemed sober."

"Thank you, Mrs. Penrose. I don't have any more questions . . . except . . . did you leave your house after Angus brought you home?"

"No, I'm quite sure I stayed in the rest of the night."

"Is there anyone who can attest to that?"

"Only Feathers, but he's not talking. I think he's lovesick."

"He wouldn't be the only one. It's almost spring you know," he chuckled. "If you think of anything else, be sure to call me." Officer McGraw gave her his card and left.

Eleanor wondered if there was any evidence her friends might have left at the scene that could incriminate them and if she was wrong not telling Officer McGraw about the journals and the ring. She worried that Angus might be wrongly convicted of killing Virginia. Perhaps they found his fingerprints on her doorknob. Certainly he couldn't have left any inside, unless he had gone inside at another time . . . unless he had killed her.

Eleanor and the ladies of the coffee group met at the Babbling Brook golf course for their first golf lesson. Cleo brought the clubs she inherited from her Aunt Lena, but the others used the ones offered by the instructor, Joe Bean, an older man with a thick head of white hair and an enormous amount of patience. After introducing himself he introduced them to some of the clubs in Cleo's bag. Aunt Lena had a sense of humor and had knitted cozy covers for her clubs—they looked suspiciously like the private parts of a man with two sacks attached for golf balls.

"Honestly, I didn't notice that until now," Cleo claimed red-faced. "Why did he pick my bag?" she whispered.

"Don't worry, it's not like I haven't seen that before," Joe said calmly—never having seen the like on a golf club.

He removed the cover gingerly and explained the use of the club, but left the cover in Cleo's bag evidently reluctant to touch it again when he was finished. He spent most of the lesson informing them about the rules and etiquette of golf. He showed them how to respect the course by repairing divots and raking the bunkers. Then he took them to the driving range and explained the use of a tee, the grip on the shaft, and the stance and necessary followthrough of driving the ball. He explained the "sweet spot" and then let the ladies try their hand at hitting the ball.

All in all they did fairly well except for the incident when Dede let go of her driver and it flew farther than any of her balls ever went, or the time when it flew out of her hands backward and nearly beaned Joe Bean.

"This is obviously a game invented by men for men," commented Pearl as they returned to the parking lot.

"Why do you say that?" asked Dede.

"It's all about sex. Just look at all the terms: shaft, head, balls, holes, sweet spot, thrust, and posture," she said. "You are even supposed to put the ball in the hole."

"I think you have sex on the brain," Josephine laughed.

"I remember something about the term GOLF meaning: Gentlemen Only Ladies Forbidden," Eleanor said.

"I can see why, no lady would want to play this game back in the day," Pearl continued.

"It's a good thing we're not ladies," Cleo remarked as she loaded her clubs with their obscene covers into the back of her car.

"You may want to check all the other covers and censor them before our next lesson," suggested Dede.

They piled into Cleo's car and headed into Waterton for lunch at the Blue Lagoon where they ordered salads and sandwiches and giggled over the previous events of the morning.

"What a beautiful day this turned out to be," Eleanor exclaimed. "It was foggy when I left Sand Beach this morning, but now the sun is out and it feels almost like spring."

"I absolutely hate this time of year," responded Dede. "It smells like mud and dog poop."

"You know they say that witches think children smell like dog droppings," Cleo said as she glanced around the restaurant looking for any offending children."

"They also say that witches don't have toes. Take off your shoes and show us your feet," ordered Eleanor.

"Don't look now but Angus is in that booth over there," whispered Cleo.

Immediately they all swiveled their heads in his direction. Angus smiled and waved good naturedly and they all turned their heads back.

"Is he with someone?" asked Dede. "I couldn't tell."

"Yes, there is clearly a woman sitting in that booth with him, and another man." Cleo said.

"Who is it this time?" asked Josephine who was obviously irritated by what she considered his immature behavior.

"I don't know. It's someone I've never seen before," Cleo said.

"I have to use the restroom," said Pearl. "I'll check her out as I pass by." None of the women seemed to recognize their own junior high school behaviors as they whispered and peeked periodically at Angus and his companions.

"I've never seen that woman before either," Pearl reported on her return, "but the man is a dead ringer for Angus so I think it must be his son."

"That makes sense," said Eleanor. "He's here to get his mother's body. Maybe that's his wife with him."

"I don't think it's his wife, too old," said Pearl, "unless he's one of those abandoned boys who try to marry their mothers."

"Do you remember Harold Scot? His mother left him when he was two and when he grew up he searched the country for her," Cleo said. "When he finally found her he discovered she was a drug addict so he left her and married a woman even older than his mother."

"So now he has a wife who's also his mother," Eleanor said. "Why is it that women always end up taking care of men?"

"In your case, it's because you won't let any man take care of you, Eleanor," Josephine said.

"Ouch, do you really think that's true?" Eleanor's discomfort proved that Josephine had indeed hit a nerve.

"Maybe, have you tried being the queen of everything and letting someone serve you?" asked Cleo.

"I am the queen of everything already. I just don't want to be demoted to servant," Eleanor defended herself.

"Relationships are always a two-way street," Dede added. "Sometimes you're the queen and he's the servant and sometimes he's the king and you're the servant."

"You've just forgotten, Eleanor, because you've been taking care of yourself for a long time," Josephine added.

"It might be time for a change. Let someone take care of you," Cleo said.

"This is beginning to sound like an intervention," Eleanor said.

"No, no," Josephine protested. "We all love you . . . and Angus, but if you're not ready for the kind of relationship Angus wants, just tell him you need more time."

"Really, why burn your bridges?" Pearl added. "You could string him along forever. From what I can see Angus isn't going to commit to anyone else."

"That's my point exactly. I don't want to string him along. He may be missing opportunities by hanging on to me when I have no intention of ever marrying," Eleanor spoke decisively.

"All I'm saying is give it some time, Eleanor," Josephine advised. "You may still be grieving now and might change your mind later."

"The experts say you shouldn't make any major decisions within a year after suffering a loss. Walter has only been gone for a few months," Dede said.

"If you want me to, I could talk to Angus," Josephine offered.

"Shhhh, he's coming over here," whispered Cleo.

"Good afternoon, ladies," Angus greeted them with a warm smile and introduced them to his companions. "I'd like you to meet my son, Michael Patrick and Virginia's stepsister, Drusilla Malfoy. They're here for Virginia's remains. And these lovely ladies are my friends: Cleo, Josephine, Dede, Pearl, and Eleanor."

"I notice that all your friends seem to be women. I see nothing has changed over the years. How predictable you are,

Angus!" Drusilla's statement sounded like an accusation. Was she blaming him for Virginia's seduction years ago?

"It's so nice to meet you," Michael said, ignoring Drusilla's rudeness. He was every bit as handsome and charming as Angus, even sharing his sparkling green eyes and deep dimples. "I feel as if I already know you. Angus has regaled me with tales of your mischief."

"I don't know what you've heard, but I'm sure it's all lies," Dede responded with a twinkle in her eye.

"Well, we're on our way to Dudley's Death Palace," said Angus. "I'll catch you later."

Michael waved and Drusilla simply pursed her lips in disapproval and they were gone.

"Did anyone else feel evil emanating from that woman?" asked Cleo.

"My hair was literally standing on end," Josephine said.

"Even her name is evil: Drusilla Malfoy. It's right out of a Disney movie," said Cleo.

"I don't believe that's her real name," Eleanor stated.

"She's definitely an evil stepsister. Is it possible there could be two meanies in the same family?" asked Pearl.

"Absolutely," said Josephine, "they were probably raised in a hot bed of dysfunction and narcissism."

"I didn't think she looked too old to be Michael's wife, but she looks nothing like Virginia and much younger," Eleanor said.

"Her hair was pulled so tightly into that bun, it probably stretched the wrinkles out, not to mention the pain it must cause. That can make a person mean as well as account for that pinched appearance around the mouth—not a flattering look in any case," Cleo observed.

"Well, stepsisters don't share genes, just stepparents," reminded Dede.

"And what is Dudley's Death Palace? Is that code for, 'Help this woman is killing me'?" asked Cleo.

"I don't know, maybe he meant the morgue," Dede suggested. "They keep bodies there if they're involved in a murder investigation. The medical examiner is Dr. Dudley."

"That reminds me. Officer McGraw visited me this week and said Angus is a suspect in the murder of Virginia and he can't consult on Gloria's case either because the same weapon was used in both crimes," Eleanor said.

"Did he tell you what the weapon was?" asked Cleo.

"No, I think he had already told me more than he thought he should."

"Did you tell him about our involvement?" asked Dede.

"We shouldn't be talking here. You never know who could be listening," Josephine cautioned.

"He didn't ask, so I didn't tell," Eleanor whispered.

"I have to use the restroom," Pearl said, "I'll check out all the booths to see if they're empty."

"Now that Pearl's hearing is improved, I think her bladder is broken," Josephine said.

"What's with all those gnomes outside anyway?" Cleo asked. "Yesterday I found a rock with a gnome painted on it. On the back were some numbers. I think it's a code for something."

"I found one too. I thought it was a phone number, but when I dialed it, I got the body shop," Pearl complained.

"Yes, they're springing up all over town," Eleanor said. "Is the city promoting something with them?"

"I can't tell you yet," Dede said.

"We are the only ones left in this restaurant," declared Pearl upon her return.

They paid their bill and left curious to learn Dede's secret.

Eleanor returned home wondering what to do with the rest of her afternoon. She didn't have to wonder for long because the doorbell rang and a smiling Lola Gaines stood at her door.

"I hope I'm not bothering you, Eleanor, but I need a little help," Lola said.

"No bother, come in Lola." Eleanor opened the door and Lola stepped inside. "How can I help you?"

"I can't cook and I think Victor is growing tired of me," her voice rose into a whining cry and big tears fell from her eyes.

"Oh my, maybe I should put on a pot of tea." Eleanor disappeared into the kitchen and returned with a box of tissues.

"Sit down and tell me why you're so sad," Eleanor said.

Lola sat on one of the new couches and dabbed at her teary eyes, trying not to smear her mascara as she worked at regaining her composure.

"You probably know by now that Victor and I have an unconventional kind of relationship. I'm sure Amy has told you we enjoy an open marriage, but the truth is that Victor enjoys it and I only tolerate it. I know he loves me and never lets his other trysts come between us, but I can't seem to separate the love from the sex."

Eleanor tried not to seem surprised by these revelations and certainly didn't want to appear judgmental so she simply nodded her head.

"It turns out I'm horribly jealous!" Lola revealed. "Victor doesn't seem to be bothered by my exploits and I think it means he doesn't care about me. I thought if I could learn to cook like you, I might be more appealing to him. Maybe I could satisfy his hunger in another way. I saw the way Angus looked at you. I want Victor to admire me like that. I want Victor to be true to me the way Angus is devoted to you."

"Hmmm," Eleanor was caught off-guard. Lola obviously didn't want advice about how to keep her man satisfied sexually but wanted to learn to cook. "Do you have any experience cooking at all?"

"I can make scrambled eggs and macaroni and cheese." She smiled as she shared her limited skills.

"Are those the meals that Victor enjoys?"

"He did in the beginning, but now he's tired of them," she admitted.

"Come into the kitchen with me. I hear the teapot boiling." Eleanor pulled out a cookbook that contained basic cooking skills. "Now tell me what Victor likes to eat when you dine out."

"He likes meat and potatoes," Lola answered immediately. Eleanor nodded knowingly.

"Let's try this recipe for Steak Diane," she said as she went to her refrigerator and looked for the necessary ingredients. As she pulled pans and spices out of her cupboards she began to list the things Lola needed to keep on hand in her pantry. Lola took notes on her phone.

"Do you think all men cheat on their wives?" asked Lola.

"Absolutely not." Eleanor was certain Walter never cheated.

"Victor says it is a biological imperative for men to have sex with as many women as possible to ensure that their genes survive," Lola said. "That's his argument for swinging."

"Surely, you use some kind of protection," Eleanor said. "He can't be planning to impregnate all the women he swings with. And then there's STDs. You must protect yourselves from those."

"Of course we use protection. Victor's not interested in having children. It's just that he believes it's a biological urge that shouldn't be stifled."

They chatted about men and relationships while they worked. Lola seemed interested in Eleanor's relationship with Angus and asked some very pointed questions about their friends and neighbors. Eleanor gave up very little in the way of gossip, mostly because she truly didn't know which of her neighbors were swingers, cheaters, or sex addicts. When everything was assembled, Lola left with the cookbook tucked under her arm and a meal ready to pop in the oven. Eleanor watched her leave and shook her head. It was a new world. Eleanor didn't know if she approved, but figured it didn't really matter.

Meanwhile in the town of Waterton, Josephine was giving advice to a lovesick Angus. "I just don't understand women, Josephine. They've been throwing themselves at me my entire life and I know most of the ones I've taken out lately want more than dinner and a movie. They're eager for a lifetime commitment after the first date," Angus complained. "Even Virginia's sister is flirting with me. I don't know how to get rid of her."

"It must be very hard being so desirable, Angus. It's difficult to know if someone loves you for you or if you're just a big handsome piece of cheesecake." Josephine was having difficulty feeling sorry for the man sitting across from her picking at his hamburger and fries.

"She told me we needed to see other people. Why doesn't Eleanor want me?" he asked.

"I know that's what you heard, but she may have meant you should see other people. Are you sure you love her?" Josephine asked. "Maybe she's just the one you can't have that makes her the one you want."

Angus's bushy eyebrows lowered as he gave that statement serious thought. "Do you think I'm that kind of man?"

"I'm not sure. I thought I knew you but lately you've given me good reason to suspect that I don't. When Walter died I advised you to give Eleanor time to grieve and yet here you are pushing her to get married not even four months after her loss," Josephine chided.

"Eleanor lost Walter years ago," Angus said.

"No, Angus, you fail to realize the depth of her attachment to Walter and how grief works. She may have endured a long goodbye but it wasn't over by a long shot."

"How long does she need to grieve?" Angus asked.

"It's different for everyone," Josephine said, "and Eleanor may be ready to let you love her without committing to marriage—even now. I know she loves you."

"How do you know that? She never tells me," Angus said. "Is she seeing any one?"

"Not that I know, although you've made it abundantly clear that you are seeing several someones. She was willing to let you go find a wife because she couldn't make that commitment.

She did that because she thinks that's what you need to be happy—that's love."

"How do I fix this now?" Angus sighed.

"You need to talk this out with her. Let her know that her happiness is important to you. If you want her in your life you're going to have to give up on marriage for now. I think you are both miserable and there's no need for it," Josephine added. "Is marriage that important to you, Angus?"

"I'd like to be married, but only to Eleanor," Angus said, "You're sure she's not seeing anyone?"

"Yes, I'm sure," Josephine said with authority.

March continued to roar like a lion with an intense windstorm and torrential rains that kept Eleanor in her house snuggled under a blanket with a book. Book club was meeting tonight and Eleanor refused to go without having read the selection for the month. By dinner time, Eleanor had finished the task even after dozing off several times and was in the kitchen searching for something to eat when she heard a strange noise coming from the front door. Feathers made a frenzied flyby and landed on her shoulder as she first peeked out the stained-glass window and then slowly opened the door. Suddenly Inky, the crow, flew inside startling Eleanor and causing Feathers to cry out in alarm, "Intruders, intruders, lock the door, Ellie."

"Too late, Feathers, the intruder is already inside." Eleanor tried putting Feathers in his cage so she could open the windows to let the crow out, but he resisted and continued to fly through the house squawking madly, inciting Inky to do the same. It was chaos and mayhem. Eleanor didn't know what to do. She worried that the excited fowls would soil her new couches. Instinctively, she picked up the telephone and called Angus.

"Angus, I need help. A wild bird flew into the house and I can't get it out." Eleanor thought she sounded calm, but what Angus heard was a hysterical woman in need of rescue. It took all of two minutes for him to arrive armed with a large fishing net and backup in the form of Michael.

The two men entered the house and immediately put a plan into action. Angus methodically cornered the brazen crow with the fishing net so Michael could throw Eleanor's blanket over it and release it outside. The whole event took less than ten minutes with Feathers interfering whenever possible and Eleanor screaming obscenities as the crow flew wildly through her house knocking over precious artifacts.

"I'm so sorry to bring you out in this weather. I just didn't know how to get it out without letting Feathers out as well. Thank you so much!" Eleanor was grateful and relieved.

"Don't mention it," Michael said, "I was a fireman for thirty years, so this wasn't my first time rescuing a damsel in distress."

"We left Drusilla in the kitchen, so we better get back before she burns the house down," Angus said as he picked up his net and walked out the door. Eleanor watched them walk away in the rain. Feathers flew to her shoulder and she stroked his head as he whispered, "I love you, Ellie."

Eleanor wondered what Drusilla was cooking up in the kitchen. She wasn't hungry after imagining a pot of crow simmering on Angus's stove, so she showered, dressed and headed off to book club.

"What a horrible night to have to drive to Pearl's house or anywhere for that matter," complained Cleo as she took off her coat and greeted the members who were already there. She remembered the time she took a wrong turn and ended up on a dead-end road in a blinding rainstorm. It was frightening to get lost on the way to a friend's house, especially when you'd been there hundreds of times before. It made her question her mental capacities as well as her night vision.

"It is a nasty night, but I'm glad you made it," welcomed Pearl.

"Did anyone else notice the billboard coming into town? It said 'Game of Gnomes Coming Soon.' What does it mean?" asked Wren.

"It's a mystery," said Cleo. "Gnomes have been seen all over the city with no explanation."

"It's most likely a marketing ploy for The Creamery," said Polly.

"I haven't heard anything about it," said Kim who worked there.

"What do gnomes have to do with cheese?" asked Pearl.

"I'm sure it will all be revealed in good time. Let's sit down," said Dede, changing the subject.

The book club gathered in Pearl's living room around a roaring fire Cary had built in the fireplace. It flickered and crackled, throwing a rosy glow over the faces of the nine women. Mercedes had been the last to arrive causing a flurry of interest over her new look. Her naturally wavy locks had been trimmed and straightened and she was wearing makeup that gave her ordinarily pretty face the glamour of a movie star, but the transformation did not stop there. Instead of her usual jeans, T-shirt and Birkenstocks, she wore a pair of ballerina flats, black slacks topped with a silk polka dot blouse and classic sweater.

"Good Lord, what happened to you?" asked Dolly. "I didn't even recognize you when you came in the door!" Mercedes beamed as she sat down next to Kim, who gave her a smile but said nothing.

"You look fabulous," said Cleo.

"I suspect there is a new man in your life," Josephine prodded.

"How did you know?" asked Mercedes shyly.

"Your face is glowing. It must be love," Pearl commented, "Or the reflection of the fire."

"I can't believe it. Maybe I need a new man in my life," Dolly said. "Where can I find one?"

"Is it someone we know?" asked Dede. Mercedes remained coyly silent.

"I did see you with someone the other night at the movies. Is it him?" asked Wren.

"I'm not ready to share that information yet," Mercedes said quietly, "The relationship is still new, so I don't want to jinx it."

With that the interrogation ended and the book discussion began although there were several people who worried that the secret lover might be Angus.

The Unbearable Lightness of Being was the book up for discussion and it was definitely a worthy and timely choice. Eleanor couldn't help but draw comparisons between the characters in the book and Lola and Victor Gaines. "Do you think you can separate love from sex?" she asked.

"Not me," said Kim. "When I have sex it's because I'm in love. I couldn't do it any other way."

"I think I could," Dolly countered. "As a matter of fact, I think I have. Sex feels good even without love."

"I used to think there was a chemical in the brain that caused women to love the men they had sex with. Could someone Google that to see if it's true?" Cleo added.

"It's all lust," Wren said, "Love is what we tell ourselves it is so that we don't feel guilty. I think men have figured that out. That's why they tell us they love us, but it's all about biology and reproducing to populate the planet."

"I used to think I could make myself love someone just by wanting to. I'd see a cute boy and think, 'I love him.' I didn't believe in love the way you see it in the movies. Do you think it might have a chemical component?" Pearl asked.

"I agree that sex is a biological imperative. It's necessary for reproducing and it's pleasurable so we want to do it. There is definitely a hormonal component, but when we start looking at it scientifically, it can take the romance out of it and spoil the mood," Josephine said.

"I think there must be different types of people who see sex and love differently. There are men and women who are totally monogamous, just as some animals are. You know beavers mate for life, as well as gibbons, wolves, swans, and albatrosses. And then there are those who scatter their seeds as far and wide as they can. It's the way they're hard-wired," Mercedes offered.

"You're not actually giving people permission to have sex with multiple partners because they're made that way are you?

Don't you think humans are above animal instincts?" Wren argued.

"I think Mercedes is right. People are made differently. It's society that attempts to keep our sexual instincts under control. Maybe love is something altogether different than lust. We only confuse it when we're young, but as we age we see that love is caring deeply for someone with or without sex," Eleanor concluded.

"I've Googled it," said Dede. "According to this article, romantic love can be broken down into three catagories: lust, attraction, and attachment, and each category is characterized by its own set of hormones that come from the brain."

"What hormones are involved?" asked Eleanor.

"Lust is driven by testosterone and estrogen while dopamine, norepinephrine, and serotonin create attraction, and oxytocin and vasopressin aid in attachment," Dede informed the group.

"I'm definitely in the attraction phase," Mercedes admitted. "I know that the release of dopamine can make a person giddy and lead to a decrease in appetite and insomnia, which I am currently experiencing."

"So it's sort of true that love is chemically induced, but that didn't really answer my question," said Cleo.

"What was your question?" asked Pearl.

"The attachment hormone, oxytocin is released during sex and it says that women often confuse the positive feeling associated with this with the thought that her partner is her perfect mate. So I think the answer to your question is yes-sort of," Dede said. "It also says that other ways to keep your partner over time are to keep positive thoughts about them, forgive them, make love, do new and exciting things with them, and laugh a lot."

"So we were all partially right about our theories of love. We just didn't have the entire picture of it being different catagories created by various hormones," Kim summarized. "Lust, attraction, and attachment are different forms of love."

"Right, I love you all, but I don't lust for any of you," admitted Cleo.

"Maybe we shouldn't be so quick to judge then," Dede said. "Maybe it's harder for some people to remain faithful and stay in a relationship than it is for others because they don't have enough of the right hormones, but we all have our crosses to bear."

"Or they don't know how to create them," said Wren.

"I'm feeling like I need to go home very soon and try out some of these theories on making love last over time," Cleo said. There was a long pause in the discussion.

"It must be twenty past the hour," said Pearl, "Does everyone want dessert? I made red velvet poke cake." Everyone snickered.

Eleanor woke up exceptionally early even for her. As she looked out the window over her little village of Sand Beach she watched the white waves wash ashore as they caught the reflected light from a moon that had not yet set. Down below she noticed the lights were on at Angus's house and wondered if he was taking his son fishing. Surely they had made arrangements for Virginia's body by now and, hopefully, Drusilla had returned to her own life, wherever that was. She put on the coffee and went outside to get the morning paper. Suddenly, Inky swooped down and landed on her shoulder.

"What is this?" asked Eleanor just a little startled. "You are becoming a pest!"

"Are you talking to yourself, Mrs. Penrose?" said a deep voice from the darkness. In a flurry of wings Inky flew away. Eleanor did not recognize the voice, but as the figure emerged she recognized Victor Gaines. "I hope you don't find me a pest."

"Good morning Victor. It's early for a walk isn't it?" she asked suddenly self-conscious about standing in the middle of the lane in her bathrobe.

"I have things to do today and I promised Lola I'd return this casserole dish she borrowed from you. The meal was delicious. I have no illusions that she cooked it so don't try to delude me. Thank you."

"You're welcome, but Lola and I put the meal together in my kitchen, she did most of the work. I only coached from the sidelines." Eleanor modestly defended her new friend.

"Well thank you just the same." He handed the dish to Eleanor. "You know you are a very attractive woman, Eleanor. I must say I've enjoyed meeting your friends as well, especially the mayor."

"I understand you've volunteered to play the organ at Sunday Mass," Eleanor said.

"Make no mistake, I only did that to get close to Dede. I'm a Reformed Druid and have no link to the Catholics other than to kiss and tell," he said, smiling mischievously.

"What do you mean by that?" Eleanor asked.

"I guess she hasn't told you that we're in trouble," he chuckled. "I couldn't help myself when I saw her on Sunday.

I laid a big kiss on those pouty lips. Unfortunately, the smack reverberated throughout the church. I guess you could say I'm a loud kisser, although I did refrain from using tongue out of respect for the venue. Later, someone called the parish office and made an anonymous complaint."

Eleanor couldn't help but laugh. "Oh, Victor, you've made my day, now I'd better get inside before the neighbors complain about me outside in my nightgown with a strange man."

Of course it was too late for that. Angus and Michael drove up the hill just in time to see Eleanor's door close and a shadowy man figure disappear down the lane. What else was Angus to believe but the worst?

It wasn't long after Eleanor finished her second cup of coffee that a surprise visitor showed up at her door. Drusilla Malfoy stood looking like something out of a Grimm's fairy tale wearing a dress and a red hooded sweatshirt. Eleanor figured the sweatshirt was something she borrowed from Angus because she didn't have any clothes fit for life in the rural wilds of Oregon. Feathers was in rare form and swooped down on her crying, "Intruder, intruder, get your gun" as soon as she stepped inside. Drusilla swatted at the unruly parrot and screamed in fright until she realized what he was.

"I should have known you would have a dirty fowl living in your home," she said covering her fright with anger.

Eleanor waited. She didn't remember offering an invitation to this woman and now she was being insulted in her own house.

"Well, I wonder if you have a few minutes to talk to me about Angus," Drusilla asked.

"Would you like a cup of coffee?" Eleanor offered graciously.

"Yes, I would love a cup of coffee. I don't know what Angus does to make whatever it is he calls coffee, but it is undrinkable and I'm afraid I'm having withdrawals. Would you make a café latté with sugar free syrup, nonfat milk, and a dash of foam for me?"

Eleanor disappeared into the kitchen, poured a latté cup full of coffee and added a great deal of French Vanilla International creamer to it. She would have rolled her eyes but there was no one there to notice so she simply returned and offered the drink to her guest. Drusilla guzzled it up within two minutes and thanked her profusely, never guessing it was full of fat and calories.

"What did you want to discuss, Drusilla?" Eleanor asked.

"I never knew Angus when Virginia was head over heels in love with him and I just wondered what you could tell me about him." Drusilla looked longingly at her empty cup.

"I never knew him then either, Drusilla, but if you are asking me if he killed your sister, I'd have to say no."

"Oh, am I that obvious?" she said. "You didn't tell Officer McGraw that you thought he might have killed her?"

"Yes, you are obvious and Officer McGraw didn't ask if I thought he killed her." Eleanor had no time for coy games. "If you think he's a murderer, why are you staying at his house?"

"Does that bother you? Are you in love with Angus, too? He seems to be a magnet for lonely old women." Eleanor wondered if Drusilla knew how insulting she was and decided she was oblivious to the feelings of others.

"Are you saying that you're attracted to him? He is quite a catch, but I'm not in the market for a husband, so if you came here looking for my permission to pursue him . . . you have it."

"Oh no, you misunderstand. My interest in Angus isn't that kind." Drusilla's face turned red and her hands fluttered wildly in front of her. It was clear to Eleanor that her interest was exactly that kind. "You've known Angus for a long time. Would you lie to protect him?"

"Angus isn't a murderer, and I'm not a liar."

"I was thinking of extending my stay here. It is lovely and Angus has been very kind and generous, but I can't abuse his hospitality by overstaying my welcome and people are beginning to talk. Do you know if any of the cottages here are available?" Drusilla asked.

Eleanor took Drusilla's empty cup into the kitchen and returned with a piece of paper. "Here's the number of a real estate agent who might give you some guidance."

"Do you think I could have another cup of your delicious coffee?" Drusilla asked.

"Of course." Eleanor began to worry that this woman would never leave. When she returned with the second cup of coffee, Drusilla was wandering out of Eleanor's office. Did she have no boundaries at all?

"Your house is quite lovely. I noticed some paperwork in your office. It seems that you are financially well off. Does Angus know how wealthy you are?" she pried. "Do you have other gentlemen friends?"

Eleanor was at the end of her tether. She decided to turn the tables and ask her own questions. "Have you ever been married, Drusilla? Is Drusilla Malfoy your real name?" Eleanor watched as Drusilla's eyebrows rose in surprise.

"Virginia and I were never close. I was engaged once, but Virginia had an affair with my fiancée and then when she met 'THE ONE' she told me I could have him back. It broke me. I've always hated her and I honestly am glad she's dead." Drusilla rattled it off like a poem she had memorized.

"Wow, did you hate her enough to kill her?" Eleanor asked boldly.

"Yes, but I didn't do it. I am her only living relative and I'm set to inherit all she owned, at least I was until she found this lost son Michael. Hopefully, she didn't change her will. I'm sure she didn't because as soon as she found out about him she charged up to Seattle to stake her claim. As if she could ever be a loving mother—the idea is laughable." She paused to sip her coffee. "You know, Eleanor, I like you. I feel like I can tell you anything. I think you could be a friend to me. Angus and Michael have gone fishing and I have nothing to do today."

Eleanor felt suffocated. She had become a prisoner in her own home being subjected to some kind of friendship torture. What had she done to deserve this? Poor Angus, he had to deal with this for days. No wonder he and Michael had escaped to go fishing.

"I'd like to help, but I have an appointment shortly. Today might be a good day for you to visit the real estate office and look at some possibilities," Eleanor suggested.

"Maybe when you get back from your appointment, you'd like to cook dinner for us. Angus has done nothing but rave about your cooking ever since I entered his kitchen. I'd love to see what he finds so satisfying."

Eleanor could not believe her ears. She would not be bullied into cooking for this woman. "Angus likes to cook his own salmon and I'm sure they'll have one for your dinner tonight." She stood and walked purposely toward the door. Surprisingly, Drusilla took the hint and left. Eleanor sank down on the couch and put her head in her hands. Would the curse of Angus and his women ever end? She needed to get out of her house just in case Drusilla came back or watched to see if she really had an appointment. She looked out the window and saw a patch of blue sky. Maybe it was time for a round of golf.

The coffee group met at Dede's house and drove to the golf course where they rented two carts. The only clubs they had belonged to Cleo, which presented a slight problem.

"I'll just take half of your clubs and put them in our cart," said Josephine.

"But each club has a special purpose," Cleo protested.

"Who cares," said Pearl. "Let's make our own rules. Mr. Bean isn't watching."

"I'll race you to those driving markers," Dede dared.

Eleanor jumped in the cart with Dede and they sped off with Pearl and Josephine not far behind.

Cleo was left in their wake. When she caught up with them they were passing around the flask she had put in her golf bag. "Did I do something to make you mad at me?" she asked sadly.

"Never," soothed Josephine. "There just doesn't seem to be room for three in the cart." She handed the flask to Cleo without taking a sip. Then they each teed off taking turns with the driver. After the eighth hole, the flask was empty and their balls were all over the place.

"This is why I hate golf," said Cleo as she walked into the high grass behind some trees to look for her missing ball. The others drove off in the carts to find and play out their own. Cleo tromped around in the tall grass for ages and was about to give up when she spied her ball beside something poking up in the mud. Being Cleo, she kicked it with her foot and then pulled out an extremely dirty golf club.

"Look what I found," she said when she finally caught up with the others who, needless to say, were not impressed.

"It looks old and muddy," said Pearl. "Maybe it's an antique."

"I'll just put it in my bag and clean it up later," Cleo said. "It will be one more club we can use."

After they completed nine holes the ladies retired to the club house for a late lunch where they feasted on grilled halibut fish tacos topped with purple cabbage and fresh salsa.

"Drusilla visited me this morning," Eleanor said between bites. "She thinks I'm her new best friend and she's looking for a cottage in Sand Beach."

"You need to dissuade her," Josephine said, "I'm almost certain she's a borderline personality."

"I'm sure you're right. The woman was in my office pawing through my personal papers. She even commented on my finances without any guilt about snooping," Eleanor said, experienceing renewed outrage.

"That reminds me, I have an appointment with my financial advisor this afternoon."

The ladies finished their lunch and went their separate ways.

Angus and Michael returned that afternoon with a huge Chinook salmon. "Ewww, that's disgusting," said Drusilla as she watched Angus bring it into the house with pride.

"You won't be saying that after I grill it for dinner," Angus bragged.

"So you're cooking for me tonight, how romantic!" Drusilla said.

"I'm going to take a piece over to Eleanor. She likes salmon." Angus needed to escape and maybe this was his chance to work things out with her. Maybe she would tell him about the mystery man he saw leaving her house early this morning and alleviate his jealous fears.

"I can do that if you like," Michael offered. He had spent the day in the boat with Angus and knew about his feelings for Eleanor.

"No, I'd like to talk to her," Angus said and he bagged up a nice filet and left.

As he walked up the hill a distinguished older man passed him in a shiny Audi and pulled up to Eleanor's house. Angus watched as Eleanor opened the door and let him inside. Was he carrying a suitcase? He made a mental note of the license number. Angus let his imagination run amok as he turned around with his gift of fish. Eleanor was definitely seeing another man. Josephine was wrong.

Eleanor met with her financial advisor, Mr. Mooney, or Mr. Money, as she liked to call him, and when he left she felt excessively rich. Evidently Walter had invested in a life insurance plan that paid off a huge benefit upon his death. She was well off before, but now she could honestly say she was rolling in it. A celebration was in order and she knew exactly what to do. She needed a new car. Her old one wasn't the same since she ran it into the ditch.

Eleanor had admired the silver Audi that Mr. Money drove. She decided she would get one just like it. And then she would do something for Walter. There hadn't been a funeral or even a memorial service for him. Angus had taken Eleanor and the girls out in the bay where they let Walter's ashes float out to sea. She would throw a huge party in Walter's honor and invite everyone she knew. Salvador Dolly would cater it with Walter's favorite foods and wines. There would be a pianist who would play the songs he loved and there would be dancing, but best of all, there would be his friends and family who loved him and missed him—the way Eleanor did. Eleanor went into her office and started working on the guest list.

"It was a dark and stormy night," said Feathers, but Eleanor didn't believe him.

Eleanor was nothing if not efficient. The plans for Walter's Wake, as she had taken to calling it, were well underway with the date set, invitations out, caterer and venue booked. She still wanted to order flowers for the tables at the event, so she drove into town in her new Audi to talk to the florist. As she passed by Angus's house she noticed Michael's car was gone and assumed he had returned to Seattle. Angus's pick up sat in the driveway. Eleanor didn't think it had moved in four days. She wondered what was going on behind his door . . . was Drusilla still there? Eleanor hadn't seen her since the friendship infestation when Drusilla admitted her desire to kill Virginia and then drank all her coffee creamer. Officer McGraw might be interested to hear about her motives, including the inheritance. Virginia had been married several times. Perhaps her husbands had been generous and there was wealth to leave behind.

Eleanor took care of her errands and stopped at the grocery store to pick up a few items. She hadn't cooked for anyone in a while and she missed it. Amy, Taylor, and the children might come over if she tempted them with their favorite dinner of sweet and sour meatballs. As she put her groceries in the car she saw Angus walking down the street with Drusilla. They didn't see her as she drove away and she wondered if they were a couple now since they spent so much time together. It was hard to imagine Angus with someone like Drusilla. Eleanor thought he was a better judge of character, but evidently she was wrong.

As it turned out, she was wrong about a couple of things. Angus and Drusilla weren't really an item, and he did see her driving away in her silver Audi, only he thought it belonged to the new man in her life.

Eleanor's dinner with the kids turned out to be a party. Not only did Amy and Taylor turn up with their three children, but Erin and Ben surprised her as well with Mitch and Ruby. Eleanor had made tons of meatballs since she knew the children would eat until they exploded so there was plenty to go around and rice always seemed to multiply like loaves and fishes.

"Mom, what made you decide to throw a party for Dad?" asked Erin. Evidently the invitations had reached their destination.

"I just thought it was time. We didn't do much to celebrate his life and he had such a wonderful one." Eleanor didn't want to tell them about the money. They would learn about her wealth later. She certainly didn't want it to affect their comings and goings in any way.

"I love the idea," Amy said. "Can I help?"

"Of course, you can put together a short video with the pictures from our albums. We'll set it up in a corner so people can watch it if they want to, but I don't want this to be a sad affair."

"Gramma, where did the spaghetti go to dance?" asked Mitch.

"Where?" asked Addie.

"The meat ball," Mitch cracked up at his own joke.

"How do you keep meatballs from drowning?" asked Ben.

"I don't know," said Ruby.

"Put them in a gravy boat," said Ben.

"What's a gravy boat?" asked Mitch.

"Awww, it's not funny if you have to explain it," said Wesley who didn't know what a gravy boat was either.

"Oh that reminds me of a funny thing that happened at the baseball game," Erin said. "We were watching the Volcanos and cheering for them when this fan from the opposing team sat down next to us and started yelling for his team. It was really annoying to everyone around us too. Then this guy with a camera and a microphone came over and seemed to be awarding the fan a big serving of nachos. It was up on the big screen and everything. The fan was just reaching out to take them when the guy with the mike handed them to a little boy behind him and said, 'Nacho nachos.' It was a riot."

"Totally a setup, but very funny," Ben said.

"I don't get it," said Wesley.

"'Not yo' nachos," Ben repeated but Wesley just frowned and shook his head. "I guess you had to be there."

When the meatballs were gone, Eleanor served apple pie and salted caramel ice cream, and then they cleaned up and sat in the living room looking through the pictures for Walter's Wake while the kids played board games and Taylor played songs from Phantom of the Opera. It was a delightful evening until it wasn't.

"Have they solved that murder case yet," asked Erin.

"Which one?" asked Amy.

"There's more than one?" asked Ben. "This place is almost as bad as the city."

"There have been three mysterious deaths lately but none of them have been solved as far as I know," Eleanor said.

"I've heard there was an attempted abduction of a twelve-year-old girl on her way to school, yesterday," Amy said.

"Kids are always going missing in the city," said Erin. "We just have to watch over them carefully and be sure they're wise to stranger danger."

"Remember when we went jogging early in the morning in the dark by the river, Mom?" asked Amy.

"We had just watched the movie about Ted Bundy and how he lured women into his van." Eleanor remembered it vividly.

"There was a van parked along the road and its lights came on as we got close. It creeped us out so much that we turned around and ran toward home. It passed us going really slow and we could see the sliding door open on the side so we ran up someone's driveway and got on their front porch ready to pound on their door for help." Amy was getting goosebumps just reliving the experience.

"The van pulled into the driveway and turned around, so we took off for home," Eleanor said. "I think we ran our personal bests."

"Yeah, and when we told Dad he drove down there and discovered one of his fishing buddies waiting by the river for the sun to come up so he could fish," Amy recalled with a laugh. "He was such a good dad, always kind and so protective. I was still in high school then."

"Just the right age to be taken by those human traffickers," Taylor said.

"I think that's what happened to the girl who washed up on the beach. You know her hands were tied," Eleanor said.

"So where is Angus anyway? Isn't he the one on the case who can catch us up on the details?" Taylor asked.

"Angus isn't consulting on these cases because he personally knew one of the victims," Eleanor explained.

"Is he a suspect?" asked Erin.

"Is that why he isn't here tonight?" asked Taylor.

Eleanor was suddenly tired and needed some fresh air. She didn't want to explain any of it. "I don't know. Have you seen my new car?" Everyone hurried into the garage to see the shiny new Audi. "It drives like a dream," Eleanor stated.

"Can I try it out?" asked Taylor.

"Sure," Eleanor said, happy that the focus was no longer on Angus.

Taylor drove slowly down the hill past Angus's house where Angus watched the Audi leaving Eleanor's place. It was too dark to see the license plate, but it was clearly a man behind the wheel.

The next day Eleanor received an alarming call from Cleo. "Something's come up. Meet at my house as soon as you can. I can't tell you over the phone." Cleo said.

"I'll leave right away," Eleanor said, wondering what could possibly be so urgent this time. When Eleanor arrived at Cleo's hilltop home above the river, all the other ladies from the coffee group were there. As Eleanor looked over the panoramic view that belonged to Cleo she was struck by the pastoral beauty of the stately elm trees that lined the river and the green pastures dotted with black and white dairy cows peacefully grazing. It was like looking at a Hudson River School painting done by Thomas Cole or Frederic Church. No wonder Cleo was inspired to paint. Before she could ring the doorbell, Cleo called to her to come to her studio that was next to the house.

"Come in, Eleanor," Cleo said with a stricken look on her face.

"What's happened?" Eleanor said as she looked at each worried face in turn.

"Remember that club I found in the long grass at the golf course? Well I took it out to clean it up and I found something that is truly frightening. Just look at it and tell me what you see," Cleo said.

Eleanor looked at the dirty club that lay on a towel on Cleo's workbench. At first, all she saw was an old club covered with rust stains and bits of debris. But as she looked closer the stains turned into blood and the debris became pieces of bone, brain, and hair. Eleanor stared at her friends in disbelief. "Are you thinking what I'm thinking?" she asked.

"That this is a murder weapon of some kind . . . " Josephine said.

"The murder weapon that killed Gloria and Virginia?" questioned Dede.

"What do we do with it?" asked Cleo.

"We should take it to the police," Eleanor said without pause.

"I don't want to get you guys in trouble because I wasn't actually with you when you went into Virginia's room, but could this come back to bite you?" Pearl asked. "If they find out you were in her room the night she was killed and now you have the murder weapon in your possession, it makes you look guilty. Right now I'm wondering if you did it."

"Maybe we should take it back to the golf course where we found it," suggested Cleo.

"I bet your fingerprints are all over it," said Dede.

"I think we should turn it in to Officer McGraw. He doesn't know you were in Virginia's room that night and this may help him solve the case," Eleanor reasoned.

"Let's take it to Angus. He's our friend and he can tell us what to do," Cleo said.

"No, Angus is a suspect in the murder of Virginia because of his past relationship with her. She was causing problems for him. Having the murder weapon or even knowledge of it would only put him in deeper trouble," Eleanor said.

"Let's just hang on to it for a while," Dede suggested, "at least until we learn more about the investigation."

"How are we going to find out about the investigation?" asked Pearl, "We don't have Angus feeding us information anymore."

"Do you really think Angus isn't pursuing this case anymore now that he's a suspect? It seems to me he has even more reason to investigate so he can clear his name," said Josephine.

"But we don't have the advantage of Eleanor getting that information from Angus," Dede reminded them.

"No, but we have husbands who might go fishing with him and find out some things," proposed Josephine.

"I'm not telling Steve what we did," Cleo said. "We haven't been getting along very well lately, and he might turn me in just to be rid of me. But he could be persuaded to find out about the case just because he's curious and he likes to fish."

"I'd bet money on the fact that Angus would accept an invitation to go fishing with any of our husbands just to find out about Eleanor," Josephine stated.

"Let's all put the idea in their heads that Angus is missing Eleanor and needs a distraction and see what happens," Dede said. "In the meantime, Cleo needs to put this club back in her bag like she hasn't noticed the gore on it. It wouldn't look good if she was trying to hide it."

With that done, they went into Cleo's house for pie and coffee and to work their magic on Steve.

On Friday the members of the coffee group met at the Boat House to share the results of their probes. "There has been another murder," Dede said without emotion. She pulled out her phone and showed the ladies a photo of a gnome lying face down with a knife in his back. "Someone reported it last night. It was one of the gnomes found earlier in the front of the court house."

"This just gets stranger and stranger," said Pearl.

"It makes me curious," admitted Josephine. "Someone is going to a lot of trouble to get our attention."

"Maybe it's a distraction to take our attention away from the murders," suggested Cleo.

"I think it's funny," said Eleanor, "but it couldn't be connected to the murders. Gnomes are mythical creatures that move underground and guard gardens and livestock."

"Do they also guard gold?" asked Pearl.

"That's leprechauns," said Josephine, who knew her mythical creatures. "It must be a business promoting something. Who else would pay for a billboard?"

Dede's eyes twinkled with amusement. She could hardly wait to tell them the truth, but knew she had to keep silent until everything was ready. The mystery was all part of the hype. "Did anyone find out anything about the real murder case?"

"Steve went fishing with Angus, but it's so difficult to get the facts out of him. Evidently this Drusilla person has been taking up a great deal of Angus's time. He's been helping her find a place to live. She wants a house in Sand Beach but she can't afford view property so she's looking in Waterton and there aren't many homes available. He thinks she's impossible to please and will never find anything, but Steve said he thinks she is just stalling so she can stay at Angus's indefinitely."

"She's still staying with Angus?" Josephine said. "That has to stop. I'll offer to put her up as soon as I can. She's toxic and he certainly doesn't need that right now."

"Yet they go everywhere together. Now he's bringing her to the Wednesday night soup kitchen," said Dede. Eleanor sat quietly. Angus used to bring Eleanor to the soup kitchen.

"What did Steve find out about the investigation?" asked Dede.

"Well, Angus is still playing poker with his buddies on the force but they're not talking. Somehow he learned that the weapon is something called a niblick. I know it sounds like some kinky sexual act but it's a kind of golf club," Cleo said.

"That confirms what we already thought," Dede said.

"I looked it up on line and I learned that the one I found on the golf course is a larger iron-headed niblick that was used like a wedge or 9-iron to gouge the ball out of the rough. I think it's fairly old and may date back to the late 1800s. Who do we know that would own such a club?"

"Who do we know who would use it to gouge out someone's brains?" asked Pearl.

"We have to turn it in," repeated Eleanor. "It has to be the murder weapon and there may be evidence on it that could help the police. I'll take it to Officer McGraw. I can honestly say I was never in her room that night."

"I've done a little research myself," Josephine revealed. "Virginia Storm never had a sister, a stepsister, or any sibling at all that I can find. Drusilla Malfoy is a fake, and we need to find out what she's up to as well because I think our friend Angus is in danger."

"The day she came to my house she said she hated Virginia enough to kill her because Virginia had an affair with her fiancée, and then claimed to be her sole heir. I think everything out of her mouth is a lie," Eleanor said.

"She's definitely up to no good," Dede said.

"Is it possible she killed Virginia? Wouldn't that mean she killed Gloria too? Was she even here at the time they were murdered?" asked Cleo.

"It doesn't mean they were killed by the same person, just with the same weapon," said Eleanor.

"What if Virginia killed Gloria and left the weapon in her room and someone used it to kill her just because it was handy?" Pearl asked.

"That's possible. Did any of you see the niblick in her room that night?" asked Eleanor.

"I don't remember seeing it," said Cleo.

"I thought we gave that room a thorough search and I didn't see it either," said Dede.

"If Virginia murdered someone with the club, she wouldn't keep it in her room. Maybe she threw it out in the ocean and it washed up and her killer brought it back and used it on her." Josephine liked the idea of things coming full circle.

"Then all the evidence from Gloria's murder would have been washed away by the ocean," Eleanor said.

"I bet forensics could match the injuries to the club," Dede said.

"We don't have the tools to solve this mystery on our own," Eleanor said. "We're either going to have to bring what we know to Officer McGraw or draw out the killer with some clever plan."

A long silence ensued while each of them tried to come up with a clever plan. "Let's give ourselves two days to come up with a plan. If we can't then we give our evidence to Eleanor to present to Officer McGraw," Dede suggested.

"It wouldn't hurt to research more about those two women. What do we really know about Virginia Storm and Drusilla Malfoy?" asked Josephine.

"I have an idea," said Cleo. "It's dangerous and scary but I think it will give us the information we need about Drusilla Malfoy."

The coffee group met at Eleanor's that night. They were dressed in black from head to toe and they were shivering with anxiety. "I think I need a stiff drink," said Cleo.

"Absolutely not!" said Josephine who never drank, "You need your wits and physical agility to successfully execute this mission."

"We'll have a stiff drink when we get back here with some facts," Eleanor promised.

"All right, let's go over this once again," said Dede. "We know that Angus has taken Drusilla out to dinner at the Boat House."

"Our favorite waitress was eager to help us out by calling Angus and pretending he won a free dinner for two. He didn't mind that it had to be used tonight. I think she enjoyed disguising her voice and she claimed he was clueless about the deception. He muttered something about not having eaten a decent meal in weeks." Eleanor took it as a compliment.

"As soon as they leave we'll walk to his house, crawl in the downstairs window, enter the house, and search Drusilla's stuff for details. Pearl will keep watch and use her whistle to warn us if they come home early," Dede continued.

"If things don't go well, we just go to Nancy's house and pretend we've been there all evening," added Cleo.

"Don't forget that Angus has a gun and he's used it before when someone broke into his house," reminded Eleanor. A whole minute passed as each of them faced their fear and strengthened their resolve.

"Does everyone have their gloves on?" asked Dede. "Does everyone have their flashlights?"

"Wait," said Eleanor, "I think I have a key to Angus's house. Give me a minute to find it. It may save us the embarrassment of climbing in the window." She didn't know why she had forgotten the key—probably because Angus gave it to her a while ago just in case there was an emergency of some kind, but she'd never used it. Now she just needed to remember where she put it. It wasn't like her to forget a thing like that. Eleanor was the kind of person who had a place for everything and kept everything in its place, but lately things had been upsetting, to say the least.

"Hurry up, Eleanor," Josephine said, "they drove away twenty minutes ago. We're wasting valuable time."

In a moment of clarity Eleanor found the key in a teacup in her cupboard and away they stumbled down the hill in the dark like five drunken sailors. Fortunately or maybe unfortunately, the fog had rolled in making the visibility almost zero.

"Keep your flashlight beam on the ground," cautioned Eleanor as several lights flickered through the night.

"Just turn off your flashlights and follow me," ordered Dede as she took the lead and the others fell in line like baby chicks.

"Please don't trip, please don't trip," repeated Cleo in rhythm to their march. She visualized one falling friend knocking into the other as they all rolled down the hill to their deaths.

They almost passed Angus's house before they realized where they were. Pearl took up her post on Angus's deck with her whistle while Eleanor quickly unlocked the door and they quietly slipped inside.

Everything looked different in the dark but Eleanor knew the bedrooms were downstairs. Holding on to the walls and each other they navigated the stairs and found the guest bedroom. They fumbled around for some time bumping into each other not knowing what they were looking for. Finally Josephine stubbed her toe on a suitcase that was under the bed, pulled it out and began to search the contents.

"Look over here!" Eleanor exclaimed as she pointed her flashlight beam on the nightstand. "Drusilla owns a gun."

"And she's left it lying right out in the open—very bad form," Cleo chided.

"She has very bad taste in clothing too," said Dede as she inspected what hung in the closet. "Everything is dark and drab, but her shoes look extremely sensible."

"Check her pockets," suggested Eleanor as she opened the drawer to the nightstand.

"Jackpot," said Cleo who was in the closet with Dede going through pockets.

"What is it?" asked Dede.

"I found ten dollars in this blazer."

"You won't believe this," said Eleanor holding up something shiny that caught and reflected the light.

The others rushed to see that Eleanor held a police officer's badge in her hand.

"Holy crap!" exclaimed Cleo who was holding up a slinky negligee.

Eleanor carefully put the badge back in the drawer but not before she jotted down the number on the back of her hand with a pen she found nearby.

Dede picked up a book on the nightstand. "She's reading about borderline personality disorders. Do you think she's diagnosed herself? Maybe she's studying Virginia's behavior."

"Maybe she's trying to convince someone that she has it," Eleanor said.

Josephine came up with nothing from inside the suitcase except a tube of KY jelly, but was studying the ID tag attached to the handle. "According to the ID tag, this suitcase belongs to someone named Delia Parker who lives at 1500 Queen Anne Ct, Seattle, Washington."

"Do you think we have enough information?" asked Dede.

"How long have we been here?" asked Josephine.

"I didn't wear a watch," said Cleo.

"I don't want to get caught here," said Eleanor. "Let's go."

"Shhh . . . I hear something upstairs," Dede said. The floorboards creaked above them.

"We can climb out the window down here," said Eleanor suddenly in a panic to get out of Angus's house.

"Maybe it's Pearl. She didn't blow her whistle," said Cleo.

"Or maybe she fell asleep and it's Angus," Josephine worried.

Then a voice came out of the darkness, "Are you guys finished? It's really cold and damp outside and my feet hurt." It was Pearl.

The coffee club investigator squad scurried up the stairs as fast as their old legs would let them, locked the door, and disappeared into the fog just as Angus's headlights lit up the night.

They quickly hugged the brush alongside the road and remained still until they were reasonably sure Angus and Drusilla were inside. With hearts beating wildly they climbed the rest of the way back to Eleanor's house, praying they hadn't been seen by the trained eyes of the professionals.

After they caught their breath and picked the leaves and sticks off of their clothes, Eleanor poured them stiff drinks and they sat in her living room digesting their discoveries.

"Drusilla is a police officer," said Eleanor. "She must be investigating Angus."

"Do you think he knows?" Cleo asked.

"It's hard to say," Dede commented.

"Why would the Washington police be investigating Angus?" asked Josephine. "And why would she be acting like she has a borderline personality disorder?"

"Maybe she has a connection to Michael," Eleanor speculated. "He's from Seattle."

"What if she's undercover and investigating something else and Angus is helping her?" said Pearl.

"What would she be investigating here?" asked Cleo.

"Virginia was from Los Angeles, Gloria was from here. Maybe it has something to do with the girl on the beach," concluded Dede.

"There was an attempted abduction the other day. Amy told me about it. What if it has to do with human trafficking?" Eleanor asked.

"What are you suggesting?" asked Dede. "Do you think that's what's going on here?"

"I don't know," Eleanor admitted, "But the girl on the beach had her hands tied. That's not normal."

"Let's say Eleanor is right and there is human trafficking going on here. How would it play out so that Gloria and Virginia are both bashed on the head with a niblick and a teenage girl is drowned?" Cleo asked. They sat in silence pondering the possible connections. Only one of them even had a clue.

"I made some inquires," Josephine said as the coffee group sat at Dede's dining room table sampling possible entries for the upcoming Pie Night. "Delia Parker is a private detective from Seattle. The badge she had in her nightstand is bogus. There is no such number."

"So what does that mean?" asked Pearl.

"Maybe she's a friend of Angus' who wants to help him clear his name," suggested Eleanor.

"She probably uses the fake badge to get information," Dede surmised. "People are more apt to talk to a person with a badge.

"But why pretend she's Virginia's sister?" asked Cleo as she took another bite of the chocolate Oreo cream pie with brownie crust. "Do you think the personality disorder is fake?"

"I think private detectives like to be private. She's using a cover so she can gather facts without tipping her hand," Josephine said. "She might be someone different to different people."

"That won't work for long in this small community," Pearl said.

"That means that Angus must know and he's not really involved with her romantically," Dede concluded.

"We don't know that for sure. She may be an old flame that's been rekindled who also happens to be a private detective," Eleanor said, remembering the slinky negligee and the KY jelly.

"That is what Angus and Drusilla obviously want us to think," Josephine said as she sampled the coconut cream pie, "and she's younger than we first thought."

"I'm not so sure Angus wants us to believe anything," Cleo argued. "The name Drusilla Malfoy is so obviously phony. I think it's his way of telling us it's all an act."

"Or he just believes we're morons who can be easily fooled," Dede said.

"I vote for the chocolate Oreo pie," said Eleanor, changing the subject.

"Me too," said Cleo with her mouth full of pie.

"It's delicious, me three," said Pearl.

"It's unanimous, Dede, you have to take this one to the auction to benefit Food Roots," Josephine declared, "It's a winner."

"Okay! What are you bringing, Eleanor?" Dede asked.

"I'm baking an apple pie. It's very traditional but with a more decorative crust," Eleanor replied. "I think people eat first with their eyes and the intricate design will get lots of attention visually."

"Absolutely, I always admire first and then eat," said Mark as he entered the dining room and began nibbling Dede's ear.

"Time to go," said Cleo. "The first one at Pie Night must save a table for us all."

"See you there," said Pearl as she followed the others out the door.

Pie Night was held at the Pacific House Restaurant, which was closed for this special community fundraiser to support Food Roots. The coffee club ladies and their husbands were all seated at a large table when Eleanor paid for her ticket and got her paper plate with the number 125 on it. She greeted a few people on her way to the table to join the others. The restaurant was buzzing with laughter and chatter as neighbors and friends came together.

"Let's go look at the pies, so we know which ones to bid on," said Josephine.

A long table in the rear of the building held a variety of delicious looking pies, including Dede's Oreo brookie cheesecake mousse, a poached pear almond tart, apple, cherry, pumpkin, berry, coconut cream, peanut butter and pecan, as well as various savory pies. It was a feast of pies for the eyes.

"Oh, look at that!" exclaimed Josephine as she pointed to a Boston cream crepe cake pie made of 125 layers of crepes, covered with chocolate and decorated with flowers and ribbons.

"Eleanor, you've outdone yourself," cooed Cleo when she saw the intricate design Eleanor created with various cookie-cutter shapes of flowers, butterflies, leaves and stems that encircled the lattice center of her apple pie crust.

"Let's get some drinks and sit down," Pearl suggested when they had viewed all the pies. "My feet are killing me."

As they made their way back to their table, Victor Gaines grabbed Dede, planted a kiss on her, and then wandered off to do the same to Amy Ash who was following close behind trying to get the attention of her mother.

"Mom, we're sitting over near the bar with friends. Come join us," Amy said wiping Victor's kiss off her red lips.

Eleanor glanced in that direction and spotted Angus with Drusilla. They were sitting in a booth with a group of people Eleanor didn't recognize.

"I think I'll sit over here with my friends," she said. "You go have fun." The emcee began to talk and the chatter died down and the bidding on the pies began.

There were thirty biddable pies and the bidding started at $100 each. Dede's Oreo brookie cheesecake mousse went for $350 and everyone at their table cheered and clapped her on the back. As the evening went along, people drank more, the noise level rose, and the bids increased. Dede and Mark bought a savory pie for $375 and Eleanor bought a lemon meringue pie for $350. Pearl and Cary bought a peach pie for $300. When the bidding started on Eleanor's artfully designed apple pie it was as if a war had begun. It was everyone against Angus McBride.

Amy and Taylor bid $200, Angus $250, Mark and Cleo bid $300, Angus $350, Victor Gaines bid $400, Angus bid $450, Josephine and Richard bid $500 and Angus bid $550. No one knew how high he would have gone but it was a record breaker for sure.

"I guess Angus misses your cooking," someone whispered in Eleanor's ear. When she turned to see who it was—there was only a sea of people.

After the bidding there was music and dancing while everyone lined up to taste all the pie they could eat. Eleanor didn't see Angus after the feasting was over. She was certain he and Drusilla never reached the dance floor and she wondered with all she knew if seeing him with Drusilla in his arms would have hurt. All in all though, Pie Night was a slice of heaven.

Eleanor and Amy met for lunch at the Blue Lagoon and noticed a new shop had opened on the corner building that had been vacant for years because of a problem with absent owners who refused to sell it.

"I wonder if that's Lola Gaines' shop," Amy said. "She hasn't been at the Y in a while. I assumed she was busy getting her business off the ground."

"Let's go check it out," Eleanor said as they crossed the street. The old-fashioned wooden sign that hung overhead swung in the breeze welcoming them to The Curiosity Shop.

"Yes, I'm very curious to see what's inside," Amy said as they stepped through the door and heard the tinkle of a bell announcing their arrival.

"Hello," Lola greeted them before they could get a look around.

"How exciting to have your shop open!" exclaimed Amy who seemed genuinely happy for Lola.

"I am so excited, but also exhausted. It was a lot more work than I thought. Please look around and let me know what you think. I really value your opinion." Lola directed the last remark to Amy, and Eleanor wondered when the two had become friends.

Eleanor wandered around the shop and noticed how clean and well organized it seemed. There was an aura of old-world charm with wooden beams overhead and various unique items on display on antique tables, in barrels, and on shelves. Colorful masks, plaques, and paintings adorned the walls along with an odd assortment of collectables enclosed behind a glass case. As Amy visited with Lola, Eleanor picked up a golf club that rested among walking sticks and umbrellas inside an old milk can. It was a dead ringer for the niblick Cleo found on the golf course. Eleanor put it back hastily and wiped her hand on her jacket. She walked to the counter where a display of sparkling jewelry caught her eye. There were rings and necklaces with a vintage look, mostly in silver. Unbelievable! Behind the glass case sat the ruby red ring with the intricate gold setting that Eleanor had bought at the estate sale. It had to be the very one Virginia had taken from Eleanor's house. Suddenly, Eleanor was in a hurry to get away. She had to tell someone that the ring was here and figure out how it could have happened.

"Oh Amy, I just remembered an appointment. I've got to go. Lovely shop Lola, I promise to come back!"

"Is everything all right, Mom?" Amy asked.

"Yes, I'll talk to you later. You stay and shop."

Eleanor rushed to her car and drove immediately to Dede's house, but no one was home. She could hardly contain her unease. Why hadn't she inquired about the ring? She sat down on Dede's porch step and called Amy's cell.

"Hello," Amy answered.

"Amy, see what you can find out about the ruby red ring behind the glass case," Eleanor instructed. "Don't act too interested and don't tell Lola it's me."

"How very mysterious, Mom. I'll call you back when I know more." Amy hung up. Fifteen minutes later Eleanor's phone rang. "Where are you, Mom?" Amy asked.

"I'm sitting on Dede's porch. What did you find out?" she asked.

"I'm coming over." Amy was there in minutes and joined Eleanor on the step.

"So, what did you learn?" Eleanor asked.

"Not much. Lola seemed surprised to see the ring in the case, but I thought if you liked it I would buy it for you." Amy passed her a small bag that held the ring nestled in a thin paper nest.

The look on Eleanor's face gave Amy pause. "What's wrong Mom, didn't you want the ring?"

"I'm afraid it may be cursed."

Eleanor drove home full of anxiety over her latest discoveries. She had to let the coffee club know and called each one and invited them to an emergency meeting. They arrived bearing gifts of food and drink, among other things.

Eleanor made her Thai chicken curry with rice while Josephine tossed her delicious green salad and Dede brought decadent chocolate lava cakes. Pearl and Cleo were busy plotting some kind of mind-altering beverage that would cure Pearl's chronic foot pain.

With plates full and minds still clear, they sat down to eat and discuss the reason for the emergency meeting. Eleanor simply put the ruby red ring on the table.

"I found this at Lola Gaines' Curiosity Shop this afternoon," Eleanor announced. "And that's not all . . . there was also a golf club that looked like the twin to Cleo's niblick."

"How very curious!" exclaimed Cleo.

"You're kidding!" Dede said.

"What does it mean?" asked Pearl. She picked up the ring and studied the inside looking for an inscription of some kind. "Do you have a magnifying glass?"

Eleanor found one in her office and Pearl peered closely at the ring. "I think it says 18K but that's all," she said. "I haven't a clue what the stone is."

"Let's Google cursed rings," suggested Dede.

Eleanor brought out her laptop and began a search, while the others got busy on their phones. "Bingo," cried Dede. "I just found this ring. It has to be the same one. Look."

An image of the red ring appeared on Dede's phone. "It's called the Blood Ruby of Burma and it's supposed to bring the wearer a renewed zest for life. When worn it is thought to restore youth, passion, and sensuality and is called the stone of love. It was stolen from its owner in 1945 and has been seen all over the world, but has never been returned," Dede read.

"That doesn't sound like a curse to me," Josephine added.

"No I found it under stolen rings," Dede said.

"How did the ring get from Virginia's room to the Curiosity Shop?" Josephine asked.

"Aren't Victor and Lola from Seattle?" asked Cleo.

"So? What does that have to do with anything?" asked Dede.

"Drusilla is from Seattle, too. She might be here to investigate them," Cleo explained.

"If they are involved in the trafficking trade, they might be linked to Tina Mallory's death," Pearl said.

"I think the ring might be cursed. Everyone who wears it ends up dead," Eleanor said.

"Maybe everyone who steals it ends up dead," Josephine corrected. "We don't know how Tina Mallory got the ring. You wore it, Eleanor and you're still kicking."

"Besides, you bought it twice," Cleo reminded them. "That means you've paid your dues and won't be dying. Eleanor left the ring on the table and refused to put it on her finger. It was quiet while they ate their dinner and tried to make sense of this new development.

"My feet are achy. I think it's time to try your medicine, Cleo," Pearl said.

"What medicine is this?" asked Josephine suspiciously.

"My nephew gave me some marijuana gummy bears. I think they might help relieve Pearl's pain," Cleo said.

"Did you bring them?" asked Dede.

"Yes, I heard someplace that marijuana-infused gummy bears with a shot of tequila will make everything better," Cleo said.

"Did you bring enough for everyone?" Eleanor inquired politely.

"Why yes I did," Cleo replied.

"Let's clear the table," Dede ordered. "Eleanor, get the shot glasses."

In no time the dishes were washed and put away, gummy bears were eaten, tequila shots were knocked back, and five sophisticated ladies were rolling on the floor in fits of giggles. Even Josephine who skipped the tequila couldn't stop laughing at the stupidest things.

"I'm telling you," Dede was saying, "The clerk asked me for my ID." Hysterical laughter, tears falling off of faces, bodies rolling off the chairs.

"That's not even the funny part," she continued between giggles. "I told her it was sweet of her to ask since I'm obviously old enough to be her grandmother and she said, 'I'm not sweet, I just like to laugh at the photo IDs.'"

More laughter ensued. When there was a lapse, Cleo stood up suddenly, "I have an idea. It's a really great idea."

"What is it?" asked Pearl whose foot pain had totally disappeared.

"Let's call Drusilla and invite her over. We'll get her stoned and pump her for information about the case," Cleo said.

"That is the best idea you've ever had," Dede was all in.

"I'm not going to call her," Eleanor said stubbornly, "Angus might answer."

"I'm not calling," said Pearl, "You call, Josephine, you can honestly say you're not drunk."

"I'll do it," Josephine said and picked up the phone. "What's his number? Don't you have him on speed dial, Eleanor?" This caused more hysterical laughter for no apparent reason.

Cleo looked his number up in Eleanor's personal directory and read it to Josephine who carefully dialed it. "Hello, can Drusilla come out to play?" she asked. There was a long pause.

"Oops, wrong number," and Josephine began to laugh like a madwoman then hung up. The phone rang in her hand.

"Hello? No I'm so sorry. I really did dial the wrong number. No I don't want to . . . what?" and she hung up.

"I'm really sorry Eleanor, that man is going to be calling your number now until the end of time. He must think I was . . . " Josephine couldn't speak she was laughing so hard.

"Let me dial," Cleo said, taking the phone. "Red Rover, Red Rover, send Drusilla right over. Yes, it is Cleo. We are having a party and want Drusilla to join us. No, we are not drunk. No, you are not invited. There are no men allowed. Please put Drusilla on the phone. Hello Drusilla, I'm Cleo. Some of the girls are having a party at Eleanor's and would like you to come have fun with us. We have chocolate lava cakes drenched in Baily's. OK! See you soon. Wear your pajamas."

"She's coming?" asked Pearl.

"We better all get in our pajamas." Eleanor went in to her bedroom and returned with PJs and nighties for everyone, which sent them into new fits of hysteria as they made their selections and modeled each one.

"I don't remember—why did we invite Drusilla?" asked Pearl. "She might put a damper on our party."

"We are going to get information from her," Cleo reminded her.

"Should we offer her some gummy bears and tequila?" Josephine asked.

"Absofrigginlutely!" Dede answered.

"I mean shouldn't we tell her they are marijuana infused?" Josephine was forever the moralist.

"No way, let's put them out and let her eat them, but offer her the tequila," suggested Eleanor.

"What should we ask her?" Cleo asked. "Do we want to know if she's sleeping with Angus?"

"No, don't ask her that, but we do want to know that," Dede said. "Maybe she'll let it slip."

"You are all terrible," Eleanor said, "But I love it."

"Let's try to get her to confess and find out what she's doing here," Josephine suggested.

"We need to know some of the facts, like who killed Gloria. What does she know about Virginia's death and the niblick," Cleo said.

"Oh no! What if she tries to get information out of us?" Eleanor cried. "We know about the niblick and have it. We know about the ring and it's on the table. We're stoned out of our minds and she's a trained professional. What were we thinking?"

"Too late, she's here," said Dede as the doorbell rang. "Everyone ON GUARD!"

Feathers flew into the room to check out the intruder. Eleanor picked up the ring and put it in the pocket of her robe on her way to answer the door.

"Come in Drusilla." Eleanor welcomed her as if she were a friend and introduced her to each of the ladies. No one giggled.

"What a sweet gathering! What is the occasion?" she asked politely. She was not wearing her pajamas.

"Just friends getting together. Would you like a shot of tequila?" Eleanor was always the gracious hostess.

"Why not?" Drusilla said as she popped two gummy bears in her mouth. Cleo stifled a giggle. Drusilla obviously wasn't concerned about holding her liquor or her tongue, but she wasn't prepared for how potent those gummy bears would be.

Cleo brought the tequila bottle to the coffee table and refilled everyone's shot glasses while Pearl slyly removed the gummy bears from the room. There was no sense in overdosing their intended victim. It wasn't long before Drusilla was giggling along with the rest of them and spilling her guts.

"Oh my, he is a heartbreaker for sure and his son is so hot. I would love to see more of him, if you know what I mean, but things are complicated," she confessed at one point.

"So why are you still here?" Josephine asked.

"We're working a case," she let slip and then got quiet and started to giggle, "People think we're an item, but he's so old. You can't believe what complete strangers say to us: 'Robbing the cradle aren't you, Angus?' 'What does Eleanor say about your new babe?' 'If you're looking for a sugar daddy sweetheart, you'd be better off going to the candy store.'"

Suddenly Drusilla didn't seem as old as Eleanor thought. Was it just her or did everyone think people were the same age as they were?

"Are you finding out anything interesting?" asked Eleanor. "Do you know who killed Gloria or Virginia, or are you working the case of human trafficking and the dead girl on the beach?"

"How do you know about the human trafficking?" she asked and started to giggle uncontrollably.

"What's so funny?" asked Dede.

"Angus." Drusilla began to laugh, "Angus thinks you are amateur detectives and I'm supposed to distract you and keep you out of harm's way at the same time, but you probably know more about this case than we do." Now they were all giggling at how silly Angus was.

"We know you're a nosy Parker," Cleo said.

Drusilla began to giggle again, "That's not the first time I've heard that, but it is the funniest."

"Maybe we should share information and work this case as a team," suggested Eleanor.

"That sounds like a great idea," Drusilla said. "Didn't you say something about chocolate lava cakes?"

In the morning, all the ladies were sleeping in various places, Drusilla was on the floor in Eleanor's robe, Eleanor had gone to her bed with Cleo sleeping next to her, Pearl was in the guest room and Dede and Josephine were on the twin couches. No one rushed to the door when the doorbell rang, but eventually, Josephine, who was not suffering a hangover, answered it.

Angus stood on the porch peering in. It had been several weeks since he had been in Eleanor's house or in her good graces. "Is everything okay here?" he asked.

"Just hunky-dory," Josephine answered as she moved to block his view.

"I'm a little concerned about Drusilla. It seems she didn't come home last night," Angus said as he tried to see around Josephine.

"No worries, Angus. We took good care of her and we'll send her home when she wakes up." Josephine closed the door. She had no use for the games that Angus was playing. Eleanor was hurting because of it even though she put on a pretty good act. What was that man thinking?

Drusilla woke up and had no regrets about leaking her secrets to her new friends. She liked them and they seemed to like her now that she wasn't pretending to be a borderline psychotic. She even thought they might be helpful in the investigation. They had revealed a few things she and Angus didn't know. They had the ruby red ring and the murder weapon. She, on the other hand, had given up that they were investigating the possibility of human trafficking on the Oregon coast, that the murders were related in some way yet unknown, and the guilty parties were possibly a couple from Seattle where human trafficking was big business.

The coffee group sat around Eleanor's table staring at food they had no desire to eat. Drusilla had hurried home to face the "wrath of Angus" as she called it for staying out all night. She planned to share the information she gleaned from the group without telling what she had given away. After all she was a private investigator working with Angus and it was unethical for her to do what she had done, but she really liked those women. They were a hoot.

"I really don't want it to be Lola and Victor," said Eleanor, "He's so funny and she's very sweet."

"It makes me sad too," admitted Dede. "Who's going to play the organ and get me in trouble with the parish office by kissing me in public?"

"We can't deny the facts," Josephine said. "They are from Seattle. Lola had the ring in her store and access to a niblick."

"They also have money to burn." Cleo reminded them that Victor had purchased her paintings. "I'm assuming human traffickers do it for the money."

"Maybe they're being set up?" Pearl suggested.

"Yes, what was their motive for killing Gloria and Virginia?" Eleanor asked. "I can't believe they are involved in human trafficking."

"What am I supposed to do with the club?" Cleo asked. "I want to use my golf bag again."

"I'm going to turn it in to Officer McGraw. I'll do it today." Eleanor knew it was the right move.

"I guess we can still try to find out who did it. Maybe Pearl is right. The evidence points to Victor and Lola but it doesn't prove anything," Josephine said.

"I'll turn the ring in too," Eleanor said. "No one needs to know it was in Virginia's room, do they?"

"I think you should keep the ring," Dede said. "How will you explain how you got it? Don't forget that the person who killed Virginia must have taken it from the scene. We saw it the very night she was killed. The police might suspect you."

"Cleo's right. We need to learn more about how it came to be in Lola's shop," Pearl said. "Maybe she came by it honestly."

"Exactly," Eleanor said, "Why would she display it openly if she knew it came from the dead girl or Virginia, but it is a clue that connects the two deaths. The authorities should know."

"Maybe she hoped to sell it to someone and be rid of it," suggested Pearl.

"I wish we could tell Angus," Dede said. "Did we tell Drusilla about the ring? I don't remember."

"Yes, we told her Eleanor has the ring we saw in the photo of Tina Mallory, but we didn't tell her about the estate sale or that Virginia stole it," Josephine said. "I'm afraid Angus is right about us. We're interfering in a murder investigation by withholding information. We've committed crimes."

"We've broken into Virginia's room, and Angus' house. I guess we're criminals," Cleo said. "Our only redemption is to solve the case."

After retrieving the nasty niblick from Cleo, Eleanor paid a visit to Officer McGraw.

"Mrs. Penrose, what can I do for you?" he asked politely.

"I have something you might find of interest." she laid the club wrapped in a towel on his desk. "My friends and I found this club while playing golf at the Babbling Brook golf course. We noticed later that it had some gory residue on it and thought we should turn it over to you for further inspection."

Officer McGraw studied it closely and then gave Eleanor a brilliant smile that revealed his perfectly white teeth. "I'm sure it's just dirt," he lied. "But thank you for being such a civic-minded citizen, Mrs. Penrose. Where did you find it exactly?"

"I'm not sure exactly," Eleanor said thoughtfully. "I may be wrong, but I believe it was off the fairway to the right of the ninth hole partially buried under soft dirt amid the tall grass. I'm not very accomplished at the sport yet so searching for the ball is pretty much something I do on every hole."

"By the way, the manager of the Sand Beach Inn reported that an older woman dressed in black came in to the lobby the night Virginia Storm was killed. You wouldn't know anything about that would you?"

"It wasn't me. I've never been to the Sand Beach Inn," Eleanor replied.

"We also received an anonymous tip about Virginia Storm and a ruby ring. Did you ever notice her wearing a ruby ring?"

"Yes, I did see her wearing such a ring once at Suzanna's."

"Was she wearing this ring when you and Angus took her to dinner?"

"No," she wasn't.

"I see, well thank you, Mrs. Penrose."

Eleanor had been dismissed. She hadn't expected to gain any additional information from Officer McGraw. He was a friend of Angus and knew about her meddlesome interest in solving mysteries, but she did leave with a sense of relief to be rid of the gory niblick. Unfortunately, there was something new to worry about—Pearl and the ruby ring. She didn't really lie, she just didn't tell him everything she knew. It wasn't her fault if Officer McGraw didn't ask her the right questions.

Next on her list of things to do was visit The Curiosity Shop and quiz Lola about the ring. The bell on the door alerted Lola, who came out of the back room to welcome her.

"Good morning, Eleanor. You said you'd be back and here you are. May I help you find something or do you just want to look?"

"Amy bought me a ring the other day and I just wanted to know more about it," Eleanor said.

"Oh, remind me. Which ring was it?" Lola moved to the glass case that displayed the other pieces of jewelry and peered in as if she could see which ring was missing.

"It was a red stone with an intricate gold setting," Eleanor said. "Do you know what kind of stone it is?"

Lola glanced at Eleanor's hand perhaps looking for the ring. "You don't have it with you?"

"No," Eleanor answered.

"I'm sorry, Eleanor. The jewelry I carry isn't valuable. It all came in a box, and I'm afraid I was in such a hurry to put things out for the opening I didn't pay much attention to it. Did you want to return it?"

"No, Lola, I like it very much and wanted to know its history, or at least what kind of stone it is. May I have the address of your source?"

"Let me look in the back. The box may still be here," Lola said as she went into an area closed off by an exotic beaded curtain. Eleanor followed her.

"Did you have to do all this work yourself or did you have help?" Eleanor asked, eying a brilliant red and yellow rug that covered the floor.

"My mother helped me at first but she's gone home now," Lola said as she pulled a box from a stack. "This is the box. I see there are still some items in it." She rummaged around in it until she found the invoice. "You must think I'm very sloppy and you'd be right, but I'll get this all sorted out eventually."

Lola studied the list of contents that were supposedly in the shipment. "Strange, I don't see anything resembling the red ring. All of the rings from here were silver. That ring was gold, right? I can't explain it, but here's the address of my supplier." Lola wrote it on a piece of scrap paper and gave it to Eleanor who left with more questions than she had before she came into the store.

Eleanor drove home and puzzled over the ring the entire way. When she got home she made herself a pot of tea and tried to remember where she had put the ring. It had been on the table the night of the party. She remembered getting her magnifying glass out to check for an inscription on the inside of the setting.

Pearl said it was 18K gold. Then they had eaten gummy bears and chased them with tequila shots. There was so much laughing. So where was the ring now? Drusilla came over and Eleanor remembered slipping the ring into her pocket. She searched her bedroom for the ring. It wasn't there. Where was the robe she wore last night? She dug through the laundry and checked all the pockets in all the sweaters and jackets in her closet. She knew she had put it in a pocket. After an exhaustive search Eleanor had determined her robe with the ring in the pocket was no longer in her house.

Eleanor needed a walk. She looked out her window and saw the sun peeking through a thin layer of clouds and decided this was her window of opportunity. As she headed down the hill to the village a cool breeze blew in from the sea bringing with it the scent of seaweed and fish along with the shrill cries of the gulls that flew in circles overhead. Angus was outside on his deck watching her with his hands in his coat pockets as she approached.

"Good afternoon, Eleanor." He greeted her without a smile. "Do you mind if I walk with you?"

She really did mind, but was too polite to say it. "I'm not sure you can keep up," she said as she continued down the hill at a good clip. Angus stretched his long-legged stride to catch up and had no problem keeping pace with Eleanor. She felt no responsibility to converse or be amiable so they walked silently for some time.

"How have you been?" he asked finally as they stepped onto the sandy beach.

"Good, and you?"

"I've been better."

Eleanor refused to delve into any deeper conversation. What she really wanted was to be left alone to pursue her own thoughts. She needed to think about the ring and figure out what part it played in this case.

"I hope you're not jealous of Drusilla," Angus said suddenly.

"Why would I be jealous of Drusilla?" Eleanor asked.

Angus didn't answer. He just looked down at his feet and kept walking.

"She told me about the niblick," he finally said. "You really shouldn't be keeping that a secret."

"I turned it over to Officer McGraw today." Eleanor didn't know why she felt so angry with Angus but she noticed her hands were formed into tight fists.

"Good, what about the ring? Did you give that to him too?" Angus was making her furious with his probing.

"No, what do you know about the ring?" Eleanor snapped.

"I know Tina Mallory had a ring in the photo that appeared in the newspaper. I saw you wearing that ring, Eleanor. I'd very much like to know how you got it." Angus said this in his professional homicide detective voice.

"It's a long story, Angus. Since you are not working on the case in any official capacity I don't believe I have to tell it to you." Eleanor could see the muscles in his jaw clench. She wondered if she should tell him the story but something deep inside of her hardened and locked tight.

"Ellie." Angus's voice was so soft Eleanor could barely hear it over the surf. She thought he must be trying very hard not to be angry. "You are withholding evidence in a murder investigation. That's wrong. You need to tell me everything you know."

Eleanor picked up the pace and Angus reached out and grabbed her arm. For the longest time they stared at each other like two starving strangers in a battle over the last crust of bread.

"How did we get here, Ellie?" Angus whispered. He thought about the silver Audi that was most likely a gift from her new boyfriend, Mr. Mooney. Angus had been unprofessional with his investigation of Eleanor's financial advisor and assumed things that weren't true, giving credence to the rules that kept detectives from working on cases too close to them.

Eleanor shook her head. She was angry at Angus for spoiling everything they had that was good—the teasing banter, the shared meals, the tender caresses, and the companionship. He needed more than she was willing to give. She was angry that what they had wasn't enough for him and she was sad because she couldn't see a way back to it.

"We took different paths, Angus." Eleanor shook off his hand and walked back toward the village.

Angus watched her go unsure about what she meant by different paths. She had the ring and the murder weapon. What more was she hiding?

Eleanor entered Suzanna's and saw Mattie and Mavis sitting at their usual table. She wasn't in the mood to talk to them and didn't know why she had even come inside. The weather was fine, she wasn't hungry or thirsty. She just wanted to be away from Angus. Mattie waved and smiled a warm welcome and Eleanor sat down with them.

"We just had lunch," Mavis said. "What's up with you and Angus?"

"We saw you two walking on the beach. Have you patched things up?" asked Mattie even though she knew they hadn't by the way Eleanor had stormed away from him. Eleanor shook her head and ordered a cup of coffee.

"We've been worried about that hussy that's moved in with him. She's not you, that's for sure, and he's a fool to let you go," Mavis said.

"They come in here almost every morning for breakfast. I guess she can't cook," Mattie said.

"It's okay. Angus needs a wife and I don't want a husband so . . ." Eleanor sighed.

"So that's how it goes," Mattie said.

"I don't blame you, Eleanor. Who wants an old man you'll just have to take care of in the end. It's better to be free and easy during this phase of your life. Maybe you can find a younger man the way Angus has found a younger woman," Mavis suggested.

"Absolutely," Mattie agreed. "You are healthy, smart, and beautiful inside and out. Why should you settle for someone like Angus? Find yourself a man who can take care of you."

"Right now I don't want any man, just a cup of coffee. Where's the rest of your posse?" Eleanor asked.

"Sybil's visiting relatives someplace in Washington and Edwina's golfing with her Potsy," informed Mattie. "She's not really a Do Nothing. Now that the weather is improving she's out at the golf course almost every day."

"Really," Eleanor spoke mindlessly as she watched Angus walk in the door and take a seat nearby. He didn't avoid making eye contact as he sat alone and watched Eleanor from under his bushy brows.

"I think you are being stalked," Mavis whispered.

When Drusilla walked in and sat at the table with Angus, Mavis frowned and Mattie turned her back to them. Eleanor simply put money on the table and left.

None of them heard Angus give Drusilla her new orders. "I want you on her like tie-dye on a hippie. You're going to be her new best friend because she has something that could get her involved in this case and I can't let that happen."

When Eleanor made out the invitations to Walter's Wake, she included Angus. He was Walter's close friend and she didn't regret it. In keeping with her generous nature she had also added a plus one to the invitation and now assumed Drusilla would be coming with him. She suspected Drusilla's purpose did not involve a real romantic relationship but she wondered if Angus knew that she knew. Would he bring a new love to her husband's memorial, knowing how painful it might be for her? Eleanor was afraid that she was learning more about Angus than she wanted to know.

The evening of Walter's Wake found her studying her face in the mirror looking for stray whiskers and other flaws. She'd decided to wear a deep royal blue dress—one that Walter always said matched her eyes. Amy and Taylor came to pick her up and they drove into Waterton to the room above the Pacific House Restaurant that she had rented for the wake. They arrived early to make sure everything was in order. White linen cloths covered the round tables that were decorated with bright yellow daffodils and vibrant green foliage. A picture of Walter engaged in one of his many activities (most involving fish) sat next to the vases along with no-flame candles that gave off a festive glow. A bank of covered chaffing dishes filled with his favorite foods occupied a nearby table and sent a welcome aroma throughout the room. Wine and other beverages could be found next to the food. Amy and Erin had created a heartwarming video depicting the highlights of his life while a pianist played his favorite music. Taylor brought Feathers into the room and put his cage on the table with the guest book where he could welcome guests in Walter's voice with his usual insults. Eleanor looked at everything and pronounced it perfect. Erin and her family arrived and hugs were shared and a few tears shed, but Eleanor did not feel sad. A tough skin had formed over her once tender place for Walter and she felt she could get through this night without going into an ugly cry.

As guests arrived Eleanor and her family greeted them with handshakes and sometimes hugs and kisses. Angus came alone, much to the surprise of Eleanor and her friends. He took the opportunity to hold Eleanor close and kiss her cheek, but he did not sit near her group, choosing rather to mingle with Walter's fishing buddies and poker players. He didn't miss the fact that Mr. Mooney was in attendance, and sat with a group of well-dressed professional-looking men and women Angus assumed were people Walter had worked with as a wealth manager.

The evening flew by with Eleanor delighted by the small groups of people sharing stories of Walter, laughing, drinking, and eating. There was no sadness as far as Eleanor could see and when the wake was over and toasts were given, she felt a sweet affection for those who were present to share the life of Walter Penrose. He did not belong only to her and she realized how many others had loved and admired him. There were those who had come for her as well. The Do Nothings: Mattie,

Mavis, Sylvia, and Edwina with her Potsy, all the members of her book club, including Mercedes' secret plus one who turned out to be a biologist from the Department of Forestry. Even Victor and Lola, who never met Walter, showed up.

Eleanor stayed until the last guest departed and then looked directly into the green eyes of Angus McBride who offered to take her home.

"I'm pretty much going your way," he said.

"I need to stay and clean up," Eleanor protested.

"No, Mom, you should go. Amy and I can take care of the cleaning. You must be exhausted." Erin's offer was made out of genuine concern for her mother.

"Okay," Eleanor said, "It will save Amy and Taylor a trip out to Sand Beach." She hugged her girls and left with an angry parrot in his cage and Angus at her side.

"That was a wonderful tribute to Walter," Angus said as they drove away. "He had lots of friends even after all that time at Rosewood Manor."

"I know," Eleanor sighed, "Some of them came up from California where we used to live."

"Walter was a good man and a loyal friend," Angus said.

Eleanor laid her head back and looked out the window at the stars that glowed against an indigo backdrop. It was a lovely night. The moon was just rising over the mountains.

"You know how you have those moments in your life when you're just happy for no reason?" Eleanor asked. Angus wasn't sure he'd had many of those moments but he nodded anyway. "I'm happy, and I don't care if I deserve it or not." Eleanor smiled and continued to enjoy the ride home.

Angus experienced something that could have passed for happiness but he thought it was just the fact that Eleanor was in the passenger seat of his ride.

"Hey Handsome," Drusilla teased as she entered Angus's living room wearing Eleanor's robe. "I've got something for you, but you'll have to search me to get it."

Angus looked up from the show he'd been watching, and to his credit recognized Eleanor's robe. "It's not your color Drusilla. Does Eleanor know you took it?"

Drusilla stuck out her bottom lip in a fake pout, "Why are you so difficult to seduce? Here I am offering you an opportunity to grope me and you sit there watching some fishing program. I guess the romance is gone."

"It's not just some fishing program, it's *Wicked Tuna*," Angus corrected her as he continued to watch as men on a boat struggling to land a fish of unusual size. "Besides, it's bad form to try to seduce a man wearing another woman's bathrobe, especially if it makes him think of her. It probably even smells like her." Drusilla buried her nose in the sleeve and sniffed it loudly then plopped down next to Angus on his leather couch.

"The real treasure is this little bit of evidence I found in the pocket," she said as she held out the red ring.

Angus took the ring and studied it closely, then pulled out a picture of the ring from a file folder that lay on the coffee table. "This looks like the real thing," he said. "Good work, Drusilla, you've earned a reward." Drusilla followed him to the kitchen where Angus cut two pieces of apple pie.

"What, no ice cream?" she questioned.

"Some people are never satisfied," he said as he scooped up the vanilla bean ice cream.

They ate their dessert in silence.

"Something terrible has happened," Dede reported as the coffee group sat eating breakfast at the Boat House. They all leaned in. "Will Vandorff went up in the woods and shot himself this morning."

"What? Does this mean he's guilty of killing his wife?" asked Cleo.

"I don't know," Dede admitted.

"Well is he dead?" asked Eleanor.

"No, not yet, but from what I heard he may not make it," Dede continued.

"Did he go up there alone?" asked Pearl.

Dede looked at Pearl and raised one brow, "I'm sure he didn't invite his friends to go with him, of course he was alone."

"Well how did they find him then?" Pearl persisted.

"Oh, he called 911 from his cell phone," Dede explained.

"That poor man," Josephine said. "His life must have been unravelling. First his wife cheated on him then she was murdered and people can be so very cruel when they think they know what happened."

"Josephine, you sound like you know what happened and you're feeling sorry for him. Do you know something you're not telling?" Cleo asked.

Josephine did not answer directly. "Some couples have relationships that are unconventional. They think they can handle it but then their emotions take over. Swinging isn't for everyone. You know I can't talk about everything I know."

"Were they swingers?" asked Pearl. "If they were swingers you can't say she was cheating on him."

"It's not that simple." Eleanor remembered Lola's confusion over sex and love. "Maybe Gloria fell in love with someone she was having sex with and Will got jealous. They were playing a dangerous game with their emotions."

"I'm sure he didn't kill her," Dede said. "I've heard other stories about inflating prices through his real estate business and credit card debt that may have added to his depression. Murdering his wife wouldn't solve those things unless there was a life insurance policy."

"They did seem to live high on the hog," Pearl said, "but lots of people do."

"There's the problem with keeping up with your peers," Eleanor said. "You never really know what their situation is. They may have nice things but be woefully overextended. Walter always said everyone should socialize with people in the same economic class. That way there is no envy or bitterness."

"Easier said than done," Josephine argued, "Especially if your friends are using credit to keep up with you. How would you know?"

"Right, you can't just go up to someone and say, 'How can you afford that new car? Are you deeply in debt? How much do you make a year?'" Cleo said.

"Not to mention the fact that people's circumstances change, some for the better through financial windfalls and others through illness or loss," Dede added.

"I've known people who lived like paupers but turned out to be multimillionaires upon their death," Josephine said.

"Wouldn't it be horrible if one of us won the lottery and decided we couldn't be friends anymore because one of us was too rich to fraternize with the rest of us?" Cleo asked.

"We will always be friends, no matter what," Eleanor vowed. "If any of you ever need money, I hope you'll ask for help before you go up in the woods and try to off yourself."

They all looked at Eleanor and decided she was suffering an emotional moment because she was missing someone—maybe Walter . . . maybe Angus. None of them suspected she was the recipient of enormous wealth.

"I had a visit from Officer McGraw," Pearl said. "He wanted to know what I was doing the night Virginia Storm was murdered."

"He did tell me an older woman in black was at the Sand Beach Inn the night Virginia was killed. He asked me if I knew anything about it. I told him it wasn't me. I'm sorry I should have warned you Pearl, but I didn't think he would even consider you."

"I bet it was the manager. I'm sure they questioned him about that night, and you have to admit Pearl is a sinister character," Cleo teased.

"I simply told him I went there to see my son and got confused. It wasn't a lie. Officer McGraw didn't have a problem believing an old woman might get the Sand Beach Inn mixed up with the Sandman Inn."

"That's a relief," said Josephine as she pulled a copy of the *Fish Wrapper* out of her bag. "Listen to this letter to the editor about gnomes." Josephine began to read, "The recent appearance of gnomes in our community has caused a great deal of interest among my neighbors and friends. Just what in the heck is going on? I have always had gnomes in my garden because I find them a whimsical and colorful addition to yard décor, but last week my favorite one went missing and I am afraid it has been gnome-napped. So far, I have not received a note asking for ransom but in my research have discovered the existence of a number of people who call themselves the Gnome Liberation Group. These misguided individuals steal gnomes from gardens and liberate them to forests or parks. I fear this is what has happened to my little friend. I have gnome one to blame but myself for leaving him out where he could be easily taken, but I beseech anyone who finds him to return him gnome at once. — Miss Gnomer"

"That's hilarious," laughed Eleanor.

"But that's not all." Josephine continued holding up the picture of the slain gnome with a knife in its back that appeared on the front page. "The mystery continues. These mythical creatures are getting more press than the murder of real people."

"I think it's time I showed you all something," Dede said. "After we finish our breakfast I want you to come with me on a tour of Waterton's underground."

"Is this the secret you've been keeping?" asked Pearl.

"Does it resolve the gnome mystery?" asked Cleo.

"It's not just my secret. The city, along with the Chamber of Commerce, planned to reconstruct some of the passages under the city that were used for various purposes in the past and have tourists pay to tour them. The gnomes were supposed to spark interest. They're known for digging tunnels underground. Anyway, the city hit a few snags along the way with absentee owners who refused to give up their access to the tunnels. Who knew people would be so possessive about underground properties?" Dede said. "Anyway, I think they've given up on the idea so it's okay if I give you a little tour so you know what I've had on my mind lately. Who knows, maybe you'll come up with a solution to circumvent our issues."

"Do we need flashlights?" asked Josephine. "I've heard stories about these tunnels, but I've no idea what they're like or where they run."

"Remember the old sidewalks and how they had those glass tiles every once in a while?" Dede asked. "Those allowed light to seep into the tunnels, but now we have new sidewalks and there is absolutely no light down there so we will need flashlights. We can stop at my house and get some as well as a battery operated lantern."

"I'm not so sure about this," Cleo said, worried. "You know sometimes I get claustrophobia."

"You'll be fine. If you get panicky, we'll just come up," Josephine said reassuringly.

"Are there spiders and cobwebs down there?" Eleanor asked.

"Maybe, but they've done some work cleaning it up already. We won't go in the undeveloped parts. They're off limits anyway due to the uncooperative owners." Dede didn't like spiders either.

They met at Dede's house, gathered their flashlights, and walked a few blocks to City Hall where Dede used her key to access a small room in the basement with a trapdoor in the floor covered by a colorful rug. "Now take your time and be very, very careful going down," Dede cautioned. She stood at the top with her lantern lighting the way until each had descended the metal steps. Pearl took the lantern and lit the way for Dede.

"It is really dark down here," Josephine remarked. Dede turned the lantern to its brightest setting and led the way.

"Should we be dropping bread crumbs so we can find our way back?" asked Cleo.

"I'm pretty sure I can get us back," Dede said.

The tunnel was narrow and dank, but opened up to a larger cavity that had been painted a light gray. "This is the part that has been renovated," Dede said. They noticed several gnomes decorating the tunnel.

"Are gnomes the same as dwarfs?" asked Cleo. "Aren't dwarfs the ones who dig underground?"

"I don't know," Dede responded. "I think they're close enough for our purposes."

They walked on and saw several divergent tunnels that were barricaded by wooden barriers. "Those tunnels go south of town and under the buildings whose owners don't want us there. They claim there are liability issues," Dede said.

"Are we under the Curiosity Shop?" asked Eleanor.

"The Curiosity Shop is above the barricaded tunnel. We're under the Elks club now. This stone stairway goes up to a secret room where a few unlucky men were drugged and kept until they could be shipped out as slave labor on various ships. If we keep walking north we'll come out to the slough where small boats waited to take them out to sea." Dede stopped to show them a door that was locked. "Behind this door is a room like a prison where men were held for longer periods when the ships didn't come on time. Lots of men died there and some of the workers said they could hear moaning coming from inside."

"You mean recently?" asked Cleo.

"Yes, they also said they heard footsteps in the tunnels and other noises that sounded like something being dragged." Dede turned and continued toward the slough pointing out locations along the way. The others followed silently, straining to hear moaning or footsteps. When they came to a heavy wooden door Dede stopped again. "If I had the key, I could open this door to the slough."

"This is so creepy," Josephine said. "Even this little bit of a tour is fascinating. I'm sure people would pay to walk down here and learn about Waterton's past."

"Especially if there are real ghosts down here," Cleo said.

"I hope there aren't rats. I hate rats," Pearl said.

"Are you ready to go back?" asked Dede. "Could you find your way?"

"Sure," said Eleanor who was not directionally challenged.

"Then lead on," Dede ordered.

Eleanor led them back to the tunnel that was barricaded and stopped. She let her light bounce off the walls of the tunnel and peered down it as far as she could.

"What's stopping us from exploring down there?" she asked.

"Nothing really," Dede answered. "The owners are from out of state, so I'm sure they won't know, but it might not be safe." The barricade was easily moved and Eleanor walked fearlessly down the forbidden passage carefully shining her flashlight to pick out possible dangers. The others followed. No work had been done on this section and yet there were no spiders or cobwebs. Eleanor wondered if the owners stored things here. She stopped near a metal ladder that led up to what appeared to be a trap door similar to the one in the City Hall.

"Listen," Josephine whispered. Tap, tap, tap and then a sound like someone being dragged echoed through the space. They all looked at each other with terror-filled eyes, turned as if one person, and ran back the way they had come.

Dede led the way and there was no evidence that she was physically challenged in any way as she scurried up the ladder and into the basement room of City Hall. The others followed close behind and Cleo let the trapdoor slam closed as soon as she came up. Dede locked it and they walked out of the building into the light of day squinting like moles fresh from their underground burrow.

"I think I'm having a heart attack," Pearl said clutching her chest.

"Really, that's nothing to joke about at our age," chided Josephine.

"Sit down on this bench and catch your breath," advised Eleanor.

"No, I'll be okay. Let's just go slowly," Pearl said as she continued to walk.

"That was terrifying!" Cleo exclaimed.

"What do you think that sound was?" asked Dede.

"It could have been from the shop above," Eleanor reasoned.

"Or it could have been the ghosts of the tortured men shanghaied years ago," Josephine said.

"I can't imagine what we must look like," Dede said as she and her friends walked down the street with white faces, their hair standing on end carrying flashlights and a lantern.

Even at the reduced pace, they made it to Dede's house in short order. They gratefully entered her house and plopped down in her living room. "I feel like swooning," Cleo said.

"Yes, brandy is definitely in order," Dede said as she gathered glasses and poured a finger in each.

"I don't drink, but today I'm making an exception," Josephine announced. "Are you going to live, Pearl?"

"Yes," Pearl said, "but please don't make me go down there again." They were quiet for several minutes which was astounding in itself.

"I've lost the red ring," Eleanor said finally.

"Were you wearing it in the tunnel?" asked Dede.

"Oh please, we're not going back for it. We'd never find it down there," Pearl pleaded.

"No, I looked for it after our sleepover and I couldn't find it. I'm sure I put it in my bathrobe pocket but I can't even find the robe," Eleanor said.

"Well, that ring doesn't want to stay anywhere. It may not be cursed but it has some form of wanderlust," Cleo said.

"Has anything else from our estate sale disappeared?" Josephine asked.

"I left the glassware on the end of my kitchen counter and then knocked it all off with my broomstick when I was sweeping," Dede admitted.

"Did it break?" asked Pearl.

"Every last piece including the Fostoria," Dede lamented. "And it left a dent in my floor."

"Well I got a sliver from my beautiful carved box," said Pearl as she held up her finger. It was red and angry looking.

"That looks infected, Pearl. Maybe you should have the doctor take a look at that," Eleanor suggested.

"Later," Pearl said just before she fainted.

The ladies sat in the waiting room of urgent care while Pearl let the doctor remove the splinter and prescribe antibiotics for the infection.

"I remember Drusilla wearing a robe," Josephine said. "Maybe she wore it home."

"Great," said Eleanor. "She probably found the ring and gave it to Angus."

"We could always break in to his place and get it back," Cleo said."

"It's not breaking in if you have a key," Dede said.

Eleanor thought about that key. "I don't remember where I put his key. Do you think I'm getting dementia?"

"It's probably the gummy bears and tequila," Dede said.

"I distinctly remember locking the door to Angus's house with that key when we left, but I don't remember putting it back in the teacup. Do you suppose I dropped it on the way home?" Eleanor had a horrible thought. "What if I left it in his door? I'm sure I left it in the door."

"So, now Angus has his key back," Cleo said, "So what?"

"Then he'd know we used it to get in his house," Josephine said.

"That can't be good," Eleanor said. "He must know we're on to Drusilla."

"Does he have a key to your house?" asked Dede.

"No," Eleanor answered a little too quickly.

"So why don't we call a truce and work with them?" asked Josephine. "When did this become a competition?"

"I'm not sure," Eleanor admitted. "I'm not sure."

Angus looked at the red ring again. This was the ring he had seen on Tina Mallory's finger in the newspaper photo and the one Eleanor had worn on the evening he'd returned from Seattle. Why was she so reluctant to reveal how she got it? Could there be more than one? That would be too coincidental and Angus didn't believe in coincidence. Was she protecting someone? He was certain she wasn't involved in Tina's death. How could she be? She was Eleanor, prim and proper, beautiful and accomplished, smart and funny, his Eleanor, but also curious and secretive. Angus was seeing another side of this woman he thought he knew and was obsessively drawn to.

He felt an overwhelming need to protect her from whatever misfortune surrounded this ring. He dropped it in his shirt pocket, picked up her robe, and walked to her house to return it before she realized Drusilla had worn it home. He knew where she kept her spare key but didn't trust Drusilla with that information. Eleanor had gone to her coffee group so there was time to replace the robe and return home without being caught.

He chuckled to himself remembering the night the coffee group came to his house looking for clues about Drusilla. The fog hadn't concealed them in their black burglar costumes as they hurried away from his headlights. Finding the key in the door was hilarious. They must have been in such a panic to get away to commit such a totally unprofessional mistake. He wondered if they even knew they had done it. He imagined them returning to Eleanor's house thinking they had pulled one over on him. He smiled as he unlocked Eleanor's door and remembered too late that Feathers was loose inside.

"Intruder, intruder," the bird squawked as he flew at Angus's head and then finally roosted near the windows overlooking the sea.

Angus hung the robe on the back of Eleanor's bathroom door but not before he held it to his face and inhaled her scent deeply. Looking out the window he saw the crow perched outside on the deck. It seemed to be having a conversation with Feathers that involved mostly cawing. He looked at the clock and realized it was much later than he thought. He needed to get out of here before Eleanor returned. He locked her door and put the key back, but before he could make his getaway, the crow swooped down and landed on his shoulder. Startled at first by the flutter of black wings, Angus soon became charmed by the friendliness of the creature. He talked to it and stroked its sleek feathers. The bird allowed him to pet it, cocked its head one way and then the other, and suddenly reached into Angus's shirt pocket, grabbed the ring in its beak and flew off.

"Holy shit!" Angus cried. "Bring that back." The bird had flown up in a fir tree and had no intention of coming down any time soon. Angus watched for a while and decided the only sure way to get the ring back was to shoot the bird. He walked quickly back to his house to get his gun. Drusilla was working on her computer researching the ring.

"Mission accomplished?" she asked innocently. Her question was answered with a string of expletives and the loud thumping of Angus on the stairs. She was surprised to see him leaving the house with his gun and thought perhaps he intended to kill Eleanor. "What happened?" she asked as she followed him out the door.

Angus was half way up the hill when Eleanor drove by. He quickly hid the gun behind his back and waved at her not knowing what to do. He could hardly shoot the bird with Eleanor as a witness, but the bird could fly off and drop the ring anywhere and that would mean a valuable piece of evidence was lost. Angus returned reluctantly to his house continuously scanning the sky for the black crow.

"What's going on?" Drusilla asked as she joined Angus outside.

"That crazy bird took the ring out of my pocket and flew off," Angus replied testily.

"Do you mean the parrot?" Drusilla asked.

"No, the crow," he said angrily. "It must be a female. She had an eye for sparkle, saw an opportunity, and grabbed it."

"A female with excellent taste too," Drusilla said.

"What do you mean?" Angus looked at Drusilla for the first time evidently giving up on his skyward search.

"I've been doing some research. That particular ring is worth thousands if not hundreds of thousands of dollars. It's the lost Blood Ruby of Burma, stolen years ago and said to possess the ability to arouse the vitality and passions of youth. I think Eleanor has you under some kind of kinky spell."

"You have to go over there right now and get the ring. Somehow it's linked to human trafficking and possibly the deaths of three people. It's evidence and we've got to get it back." Angus was adamant.

"But what will I tell Eleanor?" Drusilla asked.

"You'll think of something." Angus almost pushed her toward Eleanor's house. "Hurry, before the bird gets away!"

Drusilla dawdled her way up the hill trying to think of a reason for visiting Eleanor while Angus watched impatiently from below.

Feathers had greeted Eleanor with a dire warning about intruders. Usually his warnings preceded their arrival or coincided with the ringing of the doorbell, so this was curiously out of character. Then there was Angus on the road looking very suspicious. Eleanor had a feeling someone had been in her house. She was just about to check her teacup for Angus's house key when the doorbell rang. Perhaps Feathers was now psychic.

"Drusilla, please come in." Eleanor was eager to get to the bottom of the missing ring.

"I really hate to ask you this, Eleanor, but could you make me a cup of coffee? Angus has no idea how to make a decent cup and I've been drooling over the thought of yours ever since you made me that delicious latté the other day."

"Sure," Eleanor said as she went in the kitchen to start the coffee pot. Drusilla took this opportunity to check for the crow on the deck. She hadn't seen any sign of it on the way over.

"Have you recovered from the twilight tequila party?" Eleanor asked coming back into the living room.

"You have the most extraordinary view, Eleanor." Drusilla sighed as she looked out the floor to ceiling wall of windows that framed the gray-blue ocean. "Have you seen an unusually friendly crow around here lately?"

"You didn't by chance wear my robe home from that party did you? I haven't been able to find it," Eleanor asked.

"That was such a fun party. I really enjoyed it. Do you and your friends do that often?" Eleanor noticed their conversation was somewhat lacking in answers to a variety of questions.

"Why are you really here, Drusilla?" Eleanor asked bluntly.

Just then Drusilla spied the crow flying from the tree to the deck railing, but when she moved closer to the window it flew away into the trees across the lane.

"No reason Eleanor, I'm sorry I don't have time for coffee. I just remembered something I have to do. Raincheck please?" And with those words Drusilla was out the door and after the crow.

"What a strange woman, Feathers," Eleanor said as she poured herself a cup of coffee and held a long and detailed conversation with her fowl friend regarding love and romance.

Drusilla spent the remainder of the afternoon searching the wooded area for the crow and the missing ring. Nothing in her private detective work had prepared her for this kind of endeavor. When she finally returned Angus was drinking Crown Royal and watching yet another episode of *Wicked Tuna*.

"I'm afraid I wasn't able to find the ring. By the time I got to Eleanor's the bird had flown off and I never even saw the ring. Do you know how many crows live near here? Not to be a bird bigot, but they all look alike to me," she complained as she shook debris from her clothing and picked sticks and moss out of her hair.

Angus simply took another sip from his glass and continued to watch as one after another giant tuna got away. When he looked out the window he noticed it had begun to rain.

Eleanor slept fitfully. Her dreams were filled with dark tunnels haunted by bloody men chained to stone walls moaning and banging on locked doors. She woke several times to look out the windows that were being pelted with heavy rain. Maybe what she needed was a melatonin pill. In the cupboard she found a dish filled with gummy bears and popped a couple in her mouth. She didn't remember buying gummy bears. On one of her visits to the bathroom she discovered her missing robe hanging on a hook behind the door. She quickly checked the pockets for the missing ring but found nothing. Surely she had checked here before.

Eleanor began to doubt her sanity. She tried several times to sleep but finally got up deciding to wrap a birthday present for Addie. The Russian nesting dolls had been stored away and almost forgotten. Eleanor tucked them in with the Easter dress she had bought and wrapped them in paper covered with purple and yellow pansies. She wrote a quick note inside a card and put the gift on the dining room table then returned to look out the window. The wind had picked up and the rain continued to pour outside—winter making its final statement. Eleanor could see a light on in Angus's house down below. She wondered if he too had trouble sleeping.

As if in answer to her question there was a gentle tapping at her front door and Angus's face appeared fractured through the stained glass window. Eleanor opened the door but Angus did not step inside.

"Is everything all right, Eleanor? I noticed your lights were on awfully early or really late." Angus looked miserable huddled inside his dripping raincoat.

"Couldn't sleep," Eleanor said, "so I figured I might as well get up and do something. Do you want to come in? It's pretty awful out there."

Angus took off his coat and shoes and left them on the porch as he stepped into the home that once welcomed him warmly.

"Would you like something to warm you up?" Eleanor offered. "I mean hot chocolate or I could heat up some soup." She didn't want Angus to get the wrong idea.

"Hot chocolate sounds good," he said thinking how he might have responded to such a remark in the past. Now he had to measure his words with care. "I'll build a fire."

Eleanor clinked around in the kitchen and returned with two mugs of hot chocolate topped with whipped cream, a hard-boiled egg, and a couple of chocolate chip cookies which she set on the coffee table. Angus wasn't surprised that she could produce his favorite cookies in the dead of a dark and sleepless night. She was Eleanor after all. They didn't talk for a long time, but simply sat and sipped their drinks and nibbled their cookies. Angus picked up the egg and ate it as well as he gazed into the fire and then at Eleanor.

"I guess we won't be able to sleep now after all this chocolate," he said at last.

"Angus, I'm surprised you didn't notice I laced your drink with whiskey. I'm sure you'll go right to sleep as soon as you finish," Eleanor said as she covered them both with their favorite snuggling blanket.

When Eleanor woke up in her bed she stretched and realized what a pleasant dream she'd had. It was late and the sun was shining. She rolled out of bed feeling happier than she had in weeks and went to the kitchen to make her coffee and then out to get the morning paper. As she settled down on the couch to do her daily puzzles she noticed the mugs half full of chocolate on the coffee table and the plate sprinkled with cookie crumbs and egg shells.

Eleanor walked the beach looking for treasures that washed ashore during the storm. The feeling of bliss and good health continued despite her mental confusion over Angus's late night visit. If he wasn't there how could she explain the two mugs and cookie crumbs. Was she sleepwalking now? Did the marijuana have residual side effects? There was absolutely no way she would ask Angus if he had been at her house last night. If it was a dream, he would think she still wanted him, which of course she did, but he wasn't to know that, at least not until he had considered his other options fully. But what if he had been there? If she saw him today she might be able to tell by his reaction to her. She would wait and see.

Several shells and rocks lay on the beach amid piles of seaweed, but nothing caught Eleanor's attention so she picked up the pace and hurried home to get ready for Addie's birthday party.

Feathers greeted her with little parrot kisses and then flew to the window where Eleanor saw Inky on the deck pecking at something shiny that had fallen between the boards. When she opened the sliders, the crow flew to a tree branch and watched as Eleanor picked up the red ring and rubbed its stone with her fingers to clean it.

"It seems like you're destined to be mine," Eleanor said to the gem as she slipped it on her finger. By now she had given up trying to make sense of how it came to be there.

Addie's party was mostly made up of little girls who giggled and disappeared downstairs to listen to music, dance, and apply various temporary tattoos and nail polishes. Amy provided several varieties of pizza and green salad for dinner followed by strawberry cake and ice cream. Taylor played a flamboyant rendition of *Happy Birthday to You* on the piano, Addie blew out the lucky 13 candles and sat down amid a plethora of gifts and began to open them. There were games and jewelry, more nail polish and makeup, some clothes, including Eleanor's fancy Easter dress and the Russian stacking dolls that Addie collected.

"We hate those Russian dolls," said Taylor as he sat on the couch watching the activity.

"Why is that? Are there too many pieces lying about?" Eleanor asked thinking about her own experiences with the endless tiny toys scattered about that always needed putting away.

"They're just so full of themselves," he responded. This opened up a whole new opportunity for jokes that the boys especially loved since they had been mostly left out of the action.

"What does a boy doll do when a girl doll rolls her eyes at him?" asked Mitch.

"Tell me what he does," said Wesley.

"He picks them up and rolls them back."

"What did the left eye say to the right eye?" asked Wesley.

"I don't know," said Mitch.

"Between us, something smells."

"I think something definitely smells in here," Amy said. "You boys should go downstairs and watch a movie." The girls had already staked out their spots below and could be heard screaming and laughing.

"Just one more," Wesley pleaded. "What did the trout detective say?"

"What did the trout detective say?" asked Eleanor.

"There's something fishy going on here," Wesley answered as his mind connected fish and detective with someone he knew. "Where is Angus? He said he would take me fishing."

"Angus is busy right now," Eleanor said.

"Mitch, you and Wesley need to go downstairs and get your pajamas on before the girls start the movie," Erin ordered.

Wesley could be heard on the stairs, "Why don't fish do well on school tests?"

"I know this one," Mitch replied as their voices faded away, "They work below C-level."

"Is there anything new in the murder investigations?" Ben asked.

"Nothing that I know," Eleanor said.

"Are you and Angus still taking a vacation from each other?" Erin asked.

"Would you like another glass of wine, Mom?" Amy offered as she filled Eleanor's glass.

"I heard Will Vandorff shot himself because he was involved in some shady real estate deals. They were working with some criminals and when the deal went south they killed Gloria," Taylor offered.

"I wish you wouldn't repeat that gossip, Taylor. There's no proof," Amy scolded. "But I heard it was a jealous wife who whacked Gloria on the head with a baseball bat because Gloria was planning to leave Will and run off with this other woman's husband."

"Do you have proof?" Taylor replied.

"I heard it from a reliable swinger," Amy said.

"Would that be Lola Gaines?" Eleanor asked.

"What have you heard, Mom?" Erin asked.

"I don't have any facts, just more rumors," Eleanor reported.

"Sorry Mom, but Lola also told me Angus and Drusilla showed up at one of their swing parties. I think maybe you're well rid of him," Amy said.

"Gee Mom, maybe you should get tested for an STD," Erin cautioned.

"What?" Eleanor was shocked and slightly embarrassed that her daughters would bring up a private matter in mixed company. "I'm an adult and perfectly capable of managing my health, thank you."

"Is that a new ring?" asked Erin as she took Eleanor's hand and admired the red stone. "It's beautiful."

"Thank you, I bought it at an estate sale," Eleanor said absently.

"No you didn't, Mom. That's the ring I bought you at Lola's Curiosity Shop," Amy corrected.

"So it is," Eleanor said, but her mind was on other things.

Driving home from the birthday party, Eleanor turned over this new bit of information about Angus and Drusilla at a swinger's gathering. It was totally disgusting but absolutely in keeping with their investigation of the couple from Seattle. She wondered just how far they would go to gather facts to clear Angus of any wrongdoing. Were they working the sex trafficking case? How were the swingers connected to the murders and sex trafficking? Were Gloria and Will members of this swingers group? Did she need to get tested for an STD?

It was all so overwhelming to Eleanor. She went home and crawled into bed.

Early the next morning while Eleanor was drinking her first cup of coffee, Dede called on the phone. "Eleanor, Mark and I have been invited to a mysterious party. It's a celebration of the vernal equinox," Dede said breathlessly.

"Who invited you?" Eleanor asked.

"Victor and Lola Gaines sent the invitation. I think it might be an opportunity to learn something about what they are doing in our town. Do you think we should go?" Dede seemed interested.

"I don't know. Where is it?" Eleanor didn't like it. She wasn't interested in swinging and it sounded like some pagan celebration where they drank witches brew, made sacrifices, and participated in an orgy in the forest.

"It's very secret. We're supposed to meet in Goodspell Park where we will be blindfolded and transported to a secret location where there will be dancing and feasting. It sounds fun but dangerous," Dede said.

"What are you supposed to wear?" Eleanor asked as if it would give a clue to the real purpose of the event.

"It just said to wear comfortable clothes," Dede said.

"It might just be an innocent party. You know like the murder mystery ones we've all hosted. There may not be anything sinister about it at all," Eleanor said. "Yes, I think you should go. It could be fun. But be sure to eat beforehand. Knowing Lola, there may not be any food."

"It's potluck. You know how I hate potluck. There's no telling who cooked what, with what, or where they prepared it," Dede said.

"When is this celebration?" Eleanor asked.

"It's on the vernal equinox which falls on Monday."

"Moon day, I wonder if there will be a full moon," Eleanor said. She toyed with the idea of telling Dede about her unusual experience with hot chocolate and cookies but decided it could wait for another time.

"Let me know if you get an invitation, Eleanor. I'd feel better about going if I knew you and Angus were going too."

"I'll be sure to let you know, especially if Angus and I are invited," Eleanor said.

"Oops, I'm sorry. It was just a force of habit. Forgive me. Goodbye." Dede hung up.

Eleanor put the phone down and looked at the ruby red ring on her finger. She had to admit it felt good to wear this ring and it looked very pretty on her hand. She rubbed the stone to polish it and felt a familiar tingle in her fingers. Eleanor knew she could not wear this piece of jewelry where anyone would see it. It was evidence that Angus wanted and maybe someone else wanted it too. The thought that they may have wanted it enough to kill for it never crossed her mind. She slipped it off her finger and locked it in the safe behind the painting on the wall in her office. If the ring was determined to stay, she would help it.

Later that day Eleanor received a mysterious invitation to a vernal equinox celebration hosted by Victor and Lola Gaines. It was addressed to the lovely Eleanor Penrose +1.

Eleanor had done her homework about vernal equinox celebrations and was prepared for anything. She had made deviled eggs as her potluck dish, dressed comfortably all in black, and selected her +1 with infinite care. As she drove down the hill to pick up her date she experienced a thrill of excitement. She was truly looking forward to a fun evening. Pulling up to Nancy's house which was next to Angus', Eleanor could see that he was not at home. She wondered if he too had been invited to the celebration and if Drusilla would be his +1. Nancy quickly opened the car door and slid inside with her bottle of wine.

"I don't think we should drink anything except what's in this bottle," she declared. "We have no idea what these people might introduce in the food or drink that could make us act like brazen hussies."

"I made deviled eggs. There is nothing in them to cause you to misbehave. You have my word on that." Eleanor put her hand over her heart as they drove to Goodspell Park. By the time they arrived most of the invitees were already blindfolded and on what appeared to be a party bus.

"We won't see who is on the bus," Eleanor said, "but I recognized Angus's truck and there's Cleo's car."

"It's too dark for me to tell," Nancy said as they got out and hurried to get on board.

They stumbled onto the bus bumping into several people until they found two empty seats near the front and fell into them as the bus lurched ahead almost upending the platter of eggs.

"It's so dark in here I don't need a blindfold," said Eleanor as she tied it on, "I guess it just adds to the excitement."

"They don't want us to know where we're going," said a voice from behind them.

"Is that you Cleo?" asked Eleanor.

"Yes, I recognized your voice, Eleanor. Dede and Mark are sitting in the very back with Pearl and Cary. Angus and Drusilla are across the aisle behind Josephine and Richard," she whispered.

"She's been peeking over her blindfold," Steve tattled.

"There are lots of people I don't know," Cleo admitted.

The bus turned east, picked up speed and drove for about fifteen minutes before it slowed and turned left onto a bumpy road and finally stopped.

"You have arrived." Victor boarded and stood at the front of the bus and directed them. "You may take off your blindfolds and disembark. You'll find a lodge nearby in case of rain or if you need to use the restrooms, but there are tables set up outside for your potluck contributions. Please feel free to mingle and check out the scenery."

"I know exactly where we are," Eleanor said as she got off the bus and headed for the picnic tables that sat along the river. "It's the Old Homestead, and what a perfect night for this."

It was a perfect night. The moon was not full but its light shimmered over the river as a thin fog rose from it in a magical way. Although cool, there were several campfires for warming up the celebrants.

Eleanor could see a million stars and heard a symphony of peepers singing their love songs. No one was wearing black sheets or their birthday suits, much to her relief. She could smell what Dede considered mud and poop, but to Eleanor it was the fecund scent of a newly awakened earth composed of moss, soil, pine needles, and leaves.

Nancy opened her bottle of wine and poured a cup for herself and Eleanor. Cleo arrived with her contribution and placed a large loaf of bread in the shape of a penis on the table next to Eleanor's deviled eggs.

"I don't know this woman," Steve said as he walked away to mingle with Mark and Dede.

"This is a celebration of renewal and fertility isn't it?" Cleo smiled and poured herself a cup of something from a keg. "This must be the nectar of the gods. I wonder when the orgy begins."

"You don't know what's in there, Cleo," cautioned Nancy.

"Do you think they put poison in the Kool-Aid?" Cleo was skeptical. "It tastes good. Check on me in five minutes. If I'm still alive you can drink it."

Eleanor shrugged her shoulders as Cleo walked away to join Steve. "Maybe we're being too cautious."

"Hello my lovelies," Edwina greeted them as she filled two cups from the keg. "Isn't this the perfect night for a celebration? My Potsy is very fond of this drink. I'm not sure what it's called but it tastes like honey. So sweet and delicious, just like my darling boy. Enjoy."

As she walked away Nancy said, "There's something strange about that couple. I've seen them around the village and out on the golf course and even though they appear old, they just don't move like they are. Do you suppose they take a supplement to keep their joints limber?"

"I bet she does yoga." Pearl interjected into the conversation.

"Some people are blessed with good health and no inflammation. I never really noticed how she moves. Every time I've been around her she's been sitting with the Do Nothings." Eleanor studied her now as she snuggled up to Potsy and offered him the drink. "She definitely has a youthful and positive attitude."

"They both do. Look at the way he slung his arm around her. It's like they're lovesick teenagers with matching white heads," Nancy said.

"Funny, I've mentally named them the cute-tips," Eleanor said.

"I think you two are just jealous," Pearl accused as she put one of Eleanor's deviled eggs on her plate. "They seem perfectly normal to me."

Others were beginning to fill their plates from the table of potluck choices. Eleanor noticed many had also chosen phallic-looking dishes. Asparagus spears were laid out in abundance along with other spring greens, shoots and sprouts in various salads including an ambrosia salad using yellow and pink peeps.

Eleanor and Nancy filled their plates and sat near a fire that overlooked the river. As they ate others joined their circle. Victor sat beside Eleanor and complimented her on her deviled eggs.

"Did you use allspice to enhance your love life?" He teased. Eleanor of course refused to divulge any of her secrets.

Angus and Drusilla sat across from them and Eleanor noticed several eggs on Angus's plate as well. She secretly hoped they wouldn't enhance his love life with Drusilla. Soon Victor was telling stories about eggs as fertility symbols.

"The rabbit has been a symbol of fertility for a long time, but it was the Germans who brought the custom of the Easter Bunny who laid colored eggs for well-behaved children to the US." Victor said.

"There's a legend that tells about Mary Magdalene going to the Roman emperor and telling him of the resurrection of Jesus. He skeptically pointed to a bowl of eggs nearby and said that was as likely as the eggs turning red and then they did. So now we color eggs," Lola contributed.

"There's a Chinese tale that the universe was formed from an egg and a deity grew inside of it. When he tried to get out, he cracked the egg into two parts: the upper became the sky and the lower the land and sea." Victor seemed to know his egg history.

"I've heard an old English superstition that if a girl wishes to see who her true love is, she places an egg in front of her fire on a stormy night. As the rain falls and the wind blows, her true love will come through her door and pick up the egg." Edwina said.

The story seemed vaguely familiar. Eleanor looked across the fire at Angus who would not meet her eye. He licked the deviled egg from his fingers before getting up and walking away.

As the evening wore on, the keg ran out of nectar and the revilers grew louder. Someone with a guitar began to sing *American Pie* and several joined him around the campfire while others wandered off in the woods to pursue different endeavors. Eleanor went into the lodge to use the facilities and met Edwina there tidying up her disheveled appearance.

"Forgive me dear, I'm afraid my Potsy is an animal. He's torn my top and messed up my hair," Edwina said as she brushed at her clothing that was covered with debris. "I must look affright, but I can't deny him. He likes it rough."

Eleanor was aghast but tried not to show her concern. "Really, Edwina, are you all right?"

"Absolutely, I just take one of these pills so that I can be what he likes." She took a handful of small orange tablets out of a beaded bag and offered one to Eleanor. "I'm sure they could help you get Angus back. They make me feel so free and easy."

Eleanor took one and slipped it in her pocket, "Thanks, Edwina but I'm not trying to get Angus back."

"I heard he was a detective," Edwina slurred. "Does he know who killed Gloria?"

"No, he wouldn't tell me if he did," Eleanor said as she picked a few leaves out of Edwina's hair.

"I heard that Gloria found out about Will's pastime and she had to be put down because she was going to tell," Edwina said.

"Did you hear what the pastime was?" Eleanor was suddenly extremely interested.

"Pornography and sex trafficking or was it sex trafficking and child pornography? Suddenly I'm not feeling so well. Do you think you could find my Potsy, so he can take me home?" Edwina asked.

Eleanor led Edwina to a chair and moistened a paper towel to put on her face. She noticed the dark roots growing out from the white hair and Edwina's unlined brow as she pressed the towel to it.

"How old are you, Edwina?" Eleanor whispered.

"Forty-seven, but tonight I feel old," she whispered back.

"How long have you been with Potsy?"

"I'm not supposed to talk to you, Eleanor. You're too nosy for your own good." Edwina's head fell back against the wall and Eleanor went for help.

It didn't take her long to find Angus who was leaning against a tree while a group sat around the campfire singing *Sweet Caroline.*

"Angus, I need you," Eleanor said in what she thought was a calm voice.

Angus shot into hero mode, "What is it?"

"Come with me," Eleanor led the way into the ladies' room with Angus close behind.

"If you're trying to seduce me, Eleanor, I can think of better places," he teased. Then he saw Edwina. "What happened?"

"My guess is a bad mix of pills and alcohol," she said and opened Edwina's bag of pills.

Angus put his ear to Edwina's chest and her hand came up to stroke his hair. "She's still alive," Angus said. "You stay with her while I get Victor. He has a car here. I think we should take her to the hospital. Depending on what she's taken, this could be fatal."

When Angus returned with Victor, Edwina was snoring. Victor carried her to the car and gave Angus the keys. "We couldn't find Potsy, so I'll stay here to let him know what happened and make sure Edwina didn't pass those pills to anyone else," Victor said. "You'd better go with her, Eleanor.

Angus needs to concentrate on driving and she may stop breathing. Do you know CPR?"

"Yes." Eleanor climbed in the back seat with Edwina and Angus sped away.

Angus and Eleanor sat in the waiting room. They had given the doctor all the information they had regarding Edwina Potts. The rest was out of their hands.

"She's forty-seven?" Angus was amazed. "Why would she pretend to be older?"

"I don't know. How old do you think Potsy is?" she asked.

"Seventy?" Angus guessed.

"She told me some interesting things while we were in the bathroom before she passed out. Do you want to know what she said, or not?" Eleanor asked.

"Shoot," he answered.

"She wanted to know about Detective McBride and if you'd discovered that Will Vandorff was into child pornography and sex trafficking. Then she said Gloria had discovered this about him so she had to be put down—like some animal. Do you think any of this is true?" Eleanor thought maybe Angus would share information but she was wrong.

"Eleanor, do you still have that red ring?"

Eleanor's eyes grew wide in amazement and her mind began to spin in an evil direction. "You know you have the red ring, Angus. It was in the pocket of the bathrobe Drusilla wore home the night of our sleepover. I know you were in my house because the robe was returned but the ring wasn't. Why are you asking?"

"Don't give me that wide-eyed innocent look Eleanor. I know you and your gang of inept wannabe detectives broke into my house because you left the key in the lock." Angus returned.

"So did you come to my house on a stormy night and eat my egg and cookies?"

Now it was Angus whose eyes grew wide in amazement. "What Kool-Aid have you been drinking?"

Eleanor must have been wrong about that night. Was it possible for her to drink two mugs of hot chocolate and eat an egg and two cookies in the middle of the night?

"I don't think I want to talk to you anymore," she said as she turned away in her chair.

"Maybe it was your Mr. Mooney who picked up your egg on a stormy night or do you have so many true loves you can't tell them apart?" Angus accused.

Eleanor got up and walked out of the hospital into the night. She walked until she came to Goodspell Park where she saw the party bus pulling into the parking lot. Perfect timing she thought. She found Nancy and together they drove to Sand Beach, sharing what they had learned about the vernal equinox.

For more than twenty years, Dede and Mark had lived in their huge vintage house on Park Avenue. Never in all those years had she allowed anyone in her basement. It was well documented that she was a packrat and her coffee friends, having shopped with her, could only imagine what treasures filled that underground space. So it was with eager anticipation that they met at Dede's house in answer to an unexpected invitation to descend into those mysterious depths.

"Mark and I were cleaning out the basement. We started months ago and I swear I've taken boxes of donations to the community pantry and Goodwill, but there's still more down there. Please don't judge me," she begged. "We cleared out this one wall and when we moved a massive wooden shelving unit we discovered something you will never believe," Dede set the stage before they actually began their descent.

It looked like a basement. It had a low ceiling and was dark with cement bricks lining the walls with a washer and dryer and laundry tray near the stairs.

"How very ordinary," Cleo said as she looked around. "I was expecting a bigger mess. You know, a trail through mountains of stuff like in those hoarding shows."

"You know I've been complaining for years that this house is haunted because of the noises I've heard coming from down here," Dede reminded them. "Now I know why." She pulled a chain that lit the larger space with a stark light bulb and pointed to the wall where the massive wooden storage structure had once been.

"It's a door," Josephine said.

"Where does it go?" asked Pearl.

"Have you opened it?" asked Eleanor.

"It's locked," Dede reported, "but my guess is that it goes to the tunnels under the city."

"Are you going to unlock it?" asked Cleo.

"We would if we had a key, but we don't want to open it if we can't lock it back up again. There's no telling how many other entryways exist and who or what moves around down there," Dede explained.

"This is so creepy!" Cleo exclaimed. "Can you have a locksmith make you a key? Maybe someone hid treasure down here or it could be another room where you can store more stuff. Maybe you could make a wine cellar down here."

"Mark remembers a ring of keys that was left here when we bought the house, but he doesn't remember where he put it, so he's searching for that. There's really no hurry. It's been here a long time and a few more days won't make much difference to anyone," Dede said. "I just never expected the tunnels to go this far and can't imagine what this might have been used for."

"Have you ever researched the history of your house?" asked Josephine. "I bet we could learn more about it at the Pioneer Museum."

"Maybe it was part of the shanghaiing of those men," Pearl speculated.

"Oh, I can see this house as a brothel where young men were seduced and drugged then led down the tunnels to boats and taken out to sea," Eleanor said dramatically.

"Yes, that makes so much sense, I bet if we looked into it we'd find that's what happened here," Josephine agreed.

"You have been so very busy, Dede. Were you able to bake anything? All this mystery has given me a craving for pie," Cleo said.

"I have some coffee cake that I made this morning," Dede offered as she led the way up to the kitchen. Dede put on a fresh pot of coffee and served the cake.

"Have you heard anything about Edwina?" asked Josephine.

"She didn't die," Eleanor said, "but that's all I know about it. However, I did learn that she is only forty-seven years old. What do you make of that?"

"Weird," Pearl said. "I think she must do yoga. You know that keeps you young and agile."

"Pearl, she is young and is pretending to be old. I think she and Potsy are up to no good," Eleanor continued. "When I saw her in the restroom she looked like she had been assaulted. Her hair was all messed up and her blouse was torn and soiled. She said she took the pills to make Potsy like her. I wonder just how old he is."

"Did anyone else have a bad reaction to the mead?" Josephine asked. "I know several people drank that brew in the keg."

"It didn't bother me, but I know not to mix drugs and alcohol unless it's marijuana and tequila," Cleo said.

"She also told me Will Vandorff was involved in child pornography and sex trafficking and Gloria was killed because she was going to report it to the authorities." Eleanor tried to remember the rest but her mind filled with images of Angus instead.

"What if it's Potsy who is involved in sex trafficking and Edwina is a victim. Maybe he's her pimp," Dede said.

"If that were true it would connect two of the murders," Eleanor said, "but how is Virginia part of that?"

"She was definitely too old to be in the sex trade," Pearl said.

"I wonder if the ruby ring has something to do with it," Eleanor said. "It may be what got Virginia killed, and Angus is very interested in it. Let's retrace the journey of the ring."

"You found it at that strange estate sale, then Virginia took it from your house," Dede said.

"Tina Mallory was found on the beach but her picture in the *Fish Wrapper* showed her wearing that ring, which must have been taken before the estate sale," Cleo said.

"I saw Virginia wearing it at Suzanna's," Eleanor remembered.

"We saw it in her room the night she was killed," Josephine said.

"Then it showed up at the Curiosity Shop where Amy bought it for me," Eleanor continued.

"We researched that ring and found out it was the Blood Ruby of Burma and was stolen but keeps turning up in various places," Dede said.

"It's supposed to bring the wearer youth, and renewed passion for life," Josephine reminded them.

"The night of our sleepover, I put the ring in the pocket of my bathrobe and Drusilla wore it home. I suspect she found it and gave it to Angus who broke into my house and returned the robe, but the ring wasn't in the pocket anymore," Eleanor said.

"Did he break in or does he have a key?" asked Josephine.

"He entered my house without permission using my hidden outdoor key," Eleanor explained.

"So where is the ring now?" asked Pearl.

"That's the strange part. I found it on my deck between two boards and put it in my safe," Eleanor said.

"How did it get on your deck?" asked Dede.

"I don't know, but Angus asked me about it the night of the equinox. I told him I didn't have it," Eleanor admitted.

"Maybe this ring is more valuable than we know," Cleo speculated. "It seems to have the power to choose its owner since it keeps coming back to you, Eleanor."

"Not to mention that two of the people we know who had it are now dead," Pearl said.

"I'm losing hope that we can solve this case," Josephine lamented. "It needs the FBI if it involves sex trafficking."

"I can see how sex trafficking might be related to a desire to own that ring. After all, it promises a renewed passion and zest for life. I can imagine how some horny old geezer like Potsy, trying to regain his youth, might kill for that kind of power," said Cleo.

"Why? When all he has to do today is buy some Viagra," Dede remarked.

"But not all old men have access to Viagra. Maybe there's a market for the ring in more superstitious countries," Eleanor said. "Besides, it's a ladies ring."

"Now we come back to Victor Gaines and his import-export business. He could be exporting young women and importing curiosities for his wife. He doesn't seem to have any scruples where sex is concerned," Josephine remarked.

"Oh, that reminds me, I heard someone say something about him at the equinox thing. Gloria Vandorff was in a swing club with him and had asked Will for a divorce because she had fallen in love with Victor Gaines. Evidently Victor's wife was insanely jealous and threatened Gloria at one of their parties."

"Pearl, how long have you been sitting on this little tidbit?" asked Cleo.

"I really don't want Victor to be guilty," said Dede.

"Is it okay with you if it's Lola?" asked Eleanor who didn't want it to be her either.

"Who did you hear say this?" asked Josephine. "Sometimes the information can be discounted if the source is suspect."

"I was listening in on a conversation among a group of women. There were at least five of them and I only recognized Edwina. The others were young, at least younger than she was," Pearl said. "They stopped talking when they saw me so I think they were all in the swing club."

"I can verify that Lola is jealous of Victor's exploits," Eleanor added, "She told me herself, but she didn't confess to murder."

Eleanor had just returned from her morning walk when Dede called. "Eleanor, I have a surprise for you. Is it all right if I come over?" Dede sounded excited.

"Sure, I'm just going to take a shower. What's the surprise?" she asked.

"I'll bring it and be there in twenty minutes." Dede hung up. By the time Dede arrived Eleanor had put on a pot of coffee and baked a batch of snickerdoodles.

"Come in and tell me what this surprise is," Eleanor ordered.

Dede went immediately to the kitchen, poured herself a cup of coffee and began eating a cookie. "You know this is killing me don't you?" Eleanor's curiosity was palpable and Dede was enjoying it way too much.

"I did a little search on the internet and found this . . . " she said as she reached in her purse and pulled out a red velvet bag and emptied the contents on the kitchen counter. Out spilled a dozen ruby red rings exactly like the Blood Ruby of Burma.

"Oh my." Eleanor gasped as she picked one up and examined it closely. "It looks very similar to the one I have in my safe. Let me get my magnifying glass."

"I know they're fakes. They were cheap but do you know what this means?" Dede asked.

"Someone is mass-producing them," Eleanor said as she inspected the inside of the setting.

"We don't know if Tina Mallory had the real ring because it may have been a fake." Dede was extremely pleased with her powers of deduction.

"Eleanor disappeared into her office and returned with the real thing. She put it down next to the fake and she and Dede could tell immediately that one was exquisitely made and the other a knockoff.

Dede put the exquisite red ring on her finger. "This is a beautiful piece. I don't want to take it off."

Eleanor played with the fake rings, putting one on each of her fingers. "They don't look that bad when they're not next to the real thing. Where did you find these exactly? I searched for a ruby ring like that when Virginia took mine but I couldn't find anything similar."

"The Asian Trading Company has lots of inexpensive items. I used to order things from them all the time for my treasure chest when I was teaching," Dede said.

"Did they call it the Blood Ruby of Burma?" Eleanor asked.

"No, just ruby rings, I think," Dede said. "Do you think we can use these in some way to solve the case?"

"I don't know," Eleanor said thoughtfully. "I wish we could use them to clear Victor and Lola."

"Oh, me too," Dede said.

"The person who took the ring from Virginia's room the night she was killed was most likely the murderer. It doesn't make sense for Lola or Victor to have put the ring in her shop if they were guilty," Eleanor said.

"It does make sense for someone to put the ring there if they wanted to frame Victor and Lola," Dede said.

"We are the only ones who knew Virginia had the ring the night she was killed. She stole it from me and when you went in her room. You saw it there. The police don't know it's connected to Virginia. Even Angus only knows it was on Tina's finger and that I had it on mine." Eleanor's mind was in a tizzy. "Wait a minute. Officer McGraw said he got an anonymous tip about Virginia wearing a red ring, so they do know about it. He even asked me if I had seen her wearing it the night she was killed."

"Do you think Angus believes you were involved with Tina's death?" Dede asked. "Maybe that's why he wants the ring, Eleanor. He's trying to protect you."

"I had the ring long before Tina washed up on the beach. I wore it to Lola and Victor's party and my dinner party too. Lots of people saw it including the Do Nothings, but not everyone would be as observant as Angus connecting it to Tina," Eleanor said. "What did we tell Drusilla the night of the tequila party?"

"I don't remember," Dede confessed. "I don't think we told her that Virginia had taken your ring, but I can't be sure."

Angus's words about inept wannabe detectives popped into her mind. She hated when he was right. "Let's go down to Suzanna's and get lunch," Eleanor suggested. "Maybe the Do Nothings will still be there with some gossip."

"Well, if it isn't the mayor!" Mattie May exclaimed as Dede and Eleanor walked in the door.

"Hi Ladies," Dede greeted them individually. "Do you mind if we join you?"

"We would be honored," Mavis said.

"Yes, tell us what's going on in Waterton," Sybil said.

"There's nothing new really except the new highway construction." Dede went on for at least ten minutes describing the changes to the traffic flow and the work schedule as well as the function of the swales and improvements for disabled pedestrians.

"We heard that Edwina was home from the hospital. Do you know how she's doing?" asked Eleanor.

"She's convalescing. Evidently she took more of her medicine than the prescribed amount, totally unintentional, of course," Mattie informed them. "Her husband won't let anyone in to see her—says she needs her rest."

Eleanor searched her pocket and found the pill that Edwina gave her the night of the equinox. "Do you know what this is?" she asked. "Edwina had a bag full of these the night she collapsed. Angus and I took her to the hospital."

As a retired pharmacist, Mattie knew immediately. "Valium," she said. "Poor thing, I thought there was something off about her. She's probably addicted."

"Have you visited Lola Gaines' shop? She has lots of interesting pieces. I thought I saw a ring like yours in the jewelry case," Mavis said.

Eleanor had forgotten to take off one of the fake rings. She put her hands under the table hoping Mavis wouldn't notice it was a fake.

"I have to be off," Mattie said.

"Look at the time," Sybil said. "I had no idea it was so late."

"Can I drop you two?" Mattie liked to drive her vintage Lincoln Town car.

"I think I'll walk, thank you," said Mavis as she got up to leave.

Dede and Eleanor sat at the table and ordered the deluxe burgers and fries and pondered the mystery of the ruby ring.

"You know, Tina's ring could have been a fake. "The photo in the newspaper wasn't very clear," Dede said.

"It's possible there are hundreds of those fake rings," Eleanor agreed. "I wonder if she was wearing it when they found her on the beach."

"I can't even think anymore." Dede clasped her head in her hands.

"Lola gave me the name of her supplier when I was inquiring about the ring," Eleanor remembered, "I may still have it." She dug in her purse and came up with a piece of scrap paper. "She ordered her rings from the Asian Trading Company."

"Interesting, but it doesn't really prove anything." Dede bit into her burger. "I did a little research into the absentee owner of the building over the tunnels. You remember the one who refused to give us access for the underground tours. He's from Seattle too. Those absentee owners infuriate me. They come to a small town like Waterton looking for a bargain, buy a building, and then just leave it empty and let it go to rack and ruin. His name is Theodore something that ends with a ski like

Polinski or Podendski. I think there's access from Lola's shop into the tunnels from that building. Do you think there's a link here to the crimes?"

"I don't know," Eleanor said, distracted by Angus and Drusilla walking on the beach. They made a romantic picture together—two figures strolling along the shore with the ocean waves in the background. Then they stopped and Angus folded Drusilla into his arms. Eleanor felt such a sharp ache that she almost cried out.

Dede saw it too and read the look of hurt on Eleanor's face. "Let's get out of here," she said.

As they walked up the hill Dede tried to distract Eleanor from her funk, "Have you seen Michael Patrick lately?"

"No, why?" Eleanor asked.

"I'm sure I saw him with Drusilla yesterday having pizza at the Fat Hog," Dede commented. "They were having a very serious conversation. It almost looked like they were a couple."

"I haven't seen his car here, and Angus wouldn't have mentioned it, of course." Eleanor's voice faded away. Intellectually, she knew Angus was not romantically involved with Drusilla, but seeing them together on the beach made her doubt everything she thought she knew.

"Let's walk by Edwina's house and see how she is," Dede suggested. A very pale and youthful looking Edwina answered the door.

"How sweet of you to visit," she said. "Potsy hasn't let me out of his sight since the equinox and I'm dying of cabin fever. Please come in. I'd offer you tea and cookies but I'm afraid I don't have any and besides Potsy might come home soon. He doesn't want me having visitors. He's so protective." Eleanor had another word for it.

"Are you feeling better now?" Dede asked.

"Yes, thank you Eleanor for taking me to the hospital. I was so stupid to mix my medications with alcohol," Edwina said. "Potsy was furious. I hope I didn't say anything silly to you."

"I'm sure you would have done the same for me," Eleanor said. "And I don't remember anything you said that was silly."

"Oh what a relief," Edwina sighed, "I thought I remembered saying something about Victor assaulting me in the woods because I knew about the sex trafficking, but that was just a hallucination. Now Victor and Lola have gone away and I can't apologize."

"No worries, I'm sure it was the drugs talking," Eleanor said reassuringly. "We'd better go, we don't want to wear you out and make Potsy angry again."

"Thanks for stopping by. Edwina blew a kiss as they left.

"Jesus H. Christ!" exclaimed Dede when they were out of earshot. "What was that?"

"Crazy talk, or she was trying to incriminate Victor, because she told me Potsy had assaulted her that night," Eleanor said. "I'm not sure I trust Edwina to tell the truth. Maybe she's still on drugs."

"Their place does look empty," Dede said as they walked by Victor and Lola's house.

Eleanor stopped in her tracks. "Let's do some snooping," she said and strode to the porch with purpose.

Dede followed and looked in the windows while Eleanor went to the lock box and punched in a code. The lock box did not open. Of course the new owners would have changed it. Eleanor hit a few random numbers and got lucky.

"How did you do that?" asked Dede when Eleanor returned with the key and unlocked the front door.

"They changed the code since Norman lived here but I just tried some new numbers and it opened." "With that kind of luck, you should buy a lottery ticket when we're finished here," Dede remarked. Eleanor quickly returned the key and they both went inside.

"I'm not sure this is a good idea," Dede protested.

"Everything looks the same as the last time I was here," Eleanor noticed. "There are still unpacked boxes all over the place."

"He is in the import-export business," Dede said, "Maybe they have to do with that."

"I bet he does most of his business online," Eleanor speculated. "You don't think they're moving do you?"

"Let's look in the boxes," Dede proposed as she checked out one near her. "This one is from a company called Dick's Pumping and here's another from Lick Her Shop. Ewwwww, I bet these are full of sex toys."

"None of them have been opened yet," Eleanor noticed, "So we can't see what's in them." She searched among some others and finally found one from a place called Dominatricks that contained a number of skimpy black outfits, whips, handcuffs, and sharp pointy objects that were unfamiliar to Eleanor and Dede. "Do you think they use this in their swing club?" she asked holding up a pair of shackles.

"I have no idea," Dede said, "but these aren't the boxes that were here during their party. These have been delivered recently and only that one box has been opened."

"Maybe Victor is planning to open his own adult shop," Eleanor said.

"Not in my town!" exclaimed Dede.

"Let's look around some more." Eleanor wandered into the kitchen.

"It's immaculate," Dede commented.

"I don't think Lola uses the kitchen, at least not for cooking," Eleanor said as she snooped through some mail on the edge of the counter—all addressed to occupant.

"What are we looking for?" asked Dede.

"I don't know, some proof that Victor isn't a sick sex addict would be good." Eleanor walked into the living area to study the titles of the two books on the bookcase while Dede did more snooping in the refrigerator. She was pleased to see her latest book of poetry on the shelf.

"Eleanor, someone just drove up. I think it's them!" Dede said as she rushed into the living room. "We're trapped!"

Eleanor found the latch on the bookcase that unlocked a secret room and they quickly slipped inside and slid the bookcase back into place.

"How did you know about that?" Dede whispered in the darkness.

"Remember, I've been in this house before," Eleanor whispered back. "Shhhh.."

"I don't believe you didn't order all this crap!" Lola's voice was shrill and angry.

"Honestly, I would never in a million years buy boxes of sex paraphernalia, although I don't see anything wrong with testing some of it now that it's here. It might be fun to try," Victor said.

"Your name is on all the boxes, Victor Gaines. Who do you think sent this to our house with your name on it?"

"The Fairy Codfather?"

"You are disgusting!"

"Come on lo- lo- Lola, lighten up. Why not try on this outfit. We can have a good time if you quit being such a spoilsport. Come here."

"Stop Victor . . . I said stop! I've got a whip and I'm not afraid to use it."

"Ouch! Why do you have to be so mean?"

"Because you don't understand that when a woman says 'NO' she means no."

"The least you could do is make me a sandwich," Victor said. "A good wife would be obedient and do what her husband tells her to do."

"NO!"

"You know your frigid attitude is what's keeping you from finding out what Angus knows," he scolded. "He has all the skills of a good detective and his partner is a private investigator. You could at least try to find him attractive."

"You mean the way you find Dede attractive?"

"She's the mayor for gripes sake. It's all part of the game."

"Have you learned anything from Drusilla or the other women at the parties?" Lola asked.

"Are you talking party tricks?"

"Get serious. You know Eleanor has the ring," Lola said. "I don't know how it got in the display case and I couldn't refuse Amy when she asked for it without arousing suspicion. I think someone planted it there to make us look guilty."

"It's better if she has it. We're going to have to act quickly now because someone is either on to us or they're trying to implicate us in these murders," Victor said.

It was very quiet and then Dede and Eleanor who had their ears glued to the wall of the secret room heard Victor laughing and footsteps going up the stairs.

"Do you think they both went upstairs?" Dede whispered. "I wish I had my phone, but I must have left it at your house."

"We have to stay in here until we're sure it's safe to leave," Eleanor said.

"What's in here?" asked Dede as she began to fumble around in the darkness.

"I found a light switch," said Eleanor, "I'm going to turn it on. I just hope they can't see it from the other side."

"Try to be quiet. If we can hear them, then they should be able to hear us. Who knows what they'll do if they find us in here," said Dede. The light that came on was dim but made it possible to see the contents of the small space.

"Hey, these are Cleo's paintings. What do you think he's going to do with them?" Dede asked.

"He is in the import-export business, so maybe he's going to export them." Eleanor didn't really know what that business entailed.

"This looks like a gun safe," Dede said pointing to a metal box on a shelf.

Eleanor found a filing cabinet but it was locked. "Why put a filing cabinet in a secret room and then lock it?"

"Maybe his business dealings are secret and he's hiding them here," whispered Dede.

"What's the matter Dede? Don't you trust Mr. Charming anymore?" Eleanor teased.

"I'm not sure. Let's try to pick the lock," Dede said. "Maybe we'll find out he's a philanthropist."

"Only if you spell that p-h-i-l-a-n-d-e-r-e-r," Eleanor snickered.

Picking the lock proved unsuccessful, so they sat and looked at Cleo's paintings.

"This one is my favorite," said Dede. It was a landscape of a swampy area surrounded by red bushes with a multitude of egrets nesting in the trees. "It reminds me of home. Every year the egrets would migrate to Minnesota and build their nests in colonies in the wetlands. " Dede looked through a few others. She noticed two of the frames that were especially eye catching. "Do you think these are the ones Cleo bought at the estate sale? They really are beautifully made. Just look at this scroll work. They're made of solid wood. I bet they're worth more than the paintings that are in them."

She looked over at Eleanor who had made a nest in the corner and was snoring softly. It looked like they were in for the night.

In her dream, Eleanor punched in the lock box code and the drawer to the filing cabinet opened. They began to search through the documents. After what seemed like hours, Eleanor and Dede touched every file and piece of paper in them. "I don't get it." Eleanor said, "All of these just look like receipts for things that he's bought and sold."

"Everything looks legit until you see this folder for Cleo's paintings," Dede said. "He claims to have sold her masterpieces for $20 million, yet here they are."

"Maybe the other receipts are lies too," Eleanor said. "My guess is Victor Gaines is into something illegal that's making him rich and he's laundering his money in various ways, including claiming to sell Cleo's art."

"I like Cleo's art, but I wouldn't pay $20 million for it," Dede said. "What are we going to do?"

"We have to get out of here," Eleanor said. "Knowing what we know, if Victor finds us here he might kill us." Just then the secret door opened and the dark figure of a man loomed over them.

Eleanor woke suddenly. Every bone in her body ached. "What time do you think it is?" asked Dede. "I must have fallen asleep."

"I don't know. It must be late, maybe they're asleep. I'm going to open the bookcase and take a peek," Eleanor switched off the light and pushed the lever that swung the bookcase open. It was very dark. Eleanor slipped out and Dede followed. They closed the secret door and tiptoed out of the house.

"I just knew we were doomed." Dede breathed a sigh of relief as they stumbled down the lane in the dark toward Eleanor's house.

"I can't believe we got out of there," Eleanor felt like dancing. "I think I'm giving up snooping forever." Neither of them noticed the camera mounted under the eaves that recorded their every move or the face at the window that watched them hurry away.

"Oh no, look at all the cars and lights at your house. Mark must have called out the National Guard when I didn't come home," Dede said.

When they walked in the door Amy and Drusilla greeted them with hugs and kisses as if they had been lost for years instead of hours.

"All the men are out searching for you. Where have you been, Mom?" Amy's face was streaked with tears of relief.

"I'm sorry you were worried, sweetheart. Dede and I got trapped in Victor Gaines secret room and we couldn't get out until he went to sleep," Eleanor couldn't think of a story that made sense so she just blurted out the truth.

"I'm calling Angus to tell him to stop searching," Drusilla said as she walked away with her phone to her ear.

"I don't know about you, Eleanor, but I've got to pee," Dede said as she raced to the bathroom.

"It's very late," Eleanor said, "We've caused such a fuss. Is anyone hungry?"

"Mom, don't bother feeding us. We're just so glad you're okay," Amy said. "I'll make you a cup of tea. By the time Dede and Eleanor had their tea, the search party returned.

"Where the hell were you? We've been all over this town and up and down the beach searching for you. Amy's called everyone she knows asking if they've seen you. Do you know how worried everyone has been?" asked Mark whose angry tone masked his fear. Angus, Michael, and Taylor merely stood silently waiting to hear how two old ladies could disappear into thin air on a sunny afternoon.

Dede merely hugged Mark and whispered in his ear how sorry she was to make him worry. "We were snooping where we shouldn't have been and we got stuck in Victor's secret room. We're okay so you can all go home and get some sleep," Eleanor announced and suddenly felt the adrenaline leave her body allowing exhaustion in.

Dede gathered her things and left with Mark by her side still letting off steam. The others followed suit except for Angus who stood like a sentinel at the door. When they'd all driven away he crossed the room and swept Eleanor into his arms and kissed the top of her head.

"I'd warn you never to do that again, but I know it would just bounce off that hard head of yours. Are you okay? Did anyone see you? Are you afraid Victor's coming after you?"

Eleanor melted into his embrace and felt her knees weaken. She was so very tired that she hadn't even thought about the risks enough to be afraid.

"I want you to tell me everything you know Eleanor. Together we can figure this out."

"I'm just tired, Angus," Eleanor pulled away. "I need some sleep. Maybe we can talk tomorrow."

"As you wish, but I'm staying here. You won't be alone tonight." Angus took off his coat and left his shoes by the door.

Eleanor slept like a dead person and woke later than usual. When she finally dragged herself into the kitchen she was surprised to find Angus sitting at the counter drinking coffee and reading the morning paper.

"So you're alive," he grinned, "I made bacon and eggs, but I'm afraid I ate them too."

Eleanor poured a cup of coffee, took the crossword puzzle section, and moved to the couch where she proceeded to carry out her daily routine. Angus gave her ten minutes before he joined her there.

"If I married you this is what it would be like. We would fight over the paper. You'd see me with bed head and then eat all the bacon. You'd go fishing and leave me to do your laundry, grocery shop, cook and clean, and then you'd expect someone to kiss you goodnight."

"Sounds good to me, except the bed head part," Angus teased while Eleanor only glared at him. "Are you always this grouchy in the morning?" he asked.

"You, my friend, will never know." Eleanor was feeling uncharacteristically mean.

"What can I do to make it better, Ellie?" Angus said. "Maybe if you tell me everything you learned about Victor Gaines and the ruby ring, you wouldn't feel so stressed."

Angus sat down next to Eleanor and glanced at her crossword puzzle, "Thirty-one across is PROPOSAL," he said. "I'm taking mine off the table. I no longer want to marry you. Now can we get back to being friends? I've missed you."

Eleanor had no words. It was what she wanted too, so why was she so reluctant to agree? "What changed your mind?" she asked finally.

"I'm sure it was the bed head," he teased. "We'll take it slow. I'm sorry if I pushed too hard, too fast, Ellie. You take all the time you need to grieve for Walter. I'm all in for you and I can wait until you're ready." Angus took her hand and kissed it.

Eleanor wanted to ask about Drusilla, but couldn't bring herself to speak. Tears were in her throat. "How would you like me to fix you some scrambled eggs while you go wash your face and comb your bed head? Then maybe you can tell me about your adventure in the secret room." Angus's gentleness was breaking her down. She got up and obeyed.

While she showered, she rehearsed what she would tell Angus. He needed to know everything she knew because he wasn't the enemy. Of all the things she knew about Angus McBride there was one thing she was sure of and that was that he was not a murderer, but someone was, and that someone was responsible for ending the lives of three people and if she could help bring some justice to the world, she would. Anything else was just wrong and selfish. This wasn't a contest —it was murder.

Angus had set a place for her at the dining room table. There was a plate of scrambled eggs and bacon with a side of cantaloupe. A napkin lay on the side next to the proper silverware and a fresh cup of coffee sat steaming in its saucer. Eleanor was impressed. She didn't know Angus paid any attention to the finer details that made life beautiful. There was even some type of flowering weed in a small vase next to her coffee.

"How lovely, Angus. Thank you," she said as she picked up her fork. Angus sat at the table and watched her eat. When she was ready she told him about the adventure in the secret room which revealed absolutely nothing about Victor Gaines.

"I'm sure he's hiding something. Why else would he have a locked filing cabinet in a secret room?" Eleanor opined. "I think he's doing something illegal and laundering the money through Cleo's art.

"Interesting theory," Angus replied.

"What do you think? Did Victor Gaines kill Gloria?" Eleanor asked. "Is he involved in human trafficking? How are these murders connected?"

"There isn't any real evidence that proves Victor is guilty of murder. He may be a lecher and a sex addict, and even guilty of money laundering and fraud, but there's no solid proof that he killed Gloria. Lola has more of a motive than he does."

"Victor said something about her trying to get close to you, Angus," Eleanor remembered. "She wants to know what you know and they know Drusilla is a private detective."

Angus's eyebrows rose in surprise. "I wonder how they learned that."

"Do you think Victor got Drusilla to tell him things at the swinger's party?" Eleanor asked innocently.

"Who told you she was at a swinger's party?" Angus asked.

"This is a small town, people talk," Eleanor said.

"That was part of our investigation, Eleanor," Angus reassured her. "Drusilla is a professional and wouldn't make a rookie mistake like that."

Eleanor remembered the tequila party but didn't say anything. "I'm sure you mean you wouldn't make a mistake like that if Lola came on to you," Eleanor said.

"She is a beautiful woman, but I've heard she has a jealous streak and she can't cook," Angus said with a smile.

"Maybe someone's trying to make her look guilty to throw us off the track. Officer McGraw told me he received an anonymous tip about Virginia wearing a ruby ring. He asked if I'd seen her wearing it the night she died, then it showed up in Lola's shop. Of course, I couldn't tell him about the coffee group seeing it in her room that night without getting them in trouble."

"Wait, wait, the coffee group was in her room the night she was killed?" Angus was seriously concerned.

"The night of Victor and Lola's party, Virginia came into my house and took my personal journals. Then she called me on the phone and read excerpts from them to me. I was furious," Eleanor explained.

"You're sure it was Virginia."

"Yes, she showed up at Suzanna's wearing the red ring I had left on my dresser."

"Who else saw her wearing the ring?" Angus asked.

Eleanor hadn't thought of it that way. She only thought about people who might have seen her wearing the ring. "I can't say for sure, but Mavis Bench, Mattie May, and Sybil Wendt were all at Suzanna's when Virginia gave us the one finger salute. Oh Edwina Potts was there too. They all noticed it. I'm sure Virginia did it to show me the ring."

"How did you come by the ring?" Angus asked.

"I bought it at an estate sale in the valley," Eleanor explained.

"And Virginia took it along with your journals, so the coffee group broke into her room to recover them," Angus said. "Why didn't you go to the police, or at least tell me?"

"I wanted my journals back," Eleanor stressed. "The police might have taken days to recover them. Plus, they're private. I didn't want Virginia reading them or take the chance that she might leave town with them."

"And you didn't trust me enough to ask for my help?" Angus seemed honestly hurt.

"I thought I could do this by myself," Eleanor said.

"So that was why we took Virginia to dinner," Angus deduced. "How did the coffee group get into her room?"

"Evidently Virginia didn't lock her door. They just walked in, found the journals, and left. For some reason they didn't take the ring but they saw it on her nightstand."

"So you think the person who killed Virginia, also took the ring?" Angus asked.

"Yes, and it turned up in Lola's shop where I recognized it. Amy bought it for me because she misunderstood my interest in it for a desire to own it."

"So do you have the ring now?" Angus asked knowing it had come to him through Drusilla and been stolen by the crow.

"Yes, it's in my safe," Eleanor said.

"Eleanor, how did it get in your safe?" Angus asked curiously.

"It's a mystery, Angus. I found it on my deck. It seems I can't get rid of it even if I want to." Angus wondered if she felt that way about him too.

"Do you think Virginia was killed because of the ring?" Eleanor asked.

"I don't know, but I'm sure Virginia was just an innocent victim here. She had no idea what she was flashing you when she gave that salute," Angus said.

"How is the ring mixed up in all this?" asked Eleanor.

"There's a cult called The Red Rapture, sometimes The Red Storm. They take young girls who are runaways—new to big cities or living on the streets, or sometimes just on their way home from school. They sexually assault them and then sell them into slavery. The ring is linked to them. They believe the ring is an aphrodisiac. Tina Mallory was wearing that ring. She was groomed beforehand, probably through the internet. My theory is that she jumped ship trying to escape, drowned, and washed up on the beach," Angus sighed.

"Just like Princess Buttercup in the *Princess Bride.*"

"Right," Angus agreed.

"That means the sex traffickers are sending these girls out to sea," Eleanor said.

"That's possible."

"How do you think the ring ended up at the estate sale?" Eleanor asked.

"Maybe Tina dropped it somewhere to be rid of it or hoped it would lead someone to help her. The ring is valuable. Maybe she used it to bribe someone. We may never know," Angus speculated.

"If she knew its purpose, perhaps she thought they wouldn't want to have sex with her if she no longer had the ring," Eleanor said. "What kind of people do this to young girls?"

Angus just shook his head. He knew there were all kinds of people who were capable of lust, deceit, and murder. He had spent most of his life pursuing them, revealing their dark deeds, and hoping to bring them to justice.

"So what do you think happened to Virginia?" Eleanor asked.

"A victim of circumstance, maybe she was in the wrong place at the wrong time. I don't think anyone would confuse her with a potential sex slave, but the ring may have signaled that she knew more than she did. It might have threatened someone, or she just pissed someone off. The fact that both Gloria and Virginia were killed with the same weapon makes no sense to me."

"How is Will?" Eleanor asked. "I can't believe he tried to kill himself. Do you know why?"

"He's still in a coma," Angus said, "but that wasn't a suicide attempt. Someone shot him, thought he was dead and then called 911 on his phone. We found footprints in the woods and tire tracks that didn't belong to him. Gloria and Will were swingers and friends of Victor and Lola, but I don't think Victor is the murderer."

"Do you think it's Lola?" Eleanor asked.

"That would make it a crime of passion and I think there's more to this than a jealous wife. Somehow all these crimes are connected to human trafficking," Angus said. "Michael and Drusilla told me police have cracked down hard on the sex trade industry in Seattle and think it's made them move to smaller ports."

"Ohhh . . . I know Drusilla is really a private detective named Delia Parker," Eleanor admitted.

Angus smiled, "Is that why you weren't jealous?"

Eleanor wasn't admitting anything of the sort. "Has she helped you in all this?"

"Delia Parker is the woman Michael's been seeing on the side. I hired her to help me clear my name. Michael came down here to break it off with her so it's been a rough couple of days for her. I think she really loves him," Angus admitted.

"Ohhh . . . I like her," Eleanor said. "Will she be leaving now?"

"I don't know. I left them alone in my house all night. Either they broke it off or they didn't. She's welcome to stay, of course, but she may not want to work this case any longer," Angus said.

"What's the next step?" Eleanor asked.

"I don't know. What do you suggest?" Angus smiled.

"We need to discover how Gloria and Will Vandorff were involved. Do you think Drusilla could snoop around in their real estate dealings?" Eleanor suggested.

"Already done," Angus said. "They were trying to obtain the building where Lola's shop is, but the absentee owners refused to sell, so they asked the city if they would use eminent domain to gain possession of it."

"Do you know why Gloria and Will wanted that building?" Eleanor asked.

"The city is undergoing revitalization and that building is in a prime location. The owners haven't done anything with it for years. My best guess is Gloria and Will saw an opportunity to capitalize on it," Angus said.

"How did Lola get in it?" Eleanor asked.

"I don't know. Maybe she pulled some strings with people in high places," Angus said. Eleanor began to have second thoughts about Dede's relationship to Victor Gaines.

Eleanor and Josephine met at the Babbling Brook golf course to play nine holes. Because neither had any clubs they went in to the club house to rent a cart and shop around.

"I'm really starting to get into this game," Josephine said. "Richard and I have come out a few times and now I think I'm ready to buy my own clubs."

"Let's do it then." Eleanor was ready to commit to the price of the clubs as well. The golf pro was very helpful and steered them in the direction of the best value.

"What kind of golf clubs are these?" Eleanor asked, pointing to several wooden handled clubs mounted on the wall.

"Those are vintage 1930s Wilson niblicks. It's the whole set so quite a collector's prize," the pro said. "They're not what you want though."

"No, are they rare?" Josephine asked.

"Not rare, but obsolete."

"So a niblick is not just one club?" Eleanor asked.

"The term niblick comes from the small nib or head. This one is a driving iron, this one a cleek, then there's the mid-mashie and the mashie iron and spade mashie, the mashie niblick, the pitching niblick, and the niblick. That's the way they were until after 1930 when the numbered sets of irons became universal." The pro pointed to each club as it hung on the wall.

"Are they very valuable?" Josephine asked.

"No, you can pick them up at garage sales. It just depends on what you're looking for. They might be valuable to a collector and, of course, some with famous names are in more demand. But you ladies should be happy with the clubs you purchased."

Eleanor and Josephine took their new clubs and drove their cart to the first tee. "Do you think we should have at least invited Cleo to join us?" asked Eleanor guiltily. "It was her idea to take up golf."

"Let's practice and get outrageously good at it and then invite her," suggested Josephine. Eleanor was impressed with Josephine's game as they continued to play.

"I think this is your sport Josephine," Eleanor complimented. "I'm not sure you'll want to play with me now that you've made such massive improvements."

"Well, Dede isn't interested since she's sports challenged, Pearl thinks the game is lewd, and Cleo is more interested in drinking from her flask, so I will definitely continue to golf with you, Eleanor. That is if you want to keep golfing with me," Josephine said.

"I'm all in. Didn't I just spend a small fortune on golf paraphernalia—including this very fashionable glove?" Eleanor flexed her gloved fingers. "I will improve too, if I continue to play regularly."

"Excellent," Josephine said.

"Isn't that Victor Gaines?" Eleanor asked as she spied a man and a woman walking away from the green ahead of them.

"It does look like Victor but it's not Lola with him," Josephine said as she drove the cart closer. "I wouldn't be surprised to find him out here with another woman. He's about as faithful as a cuttlefish."

"Stop the cart, Josephine," ordered Eleanor. "I think that's Dede."

Josephine swerved off the pathway into a thicket almost upsetting the cart.

"We can't let them see us or know that we saw them. What do you think they're doing out here together?" asked Eleanor.

"I have no idea," Josephine responded. "Maybe it has something to do with city business."

"Dede doesn't golf. Why would she be out here with Victor Gaines, for heaven's sake?" Eleanor wondered. She hadn't told anyone her suspicions about Dede and Victor, but now, seeing them together on the links gave weight to her theory that something was going on between them.

"She's been secretive about a number of things lately. Those gnomes, for one, and the tunnels under the city, and she hasn't told us more about the door in her basement," Josephine said.

"Do you think she's involved with Victor?" Eleanor was reluctant to express her thought out loud. "He's quite smitten with her."

"I don't believe it," Josephine said. "Maybe he's blackmailing her. She did attend an orgy at his house and she's the mayor."

"That doesn't explain them golfing together," Eleanor said.

"Maybe he has incriminating pictures and this is where they exchanged pictures for money. There's just something I don't trust about him. I'm sure he's up to no good and now he's involving Dede," Josephine worried.

"Should we follow them? If we were able to see them, they might have seen us," Eleanor said. "Maybe we should just confront them and see what they have to say for themselves."

"We'll let them get ahead of us and then follow at a distance," Josephine suggested.

"Oh dear, someone is behind us. We have to move,." Eleanor said. "It's Edwina and Potsy."

Josephine put the cart in gear and they sped down the path to the green where Josephine four-putted and Eleanor simply picked up her ball and refused to play claiming a lack of focus.

"Let's just follow them and pretend to play," Josephine said. But as they drove to the next tee box they had lost sight of them. They raced down the fairway to the green, but they weren't there either.

"Maybe they saw us and cleared out," Eleanor said.

"Maybe they finished what they came out here to do," Josephine said.

"I can't believe Edwina and Potsy are right behind us. How can they be so fast?" Eleanor said. "Do you think they're following us?"

"No, they've stopped and are going out of bounds. They must be hunting for a lost ball," Josephine said.

"I've had enough of this for today. What do you say we get some lunch?"

"Let's call Dede and see if she wants to meet us at the Blue Lagoon," Eleanor said. "I'd like to hear her explanation."

As it turned out, Dede wasn't home and didn't answer her cell phone so Eleanor called Cleo and Pearl to invite them to lunch.

"You went golfing without me?" Cleo acted hurt.

"I don't blame them," Pearl remarked, "I'm sure you haven't replaced your aunt Lena's golf covers."

"Have either of you seen Dede?" asked Josephine.

"No," answered Pearl.

"Not since she showed us the basement door," Cleo said.

"We saw her on the golf course with Victor Gaines today," Eleanor reported.

"Were they golfing?" asked Cleo.

"It seems so," Josephine said.

"I hope Dede isn't in trouble," Pearl said, worried. "Oh, by the way, I sold that beautiful carved box on eBay and made a sizable profit to boot."

"You know what that means don't you," Cleo said, "All of the items we bought at that estate sale are no longer in our possession, except the ring."

"I would gladly give it back if I knew where its home was," Eleanor said.

"Well, maybe we should try a little harder to find it," Josephine suggested.

"What do you have in mind?" Pearl asked suspiciously.

"Who do we know was the first to own that ring?" Josephine asked.

"Tina Mallory." Eleanor furrowed her brows. "Is it too soon to visit her parents?"

"Wouldn't the police already have interviewed them by now?" asked Cleo.

"Maybe they didn't know the ring was a key element in this case," Eleanor said.

"Maybe it isn't," Josephine said, "Let's find out. I'll Google them and find out their address. I know they live in Beaverton.

Eleanor, you go home and get the ring. We can return the ring and maybe learn something that will help solve the case."

"Should we try to find Dede?" asked Pearl.

"I think we should leave Dede out of this one," said Eleanor.

Eleanor pulled up in front of the Mallory residence later that afternoon. The two-story craftsman sat in a cul-de-sac in an upscale neighborhood packed with similar houses.

"It might be better if we don't all go in," Josephine suggested. "We can be pretty intimidating in a group."

"Pearl and I will stay in the car and watch for any suspicious activity," Cleo offered.

"When you're done maybe we can go to a movie and out to dinner." Pearl liked to take advantage of a trip to the city.

Josephine and Eleanor got out of the car, walked to the door and rang the bell. An attractive middle-aged woman with long, dark hair peeked out the window and then answered the door.

"I'm afraid I don't want anything you are selling," she said as she peered out suspiciously.

"We're not selling anything, Mrs. Mallory," Josephine said, "But we may have something that belongs to you."

Eleanor reached into her purse and pulled out the ruby ring. It caught the light and sent a crimson flash like a laser beam.

"Please come in," said Mrs. Mallory opening the door wide. Eleanor and Josephine sat on a sofa in the front room opposite Mrs. Mallory.

"We are very sorry for your loss, Mrs. Mallory. This ring came into my possession through an estate sale and I recently saw a picture of your daughter wearing it. I assume it is her ring. I just wanted to return it to you," Eleanor said.

Mrs. Mallory made no attempt to take the ring. "I don't want it," she said. "The ring belonged to my mother-in-law and my husband gave it to Tina on her last birthday. It's brought nothing but sorrow to me."

"Do you know how it came to be at an estate sale?" asked Eleanor.

"I was trying to get rid of it. I took it to an estate sale in the west hills where I planned to leave it among the other items, but the one I went to was very elegant and they even had a booklet with a description of each thing on sale, so I left. Not far away was another sale. It was low-key and no one seemed to be watching, so I left it there hoping I would never see it again," she admitted.

"Was that before Tina disappeared?" asked Josephine.

"Yes," Mrs. Mallory dropped her head into her hands. "My husband, Charles was supposed to give that ring to me. I'd always admired it when his mother wore it. Then she suffered one stroke after another. She hung on for years but finally died this winter. When he gave it to Tina I realized that his relationship with her was deeper than his bond to me. She was always a difficult child but Henry was able to handle her. I guess I mean that literally. He gave her everything she ever wanted. I have to admit that I was jealous, but I turned a blind eye to what was going on between them because I didn't want to be that person—you know the jealous mother, but I was really the other woman. Tina tried to tell me what Charles was doing to her and had been doing to her for a long time, but I didn't want to hear it. Then she disappeared."

"Did you tell this to the police?" asked Eleanor.

"No, I was embarrassed and didn't think it mattered. Tina was taken. I never suspected that Charles had anything to do with it and didn't want this to ruin our life together, thinking somehow we could get back what we had, but lately I've been tortured with my suspicions."

"Where is your husband now?" asked Josephine.

"I asked him to leave after I found the elixir," she said. "He had this bottle that promised to improve his sexual vitality when used with a young woman wearing the ring. It disgusted me. I found pamphlets about an organization that Charles belonged to—The Red Rapture. You don't think Charles had anything to do with her death, do you?"

"You need to call the police and tell them everything you told us. They can investigate this and prove that Charles is innocent of wrongdoing—or not. Could you show us the pamphlets?" asked Eleanor.

"I burned them. I didn't want them in my house, just like I don't want that ring near me. I truly believe it's cursed." Mrs. Mallory began to cry.

"Would you like us to stay with you while you call the police?" Josephine asked. Mrs. Mallory looked at Eleanor and Josephine out of her tear-filled eyes as if seeing them for the first time.

"You must think I'm an awful mother and a horrible wife to let my child be abused by my husband. If I'd just given in to his desires . . . " She closed her eyes as if trying to unsee something obscene.

Josephine was on her phone calling the local authorities. "We're not here to judge you, Mrs. Mallory, but if you cooperate with the police, it might help other victims like your daughter." When someone answered on the other end of the line, Josephine reported what she knew and requested help for Mrs. Mallory.

Eleanor and Josephine left when the police arrived. Eleanor left the ring on the table in the entry way.

Eleanor and Josephine sat across the table from Cleo and Pearl at Stanford's and shared what they had learned while they waited for their dinner.

"Do you think Charles Mallory sold his daughter to keep her from telling their secret?" asked Cleo.

"It's hard to know. Maybe Mrs. Mallory sold her to get her out of the way. She said she was a difficult child. Maybe she was just tired of dealing with her. The pamphlets she found weren't there as proof that he belonged to this group. I'm sure he will have his own story to tell," Josephine said.

"Angus told me about the The Red Rapture. It's a real cult so I believe her, but why did she tell us any of this?" Eleanor questioned. "We're total strangers and it poured out of her like water. I thought she'd never stop talking."

"Sometimes it's easier to tell a complete stranger about things like this. Then it's in their hands and not yours. I made that call so she didn't have to do what she might feel is a betrayal of her husband. It probably felt good for her to let go of everything she was holding on to," Josephine explained.

"Does this help us know who killed Gloria and Virginia?" asked Cleo, "Or is Tina's death unrelated to the other murders?" asked Pearl.

"I don't know. I'm just glad to be rid of the ring," Eleanor said.

"If that was the Blood Ruby of Burma, you may have just given away a fortune," said Cleo.

"I don't care. I suddenly feel clean," Eleanor said.

Eleanor stopped at Dede's house on her way home. The lights were on inside and Dede answered the door while Doogie barked ferociously protecting his territory.

"Eleanor, come in," Dede welcomed her. "Would you like a piece of pie? I was just having dessert."

"No thank you, I just wanted to ask you about your day. Josephine and I were surprised to see you at Babbling Brook today with Victor Gaines and wondered what was going on." Eleanor saw a look cross Dede's face, but she couldn't read it.

"He was giving me a lesson. You know I'm not good at sports and I thought an extra lesson might help me keep up with the rest of you," Dede said, but Eleanor recognized it as a lie.

"Where's Mark?" Eleanor asked.

"He's off on a rat hunt with his brothers," Dede said. "He'll be gone for a couple of weeks."

"Aren't you afraid to be here all alone?" Eleanor was concerned about her friend.

"No, I've got Doogie here to protect me. He's very good at scaring the mailman away," Dede laughed.

"Did you find the key to the door in the basement?" she asked.

"Yes, but you won't believe what was behind it. Come see." Dede led Eleanor down the stairs and pulled the chain that illuminated the basement. She opened the heavy wooden door to reveal a brick wall.

"Someone bricked the door shut from the other side," Dede said. "It wasn't done yesterday, but it isn't really old either."

"What do you make of that?" asked Eleanor.

"It needs exploring. I've been working on a map and I think I know where this tunnel comes out. Come upstairs and I'll show you," Dede offered.

Dede unrolled a large map of the city. The known tunnels were highlighted in yellow. "See this branch that goes under the absentee owner's building where Lola's shop is located? If we were able to access the tunnel through our basement, we would also have access to the tunnel under her shop."

"Do you think the owners bricked up your access door?" Eleanor asked. "They don't own the tunnels. Will this give the city the access they need to pursue their tours under Waterton?"

"I think so, but I have to be honest. I don't want my basement to become the point of entrance for tourists. Think how invasive that would be!" Dede lamented.

"Maybe you and Mark could sell your house to the city and move. You don't need a huge house like this anymore," Eleanor said.

Dede shrugged. "I can't imagine moving. Mark has renovated almost every room. It's his masterpiece."

"Yes, and it's home. I understand how difficult leaving your home can be. My house is too big for me too, but I love it," Eleanor said. "If your house has a tunnel entrance, maybe there are other unknown doors as well."

"Do you want to go exploring tomorrow?" Dede asked.

"Absolutely!" Eleanor said. It wasn't until she was half way home that she realized she hadn't told Dede about Mrs. Mallory and the red ring.

Eleanor worried about Dede alone in that big house without Mark. Before she went to bed that night she called Josephine and shared her concerns. Josephine always knew what to do.

The following morning the coffee group met at Dede's house dressed for spelunking and braced for adventure. "I brought you something to help protect you while Mark is away," said Josephine. "You'll have to come get it from my car." The ladies all followed her outside. When Josephine opened the back of her Honda CRV, a life-size blow-up man popped up. He had a dark head of hair, a mustache, curls painted on his chest, and was absolutely naked.

"His name is Lorenzo. I use him for some of my therapy work, but I thought you might put him in your car when you drive to all your meetings so you don't look like a woman alone," Josephine explained.

When Dede had recovered from the shock of meeting Lorenzo, she broke out in hysterical laughter. "Maybe you could put him near your window so it looks like Mark is home," suggested Eleanor holding back her own giggles.

When the laughing died down, Dede quickly grabbed Lorenzo and stuffed him in the back of her car. "He'll be good there for now," she said as she looked around to see if anyone was watching. "Let's get this adventure underway."

"I brought headlamps for everyone," Cleo offered. "Sorry one of them is a reindeer with a red nose, but I borrowed it from my grandson."

"Excellent," said Dede, "I'll wear it and lead the way." She also carried her battery-operated lantern and the keys that Mark had found that unlocked the basement door to the tunnel. They quickly made their way to the tunnel entrance in the basement of City Hall and climbed down into the darkness.

"It doesn't seem as scary as last time," Cleo commented.

"It's still creepy," Pearl added as they proceeded to the barricade that they had explored earlier. Eleanor moved the barricade and Dede walked slowly and carefully pointing out hazards as she lit the way with her lantern. In one place by the damp gray stone walls they could see the remnants of someone's sloppy masonry work. Buckets and trowels lay abandoned along with stacks of bricks and cement that had long ago hardened into oddly shaped clumps. There was a wheelbarrow filled with debris they maneuvered around. They passed the metal ladder that led up to a trapdoor.

"I think that goes up to the The Curiosity Shop," Dede said, "Although it's difficult to know for sure."

"I need to get some air," Cleo panted, "There's no air down her. I have to get out of here. I have to get out!"

"Just take a deep breath," urged Josephine. "I can go back up with Cleo. I promised her I would if her claustrophobia kicked in. We'll meet you back at Dede's." The two of them turned back and headed toward the City Hall access.

"Let's keep going," Eleanor said as they made their way through several twists and turns.

It wasn't long before Dede stopped and pointed to a spot where the bricks took on a different appearance.

"This must be the wall that sealed my entrance to the tunnel," Dede said. "These bricks don't match the rest of the wall."

"We'd need the proper tools to break down this wall," Pearl said. They rounded a corner and saw another door.

"I wonder if the key that opened my door will work on this one," Dede said as she pulled out the ring of keys. There were half a dozen old skeleton keys on a large ring. Dede tried a couple that didn't work, but the third one turned easily in the lock and the door swung open. The three entered a small room with what looked like a low altar in the middle of the space surrounded by several folding chairs. At one end of the room a camera stood on a tripod facing the altar.

"This looks like something out of an Indiana Jones movie where virgins are sacrificed to primitive gods," said Eleanor.

Dede had wandered into a smaller room. "I don't think you are far off the mark. Look at what's in here."

Eleanor and Pearl followed Dede's voice and saw a closet-like space where red robes hung next to shelves filled with bottles and video disks.

"Red Rapture Elixir," read Dede. "Guaranteed to lift your spirits and revitalize your libido."

"That must be the elixir Tina's mother was talking about," Eleanor said. "This must be where the cult called The Red Rapture meet to perform their assaults on the lost girls."

"What are you talking about?" asked Dede.

"Yesterday, we took the ring back to Tina Mallory's mother." Eleanor filled Dede in on the events of that day, including Charles' Mallory's part in assaulting his own daughter.

"I knew it," Dede said.

"Look at all these sex toys," Pearl exclaimed as she pulled a pair of handcuffs out of a box.

"I wouldn't touch that stuff, Pearl," Dede cautioned and watched Pearl immediately drop them and back away from the container as though it could contaminate her.

"That reminds me of the box of toys we found in Victor Gaines's house," Eleanor said. "He must be a member of this cult."

"No, I'm sure he's not," Dede said.

Eleanor couldn't believe that Dede could be so blind. "Am I missing something? Are you involved with Victor?" she asked.

"Just trust me on this," Dede said. "Victor isn't a bad guy."

Pearl found a silver bowl filled with red rings similar to those Dede brought to Eleanor's house. "This just keeps getting more interesting," she said.

"Shhhhh," Eleanor shushed, "I hear something. Turn off your headlamps."

"Maybe it's Cleo and Josephine," Pearl whispered as she too heard voices.

The three women huddled under red robes in the dark and listened to a man's voice give orders.

"Sit down over there and don't talk. Chuck, tie them up while I check on the supplies for tonight's entertainment."

Suddenly the small room was flooded with light from a large lantern. There was no hiding as the three women looked into the eyes of the devil.

"Well, what do we have here?" he asked, "If it isn't the snoop sisters, Mrs. Penrose and the mayor herself!"

"Potsy?" Eleanor wasn't as surprised as she might have been.

"I'm sorry I haven't met your friend. Will you introduce her?" Potsy indicated Pearl who was still hiding among the red robes. Eleanor ignored his request as the other man entered the room to see who Potsy was talking to.

"You must be Charles Mallory." Eleanor recognized him from a photo she'd seen at the Mallory residence.

Charles Mallory stood in the doorway with his mouth agape. "What are we going to do now, Potsy?"

"They are lovely but past their usefulness I'm afraid. We'll have to lock them up here until Edwina can deal with them. There just isn't a market for old cunts." Potsy's crudeness made Eleanor wince. "Bring the fresh ones in here. We'll come back when this mess is cleaned up and celebrate."

"I'll make sure our transportation is ready and let them know there will be two to sell and three extra bodies to dispose of," Charles said. "Hey, let's give them the elixir. Have you ever had a woman on Viagra? It might be fun to experiment."

Two young girls were pushed into the small room and the door slammed shut. There was crying and hiccupping and darkness. Dede fumbled to light her lantern that had gone unnoticed and Eleanor studied the girls with concern. They were no more than eleven or twelve years old—one dark and the other blonde. Both faces streaked with tears and hands tied behind their backs. These girls could have been Addie, Ruby, or Bootsy. Eleanor imagined how distraught she would be if they were her beloved children and cursed these vile men who valued money and their own personal pleasure over the pain and suffering of others. She hugged them and whispered words of comfort while Pearl and Dede worked on the ties that bound them.

"What's going to happen to us?" one of the girls asked.

"What are your names?" Dede asked them.

"My name is Karen," answered the dark-haired girl. "Are those men coming back?"

"I'm afraid so, Karen," answered Dede.

"What should we call you?" Pearl asked the small blonde one.

"I'm Rhonda. What are they going to do to us?" she asked.

"Nothing, we won't let them hurt you," Dede said. "How old are you?"

"I'm eleven," Karen answered.

"I'm thirteen," Rhonda said.

"Can you tell us how you came to be here?" asked Eleanor.

"I was just walking home from school, when this old lady asked me to help look for her missing dog. She said she lost it near the park, so I went with her, but as we passed by a van, she pushed me in and shut the door. There was a man inside who drove away real fast. I want to go home." Karen began to whimper.

"I ran away from home," Rhonda said. "My dad's mean. He hits me and my mom. I just wanted to get away so I took all the money I'd saved and bought a ticket to the coast. I rode the bus from Boise to Portland but when I got here I had no place to go. An old man met me at the bus stop. He was kind and reminded me of my Grandpa. He bought me dinner and told me I could crash at his place, but when we got there he locked me in the bedroom. I was there for three days before this other guy drove me here. I don't want to go home before I see the ocean, and I really don't like it down here." It was clear that Rhonda was not the crying type. She exuded grit and a toughness that belied her size.

"We're not helpless," Eleanor said. "There must be a way out of this. Does one of those keys on your ring unlock the door, Dede?"

Dede studied the door. "There isn't even a lock, here. They must have pushed something in front of the door to block it. Maybe we can push it." They put their muscle to it but the door didn't budge, so they used their minds to create a plan.

"Our best weapon will be the element of surprise," Eleanor said. "They don't expect us to fight back. They think all women are weak."

"Who will come through that door though?" asked Pearl. "They said Edwina would clean up the mess. Do you think they meant us?"

"I don't know. We'll put our plan into action as soon as that door opens."

It seemed like hours passed before they heard the outer door open and the voices of Potsy and Chuck. "I can't believe she was taking a bath. She knew a party was scheduled tonight and she's supposed to be available. Lately she's been losing it," Potsy said.

"Time to trade her in for a newer model with fewer miles on her," laughed Chuck.

"Edwina should be here soon, but we've got lots to do for the party tonight. We're going to have to deal with these busybodies ourselves," Potsy lamented. "Are you up for a snuff film? Strangulation doesn't leave the mess that the niblick did."

"I'm up for anything," Chuck snickered at his own double entendre.

They heard something heavy being dragged away from the door and each of the women got into their positions. When the door opened, Eleanor threw a robe over Potsy's head while Dede did the same to Chuck. Pearl hit them each on the head as hard as she could with bottles of elixir. The red liquid spilled out covering them with a mix of broken glass and a viscous fluid that resembled blood. Eleanor and Dede sat on them and the girls helped handcuff them. It was over in the blink of an eye.

"I didn't think it would be that easy," Pearl admitted as she tried to wipe the elixir from her hands. "Let's take their clothes off and give them a taste of their own medicine."

"Let's just lock them in this room and get out of here," Eleanor said as she ushered the girls into the larger room.

They closed the door and rolled a large stone in front of it. "This may not hold them," said Dede, "We better go quickly." The three women and two terrified children ran from the room, locked the door, and fled down the tunnel with Dede leading the way. They hadn't gone far when they saw a light bouncing off the walls ahead. Someone was coming. They ran quickly into another branch of the tunnel pressing themselves against the dark walls and dousing their lights. A shadowy figure appeared wielding a flashlight and a club.

"It's Edwina," whispered Eleanor. "She may have seen our lights. Stay here. I'll draw her away toward the locked room. When we're clear, Dede, get the girls out of here." Eleanor stepped out of the darkness to confront Edwina. She turned her headlamp directly into Edwina's eyes temporarily blinding her and headed back toward the locked room. Dede, Pearl, and the girls waited until Edwina hurried past them and then made their way toward the tunnel's exit.

"Edwina," Eleanor called s she rounded a bend, "What are you doing down here?"

"Is that you Eleanor?" she answered as she closed the gap between them. "I was hoping I wouldn't have to kill you. You've been so kind to me."

"Then don't," Eleanor said. "There really isn't any reason for you to do that. Let those men take the blame."

"If it were only that simple I would let you go and run away from here but you don't know the things I've done—the things Potsy made me do. He told me to come here and clean up a mess. I'm sorry it's you, Eleanor."

"Tell me," Eleanor stalled, "If Potsy forced you . . ."

"I killed for him. He never bloodied his hands. I prostituted myself for him and kidnapped innocent little girls and sold them into slavery for him. I can't tell you how often I wanted to get away from him, but I couldn't. I'm so disgusted by what I've become but that's what I am now. I'm everything he's told me I am: a weak obedient whore." She took a step toward Eleanor. "You must be disgusted with me too now that you know."

"Edwina, there is no way you will walk away from this if you kill me. The only way is to go with me to the police and testify against Potsy and his cult. I'm sure the authorities will go easy on you if you help them end this horrible human trafficking business," Eleanor said. "My friends and I escaped and left Potsy and Chuck cuffed in that room. They've gone for help. You won't get away."

"Maybe I will and maybe I won't. It doesn't matter to me anymore. I killed Gloria because she discovered our secret. She and Will wanted to buy Potsy's building. I bashed her head in with my golf club because she was snooping around down here. People like you and your Do Nothing friends couldn't possibly know what it's like to be me. You have everything and I grew up with nothing. I've had to work for everything I have. I've done despicable things to survive. Potsy helped me when I needed someone. He's always been there for me. He helped me move Gloria's body to the swale. He told me he wouldn't turn me in to the police and he would make it look like an accident —a hit and run. He said he would help me but I had to get rid of Will too. We couldn't be sure Gloria didn't tell Will about what she'd seen. Potsy gave me the gun and I called Will and told him to meet me in the woods because I knew something about what happened to Gloria. He was a fool for her. In his grief he never suspected an old woman would shoot him. I don't think he knew anything about what we were doing, but I tried to kill him anyway. I botched it, of course, just like I mess up everything. I thought he was dead, but he wasn't. I left him too soon. He was able to call 911 before he lost consciousness. Potsy said I was stupid."

"Did you kill Victoria?" Eleanor asked.

"I did that for you, Eleanor. She was a horrible person who took your journals and the ring and wanted to take your Angus too. That night I visited her room. I was only going to talk to her. Maybe she would give back your things if I just talked to her. Her door wasn't locked so I went inside and waited for her. She was really mad and threw a horrible fit. She didn't deserve to live, believe me, Eleanor. The world is a better place without people like her in it. I had my niblick with me just in case she wouldn't cooperate and it was a good thing too. She made me so angry, I couldn't stop hitting her.

When Potsy found out, he wasn't happy. He made me take the ring to Lola's shop. I wanted to give it back to you but he said it would make Victor and Lola look guilty instead of us. I just slipped it into the display case. That was easy. I left a golf club there too hoping the police would link the murders to Lola and Victor and then called in an anonymous tip. Potsy hid the real murder weapon on the golf course, but when we went to look for it later, it was gone. I saw you there that day. Did you take our niblick, Eleanor? We planned to plant it in Lola's shop to further incriminate them. Potsy collects old golf clubs so we have lots of them. Do you like this one, Eleanor?" Edwina held up her club. "I really don't want to kill you. You and the Do Nothings made me feel so welcome here almost like I was one of the wholesome ladies and then you took care of me the night of the equinox after Potsy punished me for my stupidity. I just wanted to die that night. I took the pills on purpose, because I've made such a mess of my life.

From the very beginning, I've made a mess. Potsy found me after I ran away from home and I thought he was saving me but he was just using me. That's what you think, isn't it Eleanor. I don't know what to think. I should kill you, but I don't want to kill you but Potsy will be very angry with me if I don't clean up my mess." Edwina's rambling began to ebb.

Eleanor saw a red glow coming toward them behind Edwina. She could only hope it was Rudolph's red-nosed headlamp.

"I can help you clean up your mess, Edwina. It's time Potsy was held accountable for his own messes." She continued talking hoping to distract Edwina from the figure that approached. "What happened to Tina, the girl they found on the beach?"

"Chuck brought her here to sell her because she was trouble. Tina said she would tell her mother and anyone else

she could that he was molesting her and Chuck was afraid
someone might believe her. I don't think her mother did
believe her so Tina tried to get money from him so she could
get away. That's when he decided she had to go. After they had
their fun with her they took her out of the tunnel to the slough
where a boat waited. The boat met a ship out on the ocean
where she was supposed to go to another country, somewhere
in Asia, to become a sex slave, but she jumped overboard.

"She must have drowned—after all it was dark and her
hands were tied. I'm sure no one intended to kill her. That was
an accident. Chuck didn't get his money, but she's better off
now. I know. I've been in that room. I've been one of Potsy's
hot girls. He made me dye my hair and act like an old lady.
No one suspects sweet old ladies of committing hideous sex
crimes. No one thinks they can act like sex maniacs either.

"Potsy would give his customers some of his elixir and put
the ruby ring on my finger and watch them defile me. Suddenly
I'd be younger and eager to please them in the most depraved
ways. They believed it was the ring and elixir that made us act
like animals. If I didn't act like I wanted them, Potsy would
punish me later.

"Sometimes I did like it. That's because Potsy's right about
me. I'm a whore and a murderer." Edwina gripped the club as
if readying for a drive. "I'm really sorry, Eleanor. Angus will
be sad when you're gone. He probably really loves you. I don't
think Potsy will miss me. He says I'm too old now. He needs a
younger wife."

Just as she lifted the club to swing at Eleanor, Dede came
up from behind and clobbered her with a garden gnome.
Edwina fell to the ground.

"I knew this gnome was good for something," Dede said.

"Thank goodness you got here," Eleanor exclaimed as she gave Dede a hug. "I think she was done talking."

Three figures appeared running toward them through the tunnel wielding flashlights. It was Officer McGraw along with Victor and Lola. They hurried toward Eleanor and Dede with guns drawn.

"Are you all right?" Victor asked as Lola cuffed the limp figure that was Edwina.

"We're both fine," Dede declared. "The two men are behind a wooden door just down that way. I'll show you." She lead Officer McGraw and Victor down the tunnel.

"Why are you here?" Eleanor asked Lola as she eyed her and the gun curiously.

"Victor and I are FBI agents working undercover to catch human traffickers. We've been looking at this group for a while. You have to keep this to yourself Eleanor. Undercover agents can't be exposed. Promise me," Lola ordered.

"I don't have a problem keeping secrets, believe me," Eleanor said. "There are recipes I will take to my grave, along with your identity."

"Dede's been working with us, so she knows, but you can't reveal this to your other friends or family."

"I promise." Eleanor placed her hand over her heart. "You're a very good actress, Lola. I believed you wanted to learn to cook. Why did you really come that day?"

"That's how I get information. I wanted to know who the swingers were, if they could be linked to the sex trade and maybe find out if Angus had told you anything about the case. You didn't reveal much, Eleanor. It wasn't clear to me if you knew and just wouldn't tell, or if you just didn't know anything. You really need to work on your gossiping skills," Lola smiled.

"I told you I can keep a secret," Eleanor repeated.

"You'd better watch yourself," Lola warned. "Victor and I saw you and Dede leave our house after you broke in that day. We knew you didn't find anything that would blow our cover, so we let you escape, but someone else might have hurt you. What you did was dangerous, Eleanor. This kind of work is best left to professionals."

Eleanor had heard that before.

It wasn't long before the others returned with Potsy and Chuck in cuffs. Victor threw Edwina over his shoulder and they marched down the tunnel and exited through the trapdoor that led to Lola's Curiosity Shop where Victor and Lola holstered their guns, resuming their roles as ordinary citizens and letting Officer McGraw take over.

"Mrs. Penrose and Madam Mayor, you'll have to come down to the station and make statements," Officer McGraw said and then led his collars out to a waiting car.

"I'll wait here with Edwina until an ambulance comes," Lola said. "It looks like you did a number on her, Dede."

"Dede, you saved my life," said Eleanor. "What happened to Pearl and the little girls?"

"Pearl and I came up the metal steps into Lola's shop and immediately called the police. I went back down to see about you, Eleanor," Dede explained.

"Dede insisted on going back down to help you, against my advice. I sent Pearl and the girls to Dede's house to wait for social services with Josephine and Cleo. Victor was with Officer McGraw at the station and they got here as soon as they could. I thought we might need backup. We went down into the tunnel and you know the rest," Lola said. "We have you to thank for giving us all the evidence we need to lock up those perverts."

"Yes," said Dede, "there should be enough evidence there to put them away until the resurrection of the dead."

"I've never been so glad to see anyone ever!" exclaimed Dede as she returned to her house and looked into the faces of Cleo, Pearl, and Josephine. There were hugs all around.

"Where are the little girls?" asked Eleanor.

"Someone from DHS came and took them to get their stories," Josephine said. "They were traumatized, but alive and eager to go home. I'm sure they were hungry too."

"I hope someone takes Rhonda to see the ocean before they send her home," said Dede.

"I guess we missed all the action," sighed Cleo.

"I'm not sorry," Josephine said. "I didn't like being underground either, Cleo."

"So tell us everything," said Cleo.

"We have to go to the police station to give our statements before we forget and then let's get something to eat," Dede said.

"I'm sure I'll never forget this day. We'll fill you in when we get back," Eleanor promised, knowing she could tell them everything except the part Victor and Lola played in the whole affair. Dede just gave her a wink.

By the time Eleanor got home it was dark. Several members of the cult of The Red Rapture had been rounded up and taken into custody locally, and many more were in the process of being apprehended in Portland, Seattle, and other cities along the West Coast. The two little girls were in foster care until they could be reunited with their families, and in the case of Rhonda, visit the ocean. Statements had been given and all the details that could be shared were shared with the members of her coffee group.

Eleanor was exhausted. All she wanted was a hot bath to wash away the residue of evil stench that had permeated the places where she had spent her day. Feathers greeted her with enthusiasm, landing on her shoulder and pressing his parrot head against her face.

"Feathers, you wouldn't believe the day I've had!" Eleanor said. "You don't want to know either."

Eleanor hid some food in his toys so he could forage for it, then filled her tub with hot water and a soothing aromatherapy ball that smelled like lemongrass and ginger. She breathed in the clean scent and scrubbed away what she perceived as a film of filth from the underworld, but when she closed her eyes she saw the devilish leer of Theodore "Potsy" Potsinski and the terrified and wounded eyes of two innocent little girls. The things that happened to them and hundreds of other lost girls were unacceptable to Eleanor. When she felt as clean as she could get, she wrapped herself in a pink fluffy robe, poured a large glass of pinot noir, and called her children to make sure everyone she loved was safe.

Angus came calling later. He had heard about the ordeal from Officer McGraw, who was basking in the glory of collaring a network of criminals involved in human trafficking, not to mention solving three murders and one attempted murder almost single handedly. It had been a good day for the Waterton police.

"Are you okay?" Angus asked as he hugged Eleanor's pink fluffy covered body and breathed in the scent of lemongrass and ginger.

"Yes, where were you today?" she asked as she pulled away to look into that beloved face.

Drusilla and I spent the day with Mrs. Mallory finding out what you already knew about Charles and his connection to The Red Rapture. I can't believe your coffee group got her to rat him out. The Beaverton police were very impressed by the way," Angus said.

"It was mostly Josephine," Eleanor admitted. "She has a way of getting people to speak their truth."

"Yes, Drusilla and I were able to help compile a list of other members of the cult. Some of them are already in custody. It was just the tip of the iceberg. An entire network of human trafficking will be exposed because of this. Officer McGraw said the FBI will be involved. It's reassuring to know that none of the culprits implicated were people from Waterton. They were using the underground as a destination for their bad behavior, much like fraternity boys who go away for spring break. I don't know what it is that makes them feel free to act badly in someone else's hometown," Angus said.

"It must be like birds who don't want to poop in their own nests," Eleanor said. Angus instinctively looked overhead to see if Feathers was there.

"Would you like a drink?" Eleanor asked as she led him into the kitchen. "I think tonight I'll have one too."

"Sounds good," Angus said.

"When are you going to stop calling Delia Parker, Drusilla Malfoy? We've known for a long time that was a phony name," Eleanor asked as she poured two glasses of Crown Royal. "You really didn't give us much credit by choosing such an obvious one."

Angus laughed, "We thought it was very clever to have a stepsister named Drusilla. Solving her mystery was supposed to keep you out of trouble, and you must admit it worked for a short time. Your detecting skills are improving."

"Do I detect a compliment?" Eleanor asked.

"Certainly, you and your cohorts went for the real criminals while Drusilla and I were led astray into thinking Victor and Lola were the culprits. I guess now we'll have to endure their ridiculous dinner parties and pagan celebrations," Angus sighed and took a sip of his drink.

"I don't think they'll stay in Sand Beach. Word is they're splitting up and moving out of town," Eleanor said.

"That's strange," Angus frowned. His baloney sensor was working overtime. "I thought there was something false about them. Couldn't put my finger on it, but maybe it was that they weren't really in love."

Eleanor hoped he wouldn't pursue it. She wrapped her arms around him and hugged him tight. They snuggled under a fleecy blanket on the couch and sipped their drinks. Neither said anything about their past separation, or future marriage, or even how much they loved each other. Being together now was all that mattered. When morning broke they were still in each other's arms.

April arrived and brought Easter Sunday along with it. Eleanor and Bootsy had spent the day before baking her signature butterfly cinnamon rolls for the occasion. They chatted and giggled about girl stuff as they worked. Bootsy shared her adventures while traveling on the bus to visit.

"I made up stories about the other people on the bus. One of the ladies was a famous movie star. She wore a huge hat and the biggest sunglasses I've ever seen. They covered most of her face so I know she was traveling incognito. When we got to the bus depot, there was a man in a green suit who picked her up in a fancy car and drove off in the direction of Sand Beach. I bet she's staying here and we'll see her on the beach. There was another interesting person too. I'm sure he was a member of the paparazzi. He sat behind her and was always talking into his phone—secretly taking pictures of her too."

"Was the bus full?" asked Eleanor.

"Yes, there were lots of people on it," Bootsy continued. "One of them was a hitman for the Mafia. I could tell because he was wearing dark glasses and looked just like Arnold Schwarzenegger in *The Terminator* movie. He carried a long suitcase for his high-powered rifle and he smelled like something oily. He was coming to Watertown to hunt down the paparazzi guy who owed money to the Mmafia because he gambled away his money at the casino. The paparazzi guy was trying to get the money shot of the movie star so he could pay back his debt and the mafia guy was trying to get a different kind of shot. You will probably read all about it in the next issue of the *Fish Wrapper.*"

Eleanor smiled at Bootsy's active imagination.

"You better pack up your things and make sure you have everything for your stay with Amy," Eleanor urged. "Don't forget your Easter basket. Angus will be here soon."

Bootsy hurried off to the guest room to gather up her things while Eleanor went to work on filling Easter eggs. She just finished loading the last of the plastic eggs with dollar bills for their annual Easter egg competition when Angus rang the bell.

"Are you ready?" he asked as Feather's dive-bombed him.

"Get out, you swine!" Feathers squawked.

"Let me get my sweater," Eleanor said.

"What, no Easter bonnet?" he asked. Eleanor ignored him and handed him the shopping bag full of eggs.

"Did you bring your Easter basket?" Bootsy asked as they loaded everything into his truck.

"No, you didn't tell me I needed one." He seemed truly concerned. "Should we stop on the way and pick one up?"

"Since this is your first Easter spent with us, you may just want to watch from a safe distance when the signal is given to start the hunt," Eleanor explained.

"This sounds dangerous," Angus said. "Should I be worried?"

"I don't know. It seems like every year Erin injures Taylor. They're very competitive. One year she shoved him at the starting gate and he fell down on his Easter basket bruising his tailbone. Now it's all held together with duct tape. I mean his basket not his tailbone. Another time Erin pushed him into the sticker bushes. I'm not really sure if they dislike each other or if it's all in fun. Fortunately, Taylor has been a good sport and never taken revenge on her since he's twice her size," Eleanor continued as they drove to Amy's house.

"I thought Easter was a peaceful, Christian holiday," Angus said.

"Not really, it involves torture, murder, and rising from the dead," informed Bootsy.

"Of course Christians celebrate Jesus rising from the tomb and everlasting life on Easter, but they took many of their traditions from the pagans. Eggs represent rebirth and life so you can see why Christians took the pagan tradition of decorating them and infused it into their own festivities. Pagans also celebrated the goddess of fertility, Eostre, by using a fertility symbol—the rabbit—who laid eggs in a nest. There you have the Easter basket that resembles a nest to lure the Easter rabbit in to lay eggs." Eleanor was a wealth of information.

"I see," Angus said. "It sounds like something the Reformed Druid would enjoy hamming up."

"Even the traditional ham is from pagan rituals honoring spring. The hogs that were slaughtered in the fall took all winter to cure and were the only meats available for the spring festivals. Christians adopted this tradition as their own too. It made it easier to convert the pagans."

"So I guess we're having ham for dinner," Angus deduced.

"It's really brunch, Angus," Eleanor said.

"Then it's ham and eggs, huh?" Angus said. "I like ham and eggs."

By the time they arrived at Amy's house, Angus was a very hungry expert on Easter, and Bootsy was eager to be with her young friends.

Erin and Ben were already there with Ruby and Mitch. Amy poured each adult a mimosa and floated a raspberry in it giving it a festive flair. The grownups sipped their drinks and chatted while the children, including Bootsy, went downstairs plotting their strategies to get the most eggs. They had reached the age where cash trumped candy and no one believed in the Easter bunny anymore.

"Who's hiding the eggs this year?" asked Eleanor.

"We were hoping Angus would do it," Amy said and they all looked at him and waited for his response.

"I'd be honored," he said without missin a beat. "But you'll have to play by my rules. There will be no pushing or shoving or foul play of any kind."

"You need to tell that to the kids," said Ben.

"No, I'm telling you. The kids will learn from your example." Angus looked at Erin. Erin cut her eyes to Taylor who smiled from ear to ear. Surely he thought he had a friend in Angus.

"Why don't you hide them while we put the finishing touches on brunch? Then we can go out and hunt after we eat," Amy suggested. Angus saluted and went outside with the bag of eggs.

"Who made him the boss?" Erin scowled. "This isn't going to be as much fun if I have to be careful not to hurt Taylor."

"It breaks with tradition," Ben joked.

"Maybe it's time for me to get a new basket." Taylor picked up his battered basket and studied it closely.

Everyone helped put the food out and soon they all gathered around the table, except Angus who was still outside. "I better go find him," Eleanor said, "he's new to all this, so be kind."

"Gee Mom, we like him. He's not all that new to us," Erin said just as Angus appeared with an empty bag.

"Sorry, I didn't mean to be late but that was quite a challenge." Angus washed his hands at the kitchen sink and sat down at the table. "What a feast!" he exclaimed. Everyone dug in and soon the room was full of chatter and laughter.

"How did the Easter bunny rate his favorite restaurant?" asked Wesley.

"I don't know," said Mitch.

"Egg-cellent!" Mitch laughed and milk sprayed out of his mouth. That sent everyone else into hysterics.

"How do you kill a unique rabbit?" asked Elise.

"I don't know. How do you kill a unique rabbit?" asked Ruby.

"You neak up on it."

"How do you kill a tame rabbit?" Elise asked. "The tame way," she answered before anyone could guess.

"I know one," said Addie, "How does Easter end?"

"It ends with an Easter egg hunt," said Mitch.

"It ends when Uncle Taylor falls down," guessed Ruby.

"No, it ends with an R," Addie giggled and her laughter was contagious.

"Amy, I think your cooking is every bit as good as your mother's," Angus complimented.

"Thank you Angus, that's because it's her cooking," Amy confessed.

"No it isn't," Eleanor argued. "I simply shared some of my recipes, but Amy did all the work."

Angus's eyebrows rose in surprise. Eleanor wasn't known to share recipes, but maybe passing them down to family was another matter.

When everyone had filled up on ham, egg frittata, fruit salad and cinnamon rolls, the great egg hunt began. Angus stood on the patio and blew a whistle to signal the start. Everyone raced to fill their baskets with the most eggs, while Eleanor and Angus watched and laughed at the antics of grown children at play with their own kids.

"This must be what heaven is like," mused Angus as he took in the scent of freshly cut grass and wild roses. He reached in his pocket and took out a pink, plastic egg and gave it to Eleanor.

"Thank you, Angus."

"Open it," he ordered.

Eleanor opened the egg and was surprised to see the ruby ring. "I thought I had seen the last of this thing," she said. "How did you get it?"

"Not me—must have been the Easter Bunny," Angus teased. "What's the matter? Don't you like it?"

"Really Angus, how did you get it?" Eleanor persisted.

"I found it in my pocket after visiting Tina Mallory's mother. I'm pretty sure she slipped it in my jacket before we left that day. It was obvious she was eager to be rid of it."

Eleanor slipped it on her finger and admired its blood red hue. "It is a beautiful piece," she admitted as she took it off again. "I really can't wear it knowing its history."

"If it really is the Blood Ruby of Burma it could be worth an enormous amount of money," Angus said. "Maybe you could sell it and do something to help others with the funds."

The seed of an idea was planted in Eleanor's mind. "Maybe . . ." She was interrupted by loud raucous laughter and looked up to see Taylor lying on the ground surrounded by his broken basket and a multitude of eggs. Erin stood several feet away shrugging her shoulders.

"I swear I didn't do it!" she protested. "He just tripped over his own feet." Of course, no one believed her, but Ruby was right when she said Easter ended when Uncle Taylor fell down.

They got Taylor into the house and Erin ministered to his sprained ankle (maybe out of guilt or because she was a registered nurse) while Taylor gave a multitude of needless instructions which Erin ignored. The rest of the brood greedily counted the money found inside their eggs and bragged about who had the most.

"Is Easter over now?" asked Angus.

"No," shouted Addie, "we haven't performed our Easter dance recital." Suddenly all the children raced downstairs to get into their costumes. They performed the passion of Jesus, his crucifixion and resurrection through dance and impressed all the grownups. When the dancing was over and Ruby had declared this the "best Easter ever," Angus and Eleanor said their goodbyes amid repeated hugs and kisses leaving Bootsy with her adopted cousins and drove home to Sand Beach.

"Aren't children wonderful?" asked Eleanor on the drive home.

"Absolutely," Angus agreed, "Especially when they belong to someone else."

"Walter always said he loved to see them come and he loved to see them go," Eleanor said. "They grow up so fast. I hate to see them go. It won't be long and Elise will be off to college."

"Let's just take one day at a time," Angus said wisely. "I could use a nap. Being the Easter Bunny is 'egg-hausting' and that's no yolk."

"I think those kids are rubbing off on you," Eleanor laughed.

"I'd rather have you rubbing off on me." Angus said. "Why don't you put that ring on and see if you feel like a nap."

Eleanor blushed and swatted him, "Angus that was very naughty. I'm sure the Easter Bunny would never say such things."

Angus just smiled and twitched his whiskers.

The seed of the idea Angus planted in Eleanor's mind began to grow. She had more money than she needed, thanks to Walter's thoughtful investments. Surely he would want her to leave most of that to their children and grandchildren, but if she sold the ruby ring she could make a sizable donation to a nonprofit organization that worked to recover missing children. Without giving the matter much thought, Eleanor took the ring to a trusted jeweler in the city to have it appraised.

Mr. Smyth greeted Eleanor warmly. He was the son of Walter's college friend and had advised him on most of his jewelry purchases and repairs for many years. Eleanor knew he could be trusted. She handed him the ring and watched as he studied it through his loupe.

"What do you know about this ring, Mrs. Penrose?" he asked.

"Absolutely nothing," she said. "I purchased it at an estate sale and was wondering about its makeup and value."

"It's very interesting," Mr. Smyth murmured and excused himself. After some time he returned with an amazed look on his face.

"Mrs. Penrose, you have stumbled on a rare find. Rubies are the most valuable members of the corundum family and this is a ruby. Six carat gem rubies like this can be more valuable than comparably sized diamonds and are rarer. This one appears to be a Myanmar or Burmese ruby due to its intense flouoresce and pigeon blood-red color. I've seen some rubies from the Mogok region of Myanmar that resemble this,

but nothing of this size or quality. This is by far the finest stone I've ever seen. I could sell it for you if you'd like. I know of a buyer who would gladly pay you $15,000/carat or perhaps more. "

Eleanor did some quick calculations in her head and figured that $90,000 could go a long way toward helping lost girls. She left the ring with Mr. Smyth with a plan and no regrets.

Within a few days Eleanor received a box containing the ring along with a letter that explained its return.

Dear Mrs. Penrose,

The person who purchased your ring wishes to return it without repayment. He claims it is cursed because the moment his wife put it on her finger they have experienced one tragedy after another. He would gladly double the payment just to be rid of it. They are a very superstitious couple and request you do good works with their offering.

I could try to sell it for you again, but buyers for rings in this price range are rare and it may take some time, so I am returning it to you in the hopes that you can enjoy it in the meantime.

Sincerely,

Myron Smyth

Eleanor picked up her phone and called Mr. Mooney. She needed assistance putting her plan into action. When she told him what she wanted to do he suggested they try to find the original owner of the ring before selling it to avoid any unwanted legal action in the future. He would contact her lawyer and set up an endowment to assist the lost girls. Meanwhile, Eleanor worked on her poetry, read, and met with her coffee group.

"What did Erin do to Taylor this Easter?" asked Cleo as the ladies waited for their coffee at the Boat House.

"Just a sprained ankle," Eleanor responded absently.

"Do you ever feel guilty celebrating Easter when you don't incorporate the religious aspects into it?" asked Cleo who still carried Catholic guilt.

"No," answered Eleanor. "Celebrating spring was pagan long before the Christians made it theirs."

"I heard a nun speak about religion once. She offered a beautiful metaphor for religion and spirituality. Imagine several boats on the sea. Each boat is a different religion floating on the sea of spirituality and all the boats go to God, whatever your perception of God might be," Josephine said.

"I think I have fallen out of my boat. Do you think I can still get to God?" Cleo fretted.

"Don't worry," Dede said, "I've got you covered. I've been praying for your soul for years." There was a long pause when no one spoke. It felt strange and awkward.

"Now that the criminals have been captured, I guess we have nothing more to talk about," Pearl said finally.

"I'm sure everyone will soon be talking about the boxes that were delivered to my house the other day," Dede said.

"Why is that?" asked Josephine.

"Several boxes filled with sex paraphernalia were left on my porch," Dede said. "I'm sure they came from Victor Gaines."

"What did you do with them?" asked Cleo as she leaned in with interest. "Maybe we should pick through them before you get rid of them."

The others simply looked at her with raised brows as Dede continued. "The boxes are in the basement until I can figure out what to do with them, but something strange has happened to Lorenzo."

"Do tell," urged Josephine who had a vested interest in the blow-up guy.

"I went to Kroger's to pick up Easter lilies for the church and totally forgot Lorenzo was in the back of my car. When I opened the hatch Lorenzo popped up and the lady helping me with the lilies screamed which caused almost everyone in the parking lot to run over to see what was wrong. It was slightly embarrassing, but after, that someone stole him out of my car along with my mother's rosary. What do you make of that?"

"Sin first and pray for forgiveness later is my guess," Pearl said.

"Did you report the theft to the police?" asked Josephine.

"Only the part about the rosary," Dede confessed. "The police don't have to know everything."

"Right," Eleanor agreed. "Is there any news about Will Vandorff?"

"I heard he regained consciousness but he doesn't remember anything," Dede said.

"Does that mean he won't be able to testify against Edwina?" asked Cleo.

"It's possible he might regain some of his memory in time," Josephine said.

"Even if he doesn't, the authorities have enough evidence to prosecute Edwina and Potsy for other crimes that should send them away for a long time," Eleanor said.

"Will he make a full recovery?" asked Pearl.

"It's too early to tell," Dede said.

"I heard about a man who suffered a significant brain injury when a steel rod went though his head. He survived but his entire personality changed. After his accident he was mean and had no conscience whatsoever," Cleo said.

"That sort of goes against the idea of free will doesn't it?" Josephine mused.

"Yes, accidents and chemistry can change a person, I guess, but I still believe most of us have the power to choose right from wrong," Dede said. "It would be a sorry world if we gave everyone a pass because nothing was their fault."

"I didn't know Will Vandorff. Was he a decent man before he was shot?" asked Pearl.

"I think so," Dede said. "He and his wife may have made some mistakes dealing with Edwina and Potsy but when they learned what they were really up to they tried to do what was right."

"And it got Gloria killed and Will shot," Pearl added.

"I heard Edwina and Potsy made a great deal of money selling children into the sex trade and they were using real estate to launder it," Eleanor said.

"Are you saying Will and Gloria were knowingly involved?" asked Dede.

"We may never know," Josephine said. "No one is perfect. It could be they were just trying to make some extra money, knew Edwina and Potsy were up to no good, but didn't know exactly how they got their money and didn't want to know."

"I suppose more information will come out during the trial," Dede said. "It may be to Will's benefit if he never recovers his memory."

"I wonder what will happen to all their money," Cleo said. "It seems like it should be used to help those they hurt the most."

"I understand forfeited money involved in criminal activity usually goes to law enforcement and can easily be abused, so there have to be protections in place—probably lots of red tape," Eleanor said. "That's why it isn't commonly done."

"You would have to be a lawyer to understand how all that works," Pearl added.

"Nothing is ever easy," lamented Cleo.

"Isn't that the truth?" Eleanor related her experience trying to rid herself of the ruby ring. She didn't want to go into the part about the endowment, so she left that part out.

"The ring must belong with you," murmured Josephine.

Eleanor carried the box of journals into her house and put them in her office. With everything else that had happened they had sat forgotten in the back of her car. She went in search of Feathers who usually greeted her. He sat looking out the window at the black crow, Inky, who was perched on the deck.

"Caw, caw," Feathers said as he danced on his perch.

"Caw, caw," responded Inky.

"I wonder what you two are talking about," Eleanor said as she watched and listened to their love song.

Suddenly the tree outside was filled with crows and a loud symphony ensued. Inky cocked her head first one way and then the other and took flight along with a murder of crows while Feathers watched silently.

Parrot Love

What have I done, my feathered friend?
But locked you up for days on end.
If I should set you free today,
You'd spread your wings and fly away.
Some other fiendish bird of prey
Might strike you down and there you'd lay.
What have I done my loyal mate?
But kept you from your rightful fate
To fly among the forest trees
And forage for what food you please.
What shall I do to right this wrong?
Put you back where you belong?
Open the door let in the breeze
The scent of ocean air and trees.
Shut the screen to keep you in.
Play for forgiveness for my sin.
Open the window, open it wide,
But keep my companion safe inside.

Eleanor wandered to her office to put the journals back on the shelf where they belonged. It had been a long time since she had opened any of them. As she leafed through several, she relived some of the best and worst times of her life. Memories she had forgotten were documented here filled with details and emotions colorfully painted in words.

A slim book squeezed among the journals fell to the floor. It was one she didn't recognize—old and bound with an intricately designed leather cover. Eleanor had never seen it before. Maybe it belonged to Dede, and Mark had put it in the box mistakenly thinking it belonged to her. She opened it and saw the name Olivia Evans Penrose written in the most beautiful script. It was a diary and from the date it must be that of Walter's great grandmother. Eleanor read several pages that described the time Olivia's husband served in the British army in Burma after the third Burmese War. It detailed her distress and boredom as a soldier's wife as well as her fear that he might be unfaithful to her while away for such a long period of time.

Dear Diary,

Thomas has come home to me at last. I must say I am very pleased to see him again although after all this time apart I sense a tension and awkwardness between us. I've had my doubts about his faithfulness to me and am almost certain he has kept the company of other women because his behavior is so strange. As if to make amends he has given me a token of his affection in the form of a rather large and garish ruby ring—further evidence of his guilt. He claims to have found the ruby in the ruby mines in Upper Burma and says it will revitalize our passion for one another after our time apart. I must admit the ring is perfectly cut and set beautifully in gold. Thomas says it will make a fine heirloom to pass down to our son, Roger, when he marries. He has already christened it the Penrose Ruby and insists that after a man gives this ring to his woman, they will never part. I will wear it for him and hope in time we can once again feel the love we felt for each other.

Olivia

Eleanor was intrigued. As she read on, the diary became more mundane and finally ended with the birth of the last of Olivia and Thomas' daughters. With her husband home and many children to care for, it must have left little time for writing in her diary. Several news clippings slipped from the blank pages of the diary. Brittle and yellow with age, one told of a burglary at the home of Lena and Roger Penrose, Olivia's son, in which most of Lena's jewelry had been taken. Another showed a picture of the two at a gala event in New York where Lena was wearing the Penrose Ruby. "I regret that I won't be able to pass the ring on to my son, Arthur, as his mother intended," Lena was quoted. "I hope it brings as much misfortune to whoever took it as it has brought joy to our family."

This was too much. The ring was cursed by Walter's grandmother. Eleanor knew Arthur Penrose was Walter's father, but Walter had never mentioned this Penrose Ruby— maybe because it wasn't important to him or perhaps simply because it was lost and so was of little concern. Eleanor studied the picture closely and knew the Penrose Ruby had to be the Blood Ruby of Burma. Eleanor could hardly contain her astonishment and immediately called the coffee group to invite them over with the promise of an exciting discovery and her famous northwest salmon cakes with mustard sauce and peanut butter panache for dessert.

The ladies arrived together having carpooled out to Sand Beach. Cleo and Dede brought bottles of wine—red and white, Pearl brought a salad and Josephine carried a bag with something mysterious inside.

"What's the big reveal?" asked Cleo as she uncorked the bottle of pinot noir.

Eleanor brought out Olivia Penrose's diary and read the part about the ruby ring, then shared the newspaper clippings. A silence ensued while each of the ladies mulled over the significance of the news and sipped their wine.

"So you were the rightful owner of the ring all along, Eleanor," stated Cleo. "Walter would have given it to you, but he couldn't so Angus did—in the Easter egg. It's like karma."

"It must mean that you and Angus will never part," Josephine said. "Or does it have to be a Penrose man?"

"This is just too strange to be true!" exclaimed Dede.

"I don't get it," admitted Pearl.

"I believe it and that's not all. I want to show you something I received today." Josephine took a carved wooden box out of her bag and opened it. Inside was a wooden bead that looked like a tiny walnut with a hole drilled through it.

"That looks like the carved box I bought at the estate sale," said Pearl. "I'm sure I sold it to someone and sent it off to Hawaii. I shed blood because of that box. Do you think we are being punished or rewarded for buying those items at the estate sale? How did you get it?"

"The man I met at Cleo's exhibition sent it. He was from Hawaii and must have been your buyer. It came with a note. Let me read it to you." Josephine shared a love letter.

My Dearest,

Please forgive me for intruding on your happy life. Believe me when I tell you that your happiness is all I wish for you. I knew when I met you at the art exhibit that you were the one true love I have been seeking time after time—life after life. You had the Mala with my missing bead, but still it is not our time. I am sending you this bead so that I can find you again in the next life where I hope we can at last find our happiness together. It will be a beacon to lead me to you once again.

With infinite affection,

Omar Choden

"That is so romantic," sighed Cleo.

"How did he know where to send it?" asked Eleanor. "Did you give him your name and address?"

"I gave it to him," Dede admitted. "He asked me about her at the art show and said he was an old friend. I didn't realize just how old. I hope I didn't do anything that might cause trouble. What if it's a scam?"

"I'm glad you did," Josephine said. "This just confirms my belief that there is something after this life, but right now I feel like packing my bag and flying to Hawaii to be with him in this life."

"You mean you'd leave Richard, a man who absolutely adores you, for a man you don't know?" Dede asked.

"Obviously, we are meant to be together and I don't want to wait for another lifetime to find my soulmate when I know where he is now. You'd understand if you had looked into those eyes and felt the extreme love and warmth that emanated from him," Josephine persisted.

"Hold your horses." Cleo could not believe where the conversation was headed. Josephine was always so levelheaded except where love was concerned. "I have a story to tell too and it might make you reconsider running off to try on a new man, Josephine. Just remember where we picked up all those treasures. It was at that estate sale that made all of us uneasy. Remember we thought those items might be stolen. Well they were. I suspected it from the beginning but became concerned when I tried to put my art in the frames I'd purchased at the estate sale. After looking closely at one of the empty frames, I noticed the canvas had been cut from the frame leaving part of the previous art work around the edges. That's what thieves do when they steal art. They simply cut it out of the frame so it's easier to handle. Each of the empty frames I bought had the same thing. I took what remained of the canvases out of the frames and finished putting my art in them, but I was uneasy about it."

"Cleo, you never said anything about this. Why did you keep it a secret?" asked Dede. "We all bought items at that sale."

"I didn't know all the goods were stolen. I suspected it but I didn't know for sure and I was excited about my upcoming exhibit. There were a lot of things going on at that time if you recall. Gloria died, Virginia was murdered, a young woman washed up on the shore, journals were stolen, Eleanor and Angus split up, not to mention Drusilla, marijuana, tequila and vernal equinox parties, golfing, and a couple of break ins—and then there were those claustrophobic tours of the underworld of Waterton."

Cleo shook her head to clear it of any negative thoughts and continued. "Anyway, after Victor bought all the pieces at the show I knew I had to tell him about the possibility that the frames were stolen. He was great—just so understanding and helpful. He said he had some contacts who could work with him to discover what the paintings were by the remnants left behind. Two art experts he knew came up from Los Angeles to examine what was left of the art pieces and after some time Victor told me they had traced them to a theft that had taken place in California last fall. The three masterpieces were from a collector of George Inness' work and were valued at hundreds of thousands of dollars. I can't tell you how grateful I am to him for that. It was a heavy load off my chest. Now the authorities will have a starting place to look for those who sold the stolen items at the estate sale because I gave them the address. Now I have some good karma because I put things right."

"Victor seems to be a man with useful connections, but how does this impact my decision to go to Omar?" Josephine was obviously blinded by the prospect of long lost love.

"Josephine, the beads were stolen. Maybe they came from his real true love," Eleanor said as kindly as she could.

Josephine's face fell as she considered the implications of the stolen beads. "So you think the beads may have been stolen from his real soulmate?"

"It's possible," said Dede who didn't believe in reincarnation but wouldn't say so. The items she bought at the estate sale had met a permanent end and would not be returning to anyone in this life or the next.

"It's also possible that the beads found their way to me through the theft. He told me he found his way here because he felt a force. The universe works in mysterious ways," Josephine said.

"You don't have that much of this life left, Josephine. Even if you live to be a hundred, you'd have less than thirty years with Omar and you'd break Richard's heart. Who knows? Omar might have a wife. He didn't exactly invite you over," Cleo said.

"I think his exact words were 'it's still not our time'," Eleanor reminded her.

"Maybe you have some sins to atone for before you can be together," offered Dede. It was the best she could offer, considering her Catholic upbringing.

"I guess you're right," Josephine sighed. "I do love Richard. Who knows what bad Karma leaving him might bring? If I hurt him in this life, he may interfere with Omar and me in the next."

"Just imagine that everything that has happened is because of good or bad karma," Cleo said. "Did Virginia and Gloria get what they deserved? Did Tina Mallory? I'm sure Edwina and Potsy are going to get what's coming to them."

"I'm not sure I understand all this," Pearl said.

"I'm not sure we're supposed to," Eleanor mused. "Not all mysteries can be solved."

They savored their dinner and vowed to live in the moment. Understanding was overrated. Happiness and peanut butter panache were not.

If you enjoyed *Under A Dying Moon*, you'll want to follow Eleanor, Feathers, and the rest of the gang in the further adventures of the Coffee Club. If you missed *A Recipe for Dying* or *Dying for Diamonds* you can find them at GladEye Press!

- Visit www.gladeyepress.com for fantastic deals on these and other GladEye Press titles.
- Follow us on Facebook: https://www.facebook.com/GladEyePress/
- All GladEye titles can also be ordered online or from your local book store.

About the Author

Patricia Brown was born in Oregon City, Oregon, and was educated at Oregon State University, graduating with a degree in elementary education, a career she pursued for 28 years. She lives in a small town on the Oregon coast with her husband where she dabbles in the arts and enjoys the company of family and friends. This is her third novel.

Acknowledgments

It seems as though it's always the same people who need thanking and it is, but sometimes it's the whole world that inspires you, and sometimes it's the community of wonderful friends and neighbors who share moments from their lives as they stop to visit along the road or at the mailbox. There is no way I can name them all and they probably wouldn't want me to, although D.J. Josi might.

A special thank you to the Pioneer Museum and La Tea Dah's for helping to promote my books, and sincere gratitude to those who offer encouragement. I live in a wonderful community of people, including Diane Colcord who gave me the idea for a body in the swale.

As always, J.V. Bolkan and Sharleen Nelson of Gladeye Press deserve a shout out for their interior and cover design and copyediting. They always seem to take what I offer and make it better.

Thanks also to Dana Cunningham Anderson who led the Writing Alive workshop that inspired me to write in the first place and whose name I misspelled the last time.

www.ingramcontent.com/pod-product-compliance
Lightning Source LLC
Chambersburg PA
CBHW070556170726
48291CB00003B/629